Praise for *The Polar Bear Explorers' Club* series:

'A magical adventure.'
The Bookseller

'The most huggable book of the year. Channels everything
from Lemony Snicket to JK Rowling. An (iced) gem.'
SFX

'Wintry, atmospheric, highly imaginative fantasy.'
Metro

'A fantastic frosty adventure.'
Sunday Express

'A hugely enjoyable, fast-paced magical adventure.'
WRD

'Full of unique takes on classic tropes with some unexpected
twists and turns along the way.'
Times Educational Supplement

'A delightful read.'
The Week Junior

'I can't wait for the next one!'
Havana Brown, aged 12

ABOUT THE AUTHOR

Alex Bell has published novels and short stories for both adults and young adults, including *Frozen Charlotte*. *The Polar Bear Explorers' Club* was her first foray into middle grade. She always wanted to be a writer but had several different back-up plans to ensure she didn't end up in the poor house first. After completing a law degree, she now works at the Citizens Advice Bureau. Most of her spare time consists of catering to the whims of her Siamese cats.

ABOUT THE ILLUSTRATOR

Tomislav Tomić was born in 1977. He graduated from the Academy of Fine Arts in Zagreb. He started to publish his illustrations during his college days. He has illustrated a great number of books, picture books, schoolbooks and lots of covers for children's books. He lives and works in the town of Zaprešić, Croatia.

THE POLAR BEAR EXPLORERS' CLUB SERIES

The Polar Bear Explorers' Club
Explorers on Witch Mountain
Explorers on Black Ice Bridge
The Ocean Squid Explorers' Club

THE OCEAN SQUID EXPLORERS' CLUB

Illustrated by
Tomislav Tomić

ALEX BELL

faber

First published in 2020
by Faber & Faber Limited
Bloomsbury House,
74–77 Great Russell Street,
London WC1B 3DA
This paperback edition first published in 2021

Typeset by MRules
Printed by CPI Group (UK) Ltd, Croydon CR0 4YY

A CIP record for this book
is available from the British Library

ISBN 978–0–571–35971–4

FSC
www.fsc.org
MIX
Paper from
responsible sources
FSC® C020471

2 4 6 8 10 9 7 5 3 1

For my son, Cassidy Dayus.

I look forward to reading this book to you one day.

CONTENTS

CHAPTER ONE

Ursula Jellyfin stood on the salt-stained planks of the wooden boardwalk and watched as the submarine rose majestically out of the ocean. Frothing sea foam ran down its gleaming metal sides, which sparkled in the sunshine. A waterproof flag hung dripping from the flagpole at the rear, proudly displaying the crest of the Ocean Squid Explorers' Club.

'Ready?' the man beside her said. Ursula looked up at Chief Jonah Briggs, a tall, gangly man, otherwise known as Old Joe, who'd been her mentor for the last five years. He had kind eyes but there was a quiet sadness about him too. Joe had taught Ursula everything he knew about engineering, which was a whole lot. She hoisted the bag of equipment a little further up her shoulder.

'Ready, Joe,' she said.

At twelve years old, Ursula was the youngest submarine engineer employed by the South Seas

Navigation Company and she loved it. Not only the work but the fact that she got to live at the Ocean Squid Explorers' Club, with its sea-flower garden, jellyfish nursery, buttery stacks of pirate pancakes and – best of all – its gleaming fleet of beautiful submarines.

'Brace yourself, missy,' Joe said. He took a coin from his pocket and began to flip it over his fingers, rolling it over the knuckles in a 'coin walk'. As Joe's arthritis got worse, he'd taken to practising his coin tricks more often as a way to keep the strength and dexterity in his fingers. 'This submarine radioed ahead to say they have a problem with the air supply,' he told her. 'Reading between the lines I'd say that a flying swordfish got into one of the vents and has been stinking the place out.'

No matter how many times the engineers explained the problem to the explorers, it seemed they were determined to use flying swordfish as darts in their tournaments, and there was always one determined fish that would go racing straight into a ventilation shaft and get stuck.

'That's OK,' Ursula replied. 'I don't mind the smell of fish.'

The approaching submarine finally came to a halt and the escape hatch on top burst open, hitting the deck with a crash. There was an undignified exodus as a team of explorers pushed and shoved at one another in their frantic eagerness to be off the vessel. Some of them were quite red in the face as they slipped and slid down the ladder, and one had gone an interesting purple colour. The reek of sweating swordfish was strong, even from where Ursula stood on the docks below.

'Ah, the valets!' the purple-faced explorer exclaimed, seeing Ursula and Joe. 'I hope you'll be able to clear up this mess. I should warn you, it's quite dreadful in there.'

'We're not valets, Captain Smitt,' Joe replied mildly. 'We're engineers from the South Seas Navigation Company.'

'What, the girl too?' the explorer said. 'Isn't she a bit young?'

'I earned my first dolphin last month,' Ursula said, gesturing to the little brass dolphin badge that gleamed on the top pocket of her coverall, identifying her as an entry-level engineer.

'Sir, this is the second time we have had to remove a flying swordfish from the vents of your submarine,' Joe said, switching from the coin walk to the triple shuffle coin pass. 'My memory's not what it used to be, I guess, but I'm fairly sure we warned you about this before. The South Seas Navigation Company reserves

3

the right to confiscate any of its subs if they're not being treated with due care. They're awful particular like that. Am I right, Ursula?'

'You sure are, Joe,' she said.

'Oh, for heaven's sake, it was quite accidental, I assure you,' Captain Smitt snapped. 'Look, it's been a trying few days, I stink of fish, I can even taste it at the back of my throat a bit, and I'm certainly not in the mood for a lecture from an engineer of all people.'

He glanced self-consciously back at his waiting crew. Ursula knew from experience that while some explorers were brave, noble and decent, others were conceited, insecure and shallow. Unfortunately, Captain Smitt was one of the latter.

'Especially not some old-timer,' he went on. 'Now kindly do your job and fix the problem. Isn't that what we pay you people for, after all?'

Ursula bristled all over and felt heat rising to her cheeks. 'There'd be no Explorers' Club without the engineers,' she said.

The captain looked down at her with a startled expression, as if he'd forgotten she was there. 'What's that?'

Ursula lifted her chin slightly. 'I said there'd be no Explorers' Club without the engineers,' she repeated more loudly. She jabbed a thumb at her chest. 'We're what keeps you safe when you're all those miles under the sea. Submarines are a marvel of technology – the greatest marvel in the world. So maybe it wouldn't kill you to treat us with some respect.'

Captain Smitt stared at her for a long moment before turning back to Joe. 'Can't you control your apprentice, sir?'

With a final flick of the coin Joe slipped it back in his pocket. 'She controls herself just fine,' he said. 'Now time's a-wasting. We'd best get to that fish.'

'See that you do,' Captain Smitt snapped before turning on his heel and marching off along the boardwalk with the other explorers. Joe rubbed the back of his neck and looked down at Ursula.

'You're a smart girl,' he said. 'Beats me why you'd ever want to join that lot.'

Ursula shrugged. 'They're not all like him,' she offered.

She made no secret of the fact that she'd dearly love to be an explorer herself one day. Thanks to Stella Starflake Pearl, the other explorers' clubs were all accepting girls now. It was only Ocean Squid who were stubbornly sticking to the traditional rules of membership.

'If you say so,' Joe said. 'Now, come on. That fish won't rescue itself.'

It took them the rest of the afternoon to find the swordfish and drag it out. Having spent several days stuck in the air system, it was pretty angry by the time they got to it and it was only Joe's fast reflexes that prevented Ursula's coveralls from getting slashed in half. They released the fish up on deck and it flapped off indignantly over the side of the sub to dive back into the ocean with a loud *plop*!

'Right,' Joe said, brushing his hands together. 'That's that until next time.'

Ursula looked up at him and saw that he seemed tired. In the glow of the sunset Joe's short hair looked even greyer against his dark skin, his shoulders looked bonier and the lines around his eyes were deeper. He looked *old* all of a sudden, and Ursula felt a stab of guilt. She knew that he would have retired by now if it wasn't for her.

'Pack up the stuff and we'll go clean up,' Joe said.

Ursula gathered together the fish nets and pipe cleaners they'd used to poke the fish out of the vent and then followed Joe down the ladder to where his brown-and-white dog, Mutt, lay waiting for them on the boardwalk. He'd not been a young dog when Ursula arrived at the club with her explorer father five years ago, and was quite elderly now, with an entirely grey muzzle.

'Old dogs are the best dogs,' Joe often said, and Ursula certainly agreed.

She was giving Mutt a scratch behind the ears when she noticed a telltale ripple in the ocean to the side of the submarine and a brief glimpse of a fin. She'd know it anywhere – it was Minty come to say hello. She glanced quickly at Joe to see if he'd seen anything, but he was retying a shoelace on his work boots.

'You coming?' he asked, straightening up

'In a minute,' Ursula replied. 'I just want to look back at the club for a while.'

Joe shook his head and gazed out towards the horizon. 'You know I'm all for following your dreams, missy,' he said. 'But only if they've got a chance of coming true. If you want an old man's advice, then I say there's no sense wasting your life pining away for something that can never happen.'

Ursula knew he was talking about her failed attempt to convince Sir Percival Ollivant Verne that she should be allowed to join the club. Last week, when she had finally gathered up her courage to ask the president whether she might apply to join, he could not have looked more appalled and turned her down flat.

'The Polar Bear Explorers' Club allowed Stella Starflake Pearl to join—' she began.

'Doesn't matter,' Joe said. He sighed. 'Look, I'm just trying to do you a kindness. Sometimes you have to be realistic. Stella is an ice princess, you're an orphan. Stella's pa is a respected explorer and, more importantly, he's got money coming out of his ears. What have you got?'

Ursula wanted to say she wasn't an orphan, that one of her parents was in fact still alive, but this was a secret she absolutely couldn't share with anyone, not even Joe.

'My dad was an explorer. And I'm a good engineer,' she said instead. 'That should count for something, shouldn't it?'

'You're an excellent engineer,' Joe replied. 'But that will never be enough to get you into the club. And you've got nothing else to bring to the bargaining table.'

Ursula bit her tongue. She *did* have something else to bring to the bargaining table actually, but it was part of her secret – the most important part of all. She looked back at the clubhouse, full of maps and globes and sea monsters and fascinating curiosities from the Seventeen Seas, and to her dismay she felt tears prick the back of her eyes. She wanted to be an explorer so much that sometimes the thought of it kept her awake at night, lying in her cold, narrow bed, dreaming of big adventures.

'The Ocean Squid Explorers' Club is the most wonderful place in the world,' Ursula said, meaning every word. 'I don't care what it takes, I'm going to be a member of it one day.'

Joe thrust his hands in his pockets with a sigh. 'Well, time will tell,' he said. 'But I won't be around to see it. When that day comes – *if* it ever comes – I'll be long gone to the Pineapple Islands. No people around for miles. Just sand and surf and stars.' He glanced down at Mutt and said, 'We'll get there, won't we, old boy? If it's ever safe to leave these beautiful submarines to those idiot explorers.'

'You can leave them with me,' Ursula said. 'I can look after the submarines.'

She saw an emotion flash across Joe's face – was it worry? It was only there for a moment before he shook his head and said, 'Well, maybe you can and all. But don't hang around out here too long, all right? Those tools need cleaning before bedtime.'

'I know. I'll make sure it's done,' Ursula said.

Joe nodded before whistling to Mutt and walking down the boardwalk back to the club headquarters.

Ursula waited until he was out of sight before

crouching down at the edge of the wooden planks and dipping her hand into the cool ocean. A moment later a smooth snout poked at her fingers as a dolphin popped his head out of the water, greeting her with a series of whistles and clicks.

'Hello, Minty,' Ursula whispered. 'It's always lovely to see you, but you know I can't talk to you here. Someone might spot us.'

Dolphins were friendly, sociable creatures and it wasn't unusual for them to swim up to the club's boardwalks from time to time, or put on leaping, acrobatic displays in the waves beyond. But if anyone realised the extent of Ursula's friendship with dolphins, and this one in particular, then they might start watching her more closely. And if they watched her more closely, then they might discover her secret. Ursula could never let that happen.

'I'll come and see you tonight,' she said. 'I promise.'

Minty tossed his head a couple of times and dived back under the water, splashing playfully with his tail as he vanished. Ursula was already smiling at the thought of spending time with the dolphin later as she straightened up and looked back at the club. Fortunately, the explorers were all inside having their dinner so no one had seen anything at all.

Ursula had told Joe the truth, though, when she said how much she loved the place. She knew that the Jungle Cat Explorers' Club had a big treehouse for their headquarters and the Polar Bear Explorers' Club had some kind of igloo. She wasn't sure about the Desert Jackal or Sky Phoenix Explorers' Clubs, but it didn't matter because none of them could possibly compare with Ocean Squid as far as Ursula was concerned.

The club was positioned in the middle of the Jelly Blue Sea on Turtle Island. The main building was shaped like a gigantic starfish and perched right on the edge of the shore. A couple of its arms extended out over the sea itself and a network of boardwalks on stilts spread into the water, creating docks for the ships and submarines. Smaller outbuildings formed the engineering bay and the staff quarters and the engineering school. A forest of masts showed where the expedition ships were docked on the other side of the club. The whole place was filled with the smell of fish from the sea-monster-trophy room, mixed in with the sharp scent of Captain Ishmael's harpoon-cannon polish. The club had seemed big and a little scary to Ursula when she'd first arrived, but it had quickly come to feel like home.

Ursula took a moment to gaze at the starfish

building resting on the white sand, breathing in the scent of salt and shells, and basking in the sunset that was turning the waves pink and golden and orange. Then she grabbed her bag of tools and hurried to the engineering school.

Chapter Two

Ursula cleaned the tools and laid them out in the workshop before reluctantly reporting to Miss Soames. The schoolmistress was a tall, thin woman with a pinched mouth, and in the five years she'd been there Ursula had never once seen her smile or heard her laugh. Miss Soames was in charge of the apprentices who came to study engineering at the club. Normally, these students only came for a year, but Ursula was a special case because her father, Harry Theodore Williams, had been an explorer. He'd died on an expedition four years ago but the club had allowed Ursula to stay on, which was lucky as she had nowhere else to go.

Reporting to Miss Soames in the evening was Ursula's least favourite part of the day. The schoolmistress complained constantly about the extra work Ursula created and was always reprimanding her for not brushing her hair or having clean hands.

'Begging your pardon, but engineering is dirty work

sometimes, Miss Soames,' Joe would always say in her defence, but it never seemed to do much good.

Today, Ursula tiptoed into the empty schoolhouse, trying to get to the showers before Miss Soames could see her. When the apprentices were here they all slept in the dormitory, but the last batch of students had gone home a few weeks ago and the new ones wouldn't start until after the summer. The dormitory was now empty and quiet with its neat rows of freshly made beds.

Ursula slept on the bed at the end but the only sign of any life there was the framed photo of her parents that stood on her bedside cupboard. Everyone thought her mother was dead, but in fact she still came to visit Ursula on her birthday. It was part of Ursula's secret, and no one could ever find out, but she looked forward to that magical visit all year.

In the meantime, she had the photo. Miss Soames didn't like personal belongings cluttering up the place, which meant it was difficult for Ursula to make the little corner of the big room feel like her own. Even the photo of her parents had been a battle. For the first few months after she arrived, she'd had to hide it beneath her pillow and take it out to cry over when Miss Soames wasn't looking. Her father had always seemed to be away on some expedition and her mother was completely out of her reach. Ursula had never felt so lonely.

She'd only been allowed to display the photo on her bedside table after Joe had found out about it and intervened on her behalf. Ursula didn't know quite what he'd said to Miss Soames, but afterwards he'd set the photo on Ursula's bedside cupboard and the schoolmistress had reluctantly allowed it to stay there ever since. That was the extent of her lenience, though. When Ursula had pleaded with her to be allowed to decorate her bed with dolphin stickers, or perhaps hang a dolphin poster on the wall, Miss Soames had resolutely forbidden it.

'I'm not sure why you think you're so much better than everyone else, Ursula. Maybe it's because your father was an explorer. But all students will be treated the same under my watch,' she always replied to any request. 'It is only fair.'

But it didn't feel fair to Ursula in the least. All the other apprentices had homes and families they could return to and were only at the club for a year. Often it felt like the sole person who ever showed her any kindness at the club was Joe.

She had almost reached the showers when Miss

Soames's voice rang out sharply behind her. 'Ursula! You are trailing grease across the floor.'

Ursula sighed and turned around. 'I'm sorry, Miss Soames,' she said. 'But we had a messy job in one of the submarines this afternoon and—'

The schoolmistress held up a hand. 'I do not wish to hear your excuses. You put enough extra work on my plate as it is.'

'But I've taken off my boots.' Ursula held them up. 'And there's no other way to get to the showers so I don't know what you want me to do.'

'Don't take that tone with me, young lady,' Miss Soames replied. It was one of her favourite phrases and Ursula clenched her teeth every time she heard it. She'd never thought of herself as a naughty child before she came to the club, but Miss Soames had a way of making her feel like the most badly behaved, rude and ungrateful child on the planet. Which seemed to create a sort of vicious circle in which Miss Soames would tell her off, Ursula would try to stick up for herself, and then would be in even more trouble.

'I'm sorry, Miss Soames,' she forced out the words, wondering how many times she must have apologised over the years for things that weren't her fault.

'Just go and clean yourself up, please,' Miss Soames

replied sharply. 'We will take tea in my office after you have mopped the floor.'

Feeling her good mood start to fade, Ursula trudged to the showers. After washing, she changed into cut-off trousers and a plain white polo shirt with the South Seas Navigation Company logo embroidered on it. Finally, she took one of her headscarves – a blue one covered in tiny dolphins – fashioned it into a headband, and tied it over her head behind her fringe. It was useful for keeping her shoulder-length black bob out of her face, but more importantly hid her blue streak from view. It was something else that might give her secret away.

She retrieved a bucket from the store cupboard and washed the dormitory floor, making sure to remove every last possible speck of grease. When this was done she washed her hands again before going to Miss Soames's office – a small, cheerless room with a tidy desk, some large filing cabinets and two hard chairs set before a folding table where they took their meals. The good food was kept back for the explorers, so the engineers and other staff had to make do with whatever was simple and cheap from the kitchen. Fortunately, Ursula had befriended the chef and was sometimes lucky enough to get treats from him when she snuck into the kitchen after hours.

Tonight, though, it was gruel again, which Ursula detested. Miss Soames seemed to quite like gruel, which really told you everything you needed to know about her. Ursula was forcing it down when her eye fell on a newspaper that had been left on the desk. The headline read: *Frogfoot Island Mysteriously Reappears in the Seventeen Seas.*

'Oh!' Ursula exclaimed. 'Has there been another one?'

'Please don't speak with your mouth full,' Miss Soames said automatically, despite the fact that she hadn't been looking at Ursula and so couldn't have known whether she was speaking with her mouth full or not.

'Sorry,' Ursula said just as automatically. She gestured at the paper. 'I hadn't realised that another lost place had come back.'

When the first girl explorer and ice princess, Stella Starflake Pearl, had returned from her expedition across the Black Ice Bridge three months ago, the world had been rocked by the discovery of the Collector – a villain called Scarlett Sauvage from the mysterious Phantom Atlas Society, who had been stealing parts of the world and locking them up in her private collection of snow globes. The globes had been forged using powerful snow-queen magic and all a person had to do was unscrew the base, whisper the name of the place they wished to collect and it would be swept up inside it.

Scarlett claimed to be a conservationist, keeping the locations safe from being spoilt, but she never asked permission to take them and everyone else was horrified that the Phantom Atlas Society had been quietly stealing away lands for years without anyone realising. Fortunately, Stella and her friends had been able to rescue some of the snow globes, including the one containing the Sky Phoenix Explorers' Club, and had recently been releasing them back into the world.

'I expect that Scarlett Sauvage is running scared now that she knows she's been discovered,' Miss Soames said. 'No doubt trying to put all the places back in order to avoid punishment. It won't work, of course. She'll be brought to justice eventually.'

Ursula frowned. She'd recently come across an interview with Stella Starflake Pearl in one of the expedition journals in the club library. From what the ice princess said, Scarlett Sauvage didn't sound like the repenting type.

'I read an interview with Stella the other day,' she volunteered. 'She said that Scarlett can't take any more places because she only has a certain number of snow globes. If she wants to take a new place, she has to put something back. Stella warned that lost places might be reappearing now because the Collector is preparing to steal something new—'

'That's quite enough, Ursula,' Miss Soames cut her off. 'Stella Starflake Pearl is scaremongering. Do you know what scaremongering means?'

'Yes, it means—'

'It means she's viciously making up wild stories in order to frighten people.' Miss Soames's nostrils flared and her mouth became even more pinched than usual. 'I won't have that kind of talk here, I simply won't. Someone really ought to take that girl in hand.'

Ursula felt a new bubble of dislike rise up inside her. 'But Stella and her friends saved lots of lives!' she protested. 'All those people who were imprisoned in the snow globes. The Sky Phoenix Explorers' Club!'

'Ursula, you are very naïve but you must remember that Stella is an ice princess. That means she's dangerous. She's probably done these things in order to protect herself, but mark my words – one day her true nature will out. This is what comes from letting girls be explorers. If I had my way, she'd be in a magical prison right now.'

Ursula clamped her jaw shut. Her own secret

suddenly felt too big inside her and she had a strong fear that Miss Soames might somehow guess what it was at any moment. And then she'd really be done for. Locked up in some magical prison herself, probably.

She laid down her spoon in her empty bowl and said, 'I'm finished. Please may I be excused?'

'You may,' Miss Soames replied. 'Once you've cleared the table.'

Ursula gathered up their plates and cups on to the tray and carried them outside, glad to escape from the schoolmistress. A winding pebble path led the way to the main building of the Ocean Squid Explorers' Club, and Ursula followed this past floodlit fountains in the shape of giant shells, topiary bushes carefully fashioned into fish, trees hung with turtle-shaped lanterns that glowed softly in the dusk, and low brick walls covered in the club's famous sea-salt roses.

She walked around to the back entrance of the kitchen where the chef, Yately, was yelling at one of the explorers.

'I will not turn that puffer fish into a pie! It's poisonous, you hear? For the last time, there's no safe way to eat it.'

He thrust the fish in question back at the explorer, who left the kitchen with his head hung low. Ursula set down the tray in the washing-up area and gave Yately a sympathetic look. The chef rolled his eyes at her.

'Moronic bunch,' he said, jabbing his thumb back in the direction of the dining room. 'And they're even more fired up than usual today because the Rooks are here.'

Ursula's ears pricked up at once. 'Ethan Edward Rook?' she asked eagerly. 'The magician who's been on all those adventures with Stella?'

'That's the one,' Yately replied. He nodded towards the dining room again and said, 'He's been holding court in there for an hour now.'

The chef turned away to the sideboard and began chopping up a fish with gusto. Ursula went straight to the door. Engineers weren't supposed to be seen in the dining room but she risked opening the door a crack to peek through.

The room was a long, rectangular shape with dozens of glass bubbles hanging down from the ceiling on green ribbons. Inside each was an unusual fish, or crab, or sea-fairy specimen which had been brought back from a former expedition. One larger bubble over in the corner held a whole choir of singing cucumbers who were going through their repertoire of sea shanties. In the centre of the room, a group of explorers were all crowded around a pale boy with white-blond hair. He'd scrambled up on to a chair so that everyone could see him. Ursula immediately recognised Ethan from the photos in the newspaper.

'And then,' he went on, 'Portia the snow queen lunged after us, and the gargoyles were coming for us too, and the Black Ice Bridge had run out, so we were trapped right at the edge of the world.'

'So what happened?' an explorer asked eagerly.

'I created the most magnificent shield!' Ethan said. 'Huge and black with the Ocean Squid Explorers' crest stamped right in the middle. It protected us from the snow queen's magic and—'

'Show us!' one of the explorers cried, cutting off the magician in mid-flow.

Ethan looked uncertain. 'Now?'

'We'd all love to see it,' another explorer said. 'It must have been a tremendous shield to keep a snow queen's magic at bay.'

Ethan hesitated, but then puffed out his chest and rolled up his sleeves. 'Very well,' he said. 'You'd best stand clear, though, and mind yourselves. This is highly powerful magic.'

The other explorers took a few steps back and Ursula held her breath as Ethan threw out both his hands. But instead of a fearsome shield, he produced a little black

Frisbee that flew straight to the kitchen door and hit the wood above Ursula's head with a thump before falling feebly to the floor.

Someone in the group sniggered and then Ethan was complaining that the singing cucumbers made it impossible for him to concentrate. Ursula reached forward to snatch up the Frisbee. She saw it had the crest of the Ocean Squid Explorers' Club stamped on it, which made it kind of cool even if it wasn't a great shield. She was just wondering whether she ought to try to return it to Ethan when a hand gripped her sleeve and yanked her back into the kitchen.

'Come on, you,' Yately said, not unkindly. 'You know you're not supposed to hang around here getting under our feet.' He held out a napkin to her and Ursula saw that it contained one of the little shark cakes meant for the explorers.

'Thanks, Yately,' she said, taking it.

He winked at her. 'Now beat it.'

Ursula ate the cake as she hurried out of the club with the Frisbee tucked under her arm. It was quiet outside and she thought she was alone until she noticed a young explorer named Maxwell Xavier Clark sitting on the wall. He was tall and slim with black skin and a high shave fade haircut that turned into black curls on top of his head.

Having lived and worked at the club for five years, Ursula was on first-name terms with a few of the junior explorers, and Max was one of her favourites. He always had a grin and a friendly word for her whenever they met. More importantly, Ursula liked him for his explorer's specialities. Max was training to be an inventor, and not just any kind, but a robot inventor. He almost always had some cool new gadget with him and now was no different. He held a controller in one hand and a little robot crab scuttled around at his feet. But to Ursula's surprise he looked rather despondent, which wasn't like Max at all.

'Hello,' she said. 'Are you OK?'

Max looked up, startled. The downcast look left his face so quickly that Ursula wondered whether she might have imagined it.

'Right as rain, Jellyfin,' he said cheerfully.

'What are you doing out here?' she asked.

'I had to get away from Rook,' Max said. He gestured at the Frisbee she carried. 'Let me guess. He just tried to show everyone the amazing shield he can supposedly create?'

'Yep. The singing cucumbers ruined his concentration.'

'Well, at least he made a Frisbee this time. The other day it was a spiky starfish, and trust me, you really don't want one of those whizzing towards your head. Rook's boasting gets on my nerves. He's always been a bit stuck up but he's been insufferable since he got back from the Black Ice Bridge.'

'Well, it might have been worse,' Ursula teased. 'Jai Bartholomew Singh could have been there too.'

Jai was the same age as them and one of the Ocean Squid Explorers' Club's most renowned members. He had more medals and accolades than any other junior explorer. In fact, his achievements were so many and varied that the club had even taken to using his image in their promotional materials encouraging new members to join. Jai did everything by the book, whereas Max must have broken every rule the club had and was always getting himself in trouble for one thing or another. The last occasion the two boys had been at the club together they'd rubbed each other up the wrong way so much that it had almost turned into a duel.

'I met Jai once,' Ursula said, 'getting off his submarine. You might find him annoying, but he was very polite to me.'

Max rolled his eyes. 'Any more than five minutes in the same room and I'm tearing my hair out.'

'Speaking of hair,' Ursula said. 'I like your shark.'

Max often had a cool design shaved into his fade. Sometimes it was a kraken's tentacle, others it was a submarine, or sometimes, like today, it was a shark.

'Thanks,' he said. 'Here, check this out. I know you'll appreciate it.'

He nodded at the robot crab at his feet and pressed a few buttons on his controller, which made the crab scuttle over to the wall of the club and then climb straight up it.

'That's awesome!' Ursula said.

'Do you want to come to the submarine and see the other stuff I'm working on?' he asked. 'No one else appreciates my robots as much as you do.'

'I'd love to,' Ursula replied. 'But it's late and I'm supposed to be in the dormitory. Maybe another time?'

'Sure thing, Jellyfin,' Max said, giving her a salute. 'Goodnight.'

'Goodnight, Max.'

She gave him a wave then headed off down the path. She glanced back at Max just once and to her surprise he was staring at the crab with a gloomy expression on his face again. She was sure she hadn't imagined it this time – there was definitely something on Max's mind. She hoped it wasn't serious as she made her way back to the dormitory. When she got there, she put the Frisbee straight in the bedside cupboard before Miss Soames could see and find a reason to confiscate it. Then she quickly changed into her bikini, put on her pyjamas over the top, got into bed and turned out the lights.

Ursula hated the big dormitory when there were no other students in it. The room felt big and cold and unfriendly, more like a hospital ward than a bedroom. But she didn't intend to stay there for long this evening. She waited until she heard Miss Soames's door open, then snuggled down in the covers and pretended to be asleep. The schoolmistress appeared a moment later and walked into the dormitory to do her final checks before going to her own bedroom for the night.

Ursula waited ten more minutes, just to be safe, then threw back the covers and got out of bed. She took the Frisbee, a little flashlight and a bag with a towel in it from her cupboard and with one last check to see that the coast was clear, tiptoed from the room.

She made her way outside where the warm air ruffled over her skin, carrying with it the smell of salt and sea, and made her heart speed up in her chest with anticipation. There was no one around except for the flying fish drifting through the air, painting their blue glow through the darkness.

Ursula hurried straight to one of the boardwalks near the engineering bay. No one came here at night and it was out of sight of the main club, so it seemed like the safest place for what she was about to do. Moving quickly, she took out her towel, removed her pyjamas and stuffed them into the bag along with her flashlight, then dropped the Frisbee on to the surface of the water.

Finally, she reached her toes down towards the ocean. The moment they touched the surface, a cool, tingly feeling rushed all the way up her legs as they transformed into a sparkling blue mermaid's tail. Ursula grinned and paused a moment to run her hand over the shimmering scales, pearly and beautiful, before diving into the water with a soft splash.

CHAPTER THREE

Beneath the surface of the water there was a whole other world, and Ursula loved every inch of it. No one at the club knew she was half mermaid and they must never find out. The Ocean Squid Explorers' Club viewed mermaids as their age-old foe, convinced they were responsible for drowning hundreds of explorers over the years. Ursula didn't know how much truth there was to this. It seemed to her that most of the supposed drownings were attached to explorers who'd sailed off and simply never returned, so there was no way of knowing that mermaids were responsible. Anything might have happened to those men. They could have lived out their days on a paradise island surrounded by dancing coconuts for all anyone knew.

But Ursula had kept her identity a closely guarded secret these past five years, only going into the ocean late at night after everyone else had gone to bed. Mermaids had excellent underwater vision and she could see everything now as clearly as if it were daylight, especially since a couple of sunset jellyfish bobbed in the water nearby, casting their glowing light through the waves.

Ursula resurfaced to grab the Frisbee, then dived back underwater. As always, she went straight to the special cave where she met her mother every year on her birthday. Today was not Ursula's birthday but there was still a chance that a message from her mother would be waiting for her instead, which was the next best thing.

As soon as she swam through the cave entrance she saw the conch shell nestled on the sandy floor, a beautiful thing with a pearly pink interior. Ursula snatched it up eagerly. Mermaids could use shells to send messages to each other underwater. Any shell would work for this – the larger it was, the bigger the message it could contain, but the longer it would take to arrive, carried along by the currents.

All a mermaid had to do was whisper their message into the shell, along with the name of the intended recipient, and then release the shell into the sea where it would join the bubble tide. This was a bit like the postal service, except it was powered by mermaid magic rather than postmen and delivery carts. As soon as the shell was released, it would join the underwater tide and find its way to whoever it needed to reach.

Ursula pressed the shell to her ear now and felt a thrill of delight when her mother's voice came through as clearly as if she were floating right beside her. She told Ursula all about the little things that were happening in her life, like what her naughty pet terrapin, Ambrose, was up to, and who'd won the ocean cauliflower contest and which seahorse came first in the seahorse race at the underwater fair that week.

Ursula didn't mind what her mother talked about as long as she could hear her voice. She loved getting the messages but it always made her feel a little sad at the same time, especially when she got to the end and could hear the sorrow echoed in her mother's voice as she told her how much she loved and missed her. They both wished they could live together, but mermaids can't survive on land for very long without becoming ill, and similarly Ursula couldn't stay in a deep-sea mermaid city because the human part of her needed light and air and sunshine.

To cheer herself up, Ursula immediately whispered her own message into the shell, telling her mother about her last few weeks at the club and how proud she was to have earned her first dolphin. Once she'd finished, she kissed the shell and released it out to the bubble tide to find its way across the sea.

Then she turned her attention back to the cave. On one of her mother's previous visits, they had decorated it together so that Ursula would have somewhere nice to go, a tiny piece of the ocean that was all her own. It was a pretty space with a floor of golden sand and strings of pearls draped from the ceiling. The light from the sunset jellyfish spilled inside, illuminating the mermaid furniture her mother had brought in a sea chariot pulled by dolphins. There was a special dressing table and stool set in front of a beautiful oval mirror with mermaids carved into the frame, and a comfy armchair covered in a pattern of starfish with its own matching footstool.

Unlike regular human furniture, mermaid furniture didn't get spoilt underwater, nor did the mermaid books her mother had given her. They were lined up neatly on a shelf in the corner and the pages repelled the water effortlessly. Sometimes, if she was feeling lazy, Ursula enjoyed curling up in the starfish armchair and reading one of her books until it was time to return to the surface.

Other times she simply admired the paintings of water horses that adorned her cave walls. She'd never been lucky enough to see one of the majestic white horses in real life, but she knew from her mother that they came from the sea and that their bodies and souls were one with the ocean. People said they could see

them sometimes, racing along the surface, galloping upon the crest of a wave.

Ursula knew that mermaids had the ability to call the water horses with a song, and that magical things could happen when mermaids and water horses came together. But despite multiple attempts, she had never managed to do this, and it was a failure she found bitterly disappointing. She understood that other mermaids might be wary of her because of her mixed heritage, and she wondered if being only half mermaid caused the water horses to reject her too.

Ursula's singing was certainly different from humans', though. For a start, there were little golden musical notes that appeared around her, sparkling in the air before fizzing away into nothing. People couldn't see them but Ursula knew they could sense them. Shortly after she'd arrived at the club she'd been singing to herself in the engineering bay as she worked one day. A little later she looked up to realise that all the other workers in the room had put their tools down and were staring at her dumbstruck. She'd stopped singing at once, terrified she'd revealed her secret, and she never sang in public again after that.

Now she swam over to her dressing table where her treasures were locked away inside a chest. It contained the birthday presents her mother had brought her since she'd lived at the club. Ursula couldn't risk keeping them in the dormitory because Miss Soames regularly went through Ursula's private things under the pretence of checking she wasn't keeping anything 'unsuitable'. And it would be pretty hard for Ursula to explain any of *these* items because they all contained mermaid magic.

She sat at the stool now, enjoying the sight of her hair floating around her head in the mirror, and opened up the treasure chest. First there was the tiny wind-up harp that played mermaid music you could only hear underwater. Then there was the hairbrush that Ursula only needed to sweep through her hair once to make it suddenly grow long enough to sit on and, not only that but also thread it with tiny shells and shiny pearls too. Then there was a mermaid map showing Ursula exactly where her mother lived in the faraway Bubble Ocean.

And finally, there was the gift her mother had given her on her twelfth birthday earlier this year – a silver locket in the shape of a clam shell. Ursula picked it up, enjoying the cool weight of it on her palm. She could almost see her mother in the cave with her now – a beautiful mermaid with blue and green hair, emerald eyes and a kind, pretty face.

'You're growing up, Ursula,' she'd said. Her melodic

voice seemed to make the water around her shimmer but Ursula could understand her, and speak herself, just as clearly as if she'd been on dry land. 'If you were completely mermaid, your hair would start to change colour soon, into mermaid colours. Blue, or green, or purple, or silver, or a mix of any of those. There's also a chance you could get gills in your neck or even webs between your fingers. Then you wouldn't be able to keep your identity hidden at the club any more.'

'So where could I go to be safe?' Ursula had said. It was part of an old conversation she didn't enjoy having. 'As much as I want to, I can't live in a mermaid city with you. Am I just meant to live in a cave by myself?'

'Of course not, darling,' her mother had said, looking troubled. 'Let's hope those things never happen. There's never been a child before who's half human and half mermaid that I've heard of, so we don't know what to expect. It might not come to that. I only want you to be on guard in case you start to experience any changes. They could be physical or they could be … well, magical. Mermaid girls start to get their magic about this time. That's what the locket is for. To help you channel and control it.'

Ursula gazed down at the shell now, feeling a strange mixture of excitement and dread. She knew explorers were afraid of mermaid magic, and some of that distrust had seeped into her too. After all, it was terrifying to think that mermaids could use the magic of their voices to control humans and make them do awful things like drowning themselves. And she didn't want any part of that. Her mother had tried to tell her that the magic took more pleasant forms too – like summoning the water horses or making sea flowers grow from a grain of sand. But even so, she thought mermaid magic was probably best left well alone.

Eventually, Ursula packed up her treasures and left the cave to go in search of Minty. She began by checking the reef that flourished beneath the engineering bay – a colourful garden of rose-coloured coral, bright yellow sponges and pearly sea flowers that attracted all kinds of marine life.

Ursula swam past squirrelfish, parrotfish, several crabs and some argumentative sea cucumbers, but there was no sign of the dolphin. Many of the fish came to say hello to her, though. She may not have any friends other than Joe on land, but under the sea she had formed all kinds of friendships. And best of all, her ocean friends were always there; even though she sometimes made friends with the other engineering students, they never stayed longer than a year.

She made her way to the nearby sea caves where Minty sometimes liked to hang out, but found only a group of sea fairies decorating the place for a birthday party. It looked a very grand affair, with colourful water balloons and a tiny chandelier fashioned from coral and lit up with sparkle plankton. The fairies all had their best seaweed dresses on and pearls in their hair and had set up some sort of bouncy castle made from orange sea sponges.

Ursula paused to say hello. The sea fairies were her friends too, and she wished the birthday girl a happy birthday and presented her with a sea flower before going on with her search for Minty. Along the way she was greeted by a couple of sea turtles and a whole flock of bright pink seahorses, before at last she found her dolphin friend.

Minty was swimming in one of his favourite playgrounds – an old sunken galleon called the *Theodora*. The ship had sunk outside the Ocean Squid Explorers' Club more than a hundred years ago and was a hollowed-out husk now, but Ursula had spent many happy hours exploring it, even discovering a treasure map and some chests of pirate medallions tucked away in the captain's study.

She called out to him and Minty came splashing

through the water, delighted to see Ursula in her mermaid form. She laughed as he twisted and flipped around her, poking at the Frisbee in her hand.

'I thought you'd like this,' Ursula said. 'I don't think it will fly down here, though. We'll have to go up to the surface. Come on! I'll race you!'

They shot up through the waves so fast that they left a trail of tiny bubbles in their wake. Ursula checked to make sure they were a suitable distance away from the club. The moon was shining tonight, painting the waves silver, but if anyone saw her from this distance they'd only see her human half and would think she was just out for a late night swim.

Minty was nudging her impatiently with his nose so she drew back her arm and let the Frisbee fly across the ocean. The dolphin chased after it in delight and Ursula watched as he clamped it between his teeth and brought it straight back to her. They did this a few times before Minty suddenly decided to change the game, jerking his head to toss the Frisbee back at Ursula. One of her favourite things about the dolphin was that he was super-smart and excellent at playing games, even better than Mutt.

Ursula laughed as she jumped out of the water to grab the Frisbee, twisting slightly in the air to catch it, but the laughter abruptly stopped as she fell back into the sea with a splash. There were men running around on the docks and she could tell they were explorers by their long black cloaks. But what on earth were they doing out at this time of night? They ought to be safely ensconced in the club's trophy rooms by now, arguing over who had brought back the largest squid. It was highly unusual for any of them to be out after dark. Plus, there was a panicky edge to the way they were moving, waving their arms and yelling to each other. Ursula realised something must have happened. And then the wail of the club's alarm filled the air.

She turned to Minty, who had appeared in the water beside her.

'Something's wrong,' she said. 'I have to go back.'

That alarm meant everyone was supposed to evacuate and she knew Miss Soames would be on her way to the dormitory and that she'd be absolutely furious when she discovered Ursula wasn't in her bed like she was supposed to be. The alarm had only gone off twice before and both times it had been due to a fire in the kitchen when some foolish explorer had tried to cook a fireworks crab. No matter how many warning signs Yately put up, there was always one explorer who thought he could do it successfully. Ursula assumed it was probably the same thing now, but the timing couldn't have been worse.

She snatched up the Frisbee and handed it to Minty. 'Here, you keep this,' she said. 'I'll see you later.' She kissed the dolphin on his smooth head and waved goodbye as he disappeared into the water with the Frisbee. Then she turned her attention back to the shoreline and wondered how she was going to get back on land without anyone seeing her.

She was just considering whether it was too risky to return, and perhaps she should stay hidden out in the water instead, when she remembered her bag. If they found that, they'd know she was swimming and then a boat might be sent to find her. She could dive deeper beneath the water, but how would she explain where she'd been later?

There was no one on the boardwalk yet. If she moved quickly, perhaps she could get to her bag, dry off, turn back into a human and run to the evacuation point outside the dormitory. Her hair would still be wet, of course, but she'd just have to make up some story about going for a midnight shower and hope that Miss Soames believed her.

She ducked back under the surface and swam as fast as she could to the boardwalk. But when she surfaced, to her dismay she heard footsteps approaching and she only just had time to reach up and snatch her things from the planks before a couple of explorers came running along the boards. Ursula ducked beneath the walkway and pressed her back up to one of the wooden posts, which was wrapped in seaweed and barnacles, praying that neither of them looked down through the gaps and spotted her.

Why were they running to their submarine at this time of night anyway? Perhaps they were the ones who had set off the alarm and were now hiding from the chef. Yately could get pretty mad when explorers broke into his kitchen.

Ursula heard the men climb the ladder into the submarine. Once they were inside they'd be able to see her clearly through the portholes and then her secret would be out. She put her arms through her backpack straps and, still clutching her towel, swam around to the other side of the club. The staff accommodation quarters were located there, but her only thought was to get as far away from the subs as possible. Not only might someone see her, but the vessels' huge propellers were very dangerous to anything that got too close.

However, her towel was now soaked and that was a

problem because her tail wouldn't turn back into legs until it was completely dry.

'There you are!' a voice rang out, and to Ursula's horror she realised that Joe was on the pier outside his cabin, staring right at her. 'Miss Soames is looking high and low for you, missy! Didn't you hear the evacuation siren? Get outta there right now.'

'I can't!' Ursula gasped, cold fear flooding through her whole body.

What the heck was she going to do? She absolutely could not come out of the water in her mermaid form and she had no way of drying her tail to turn it back into legs. Joe had lost his only son to mermaids. If he saw that she was one, they wouldn't be friends any more. He would hate her – she could already imagine the disgust in his eyes and his mouth twisting with contempt.

'Mermaid!' he'd yell. 'There's a mermaid here! Send for the guards!'

In a panic, Ursula was just about to dive beneath the surface of the water but Joe must have realised what she intended. Quick as a flash, he dropped down on the side of the pier.

'Oh no, you don't!' he said, grabbing her bag.

Before Ursula could squirm out of the straps, he'd hoisted it up, dragging her from the water with it.

CHAPTER FOUR

'Joe, no!' she cried out, but it was too late.

Ursula dropped her towel and sprawled on the cold boards, streams of water running from her tail, which was now completely exposed. After all this time, her secret had been revealed and she felt a sob rise in her chest as she looked up at her friend. Joe stood gazing down at her in the light from the nearby turtle lanterns, an unreadable expression on his face.

'I ... I can explain,' she began, although she had no idea what she could possibly say. Joe now knew that Ursula was part mermaid and that she'd been lying to him about it for years. How could she excuse that? How could she make him believe that she wasn't a monster?

But before she could say anything, Miss Soames called out, 'Chief Briggs, I can't find the girl anywhere! Have you seen her?'

Ursula and Joe both turned to look at the schoolmistress hurrying along the boardwalk in her nightdress. She was far enough away that she hadn't spotted Ursula on the ground yet, but she would at any moment.

Joe leaned down and scooped Ursula up in his arms. Then he grabbed the wet towel and threw it over her tail.

'Can you turn back?' he asked.

'My tail needs to be dry first,' Ursula replied. 'I can't be human again until the last drop of ocean is gone.'

Joe muttered an oath. Miss Soames was nearly upon them now and had clearly spotted Ursula because she let out a shrill cry.

'You hurt your ankle,' Joe whispered in her ear.

Before Ursula could reply, Joe looked up at the schoolmistress, raised his voice and called, 'It's all right, Miss Soames, no need to fret. I've got the little mite.'

The teacher hurried down the path towards them, her furious face looking almost purple in the lantern light.

'Where on earth were you?' she demanded. 'I've been going out of my mind.'

'Someone decided to go for a little swim,' Joe said. 'You know what these kids are like.'

'Outrageous behaviour!' Miss Soames exclaimed. 'Please put her down at once, Chief. She will be accompanying me to explain herself.'

'No can do,' Joe replied. He nodded down at Ursula and said, 'Hurt her ankle getting out of the water. I'm just going to take her along to the infirmary.'

'Give her to me. I'll take her,' Miss Soames said, holding out her arms.

Ursula started to tremble. Her tail was still very much a tail, curled out of sight over Joe's arm. The towel felt precariously balanced and she clutched it tighter, praying that it didn't slip and expose a shining blue scale.

'It's no trouble,' Joe said mildly. 'Besides, you wouldn't want to get your nightie all wet now, miss.'

Miss Soames hesitated. At the same time, the alarm stopped abruptly and was replaced with a series of three short, sharp whistles, which meant that it was safe to return to the club.

'That's that, then,' Joe said. 'I'll take this one to the infirmary and how about you meet us there? You'll want to pop back for a cardie or something on a chilly night like this, miss.'

'Very well,' Miss Soames snapped. 'I'll see you in five minutes.'

She spun round and marched off down the boardwalk towards her quarters. Joe turned too, but instead of walking in the direction of the infirmary, he went straight to his own cabin, shouldering open the door. Mutt greeted them with some excited yaps.

'Out of the way, you,' Joe said. He went into his little bathroom and set Ursula down gently on the edge of the bathtub.

She gripped the sides to balance and the towel slipped away, exposing her mermaid's tail in the stark electric lights, her fin resting against the cool tiles.

'Well, now,' the chief said. 'Seems to me you must think old Joe is pretty stupid.'

'Of . . . of course I don't—' Ursula began.

'Save it, missy. I know all about you being a mermaid. Have done for years.'

Ursula's mouth fell open in utter shock. For a moment she wondered whether she could possibly have misheard him. Better yet, perhaps this was all some awful dream.

'Hang on a tick,' Joe said, heading out the door. He reappeared a moment later with one of his clean shirts, which he tossed over to her, along with a dry towel. 'I'll put the kettle on,' he said. 'Give me a shout when you're ready.'

He went into the kitchen and Ursula heard him clattering around. She put her backpack on the floor, picked up the towel and used it to rub her tail dry.

When the last drop of ocean had gone, her mermaid's fin transformed back into human legs. She peeled off her bikini top, stuffed it in her bag and then pulled Joe's shirt over her head. It was so big that it was more like a dress on her and almost reached her ankles. She used the towel to wring the excess water from her hair, picked up her bag and then made her way to the kitchen where Joe was pouring hot water into two mugs.

'Here,' she said in a small voice, holding out the towel.

'Put it on the table,' Joe said without turning around or looking at her. 'Then sit your butt down in the living room.'

Ursula did as she was told. She had no idea why Joe hadn't exposed her to Miss Soames. She'd always assumed he'd be furious if he ever found out she was part mermaid, and yet now he said he'd known for years and didn't seem angry at all. Perhaps he was just disappointed, which was even worse. Ursula had been to Joe's cabin before and knew the way to the living room. They sometimes played cards in front of the fire and they had spent the last few Christmases there too.

She put down her bag, perched awkwardly on the edge of an armchair and her eye fell immediately on the framed photo of Joe's son, Angus, propped up on the mantelpiece. He looked about seventeen, which meant the picture must have been taken shortly before the mermaids drowned him. Ursula had always thought he had a kind, open face. She knew his death had broken Joe's heart.

Joe walked in just then, set a mug of hot chocolate down on the table beside her and then lowered his lanky body into the armchair opposite. Mutt shuffled in and flopped down at his feet with a contented grunt.

'When she doesn't find us in the infirmary, Miss Soames will probably come here soon enough,' Joe said. 'I reckon we don't have much time. So you'd better get explaining.'

Ursula picked up the mug of hot chocolate to stop her hands from shaking.

'My mother was a mermaid,' she said.

It felt strange to say the words out loud like that after so long keeping them locked up inside.

'And you already know my dad was an explorer. They fell in love,' she went on. 'And that's ... well, it's forbidden on both sides. So my mother used a sea witch's enchantment to turn into a human and my dad left the club so they could be together. Then they had me, and even though the enchantment made Mum look like a human, she was still a mermaid underneath. So I'm both.'

'You turn into a mermaid when you touch water?' Joe asked.

'It has to be seawater,' Ursula replied. 'It wouldn't work with bath water, or a river.'

'Who knows the truth about you?'

'No one. My parents said we had to keep it a secret. When I was born we moved to Peekaboo Island, which was deserted, and we lived there by ourselves.'

For a moment Ursula was back there, in the little cabin her father had built by the sea – an idyllic place full of seashells and laughter and love. But something like that couldn't last forever.

'But the enchantment only let my mother be human for five years,' Ursula said. 'Then she changed back into a mermaid. She tried to live in the shallow water around the island. She tried really hard so we could all stay together.'

Ursula felt tears suddenly sting her eyes. She'd never been able to talk to anyone about this, and the memories brought a powerful rush of sadness with them. She recalled how her mother would take her into the sea for the day – the delicious feel of the cold, salty water against her mermaid's fin, the joy of swimming through the underwater world and searching together for pale pink pearls on the seabed.

'But then she got ill,' Ursula said. 'Mermaids are

supposed to live in deep water and only come up to the surface occasionally.'

She recalled how her mother's beautiful blue-and-green hair had started to turn lank and lose its colour, fading into grey strands. Her skin took on a sickly sheen and her tail started to bleed and shed its shimmering scales.

'It got so bad that Dad thought she was going to die,' she said. 'So they agreed that Mum would return to her mermaid city and Dad would take me to the explorers' club.'

'So your father enrolled you in the engineering course?' Joe asked.

Ursula nodded. 'It was the only way for me to stay here. And he came to see me when he could.'

'What about your mother?'

'She comes to visit me every year on my birthday,' Ursula said. She risked a look at Joe. 'How long have you known about me?' she asked.

'Couple of years,' Joe said.

'How did you find out?'

Joe rubbed the back of his neck. 'Those explorers might tuck themselves up early in the evenings,' he said. 'But when you get to be my age you don't always sleep so good. There's all these aches and pains that keep you up at night. So I sit out on my veranda sometimes, or go for a walk through the grounds. And that's when I saw you playing with that pet dolphin of yours.'

'Minty . . . He's not my pet,' Ursula said. 'He's a wild dolphin who lives in the sea. We're friends, that's all.'

Joe put his mug down on the table. 'What I don't get,' he said slowly, 'is why you'd take such a risk in the first place. You've seen the mermaid's tail that's pinned up on the wall in the trophy room. You know mermaids are monsters to the club.'

Ursula flinched. 'I know. I . . . I tried to keep away from the ocean when I first arrived here, but it makes me sick, just like it made my mum. I have to go into the water sometimes. I just have to.'

Ursula thought back to the early days when she'd not set foot in the ocean for weeks. Her skin had taken on a sallow look, her hair had started to fall out. She'd even found a couple of scales in her bed.

'Hmm,' Joe said. 'I figured it must be something like that.'

'I'm sorry.' The words suddenly burst out of her. 'I didn't want to lie to you. But I always thought you'd hate me if you ever found out . . .'

'Hate you?' Joe repeated. 'Missy, in all my life, I can honestly say that I've never hated anyone and I certainly don't hate you. What would make you think something so dumb? We're friends, aren't we?'

Ursula looked up at him, startled. 'Y-yes, but ... I mean, mermaids drowned your son, so ...'

Joe shook his head. 'Ursula, I don't hold you responsible for what happened to Angus,' he said. 'Why would I? It was nothing to do with you. You don't want to drown anyone, do you?'

'No!' Ursula said. 'Of course not.'

'That's what I thought. You know, I've always been a pretty good judge of character.'

'But ... I thought you'd hate all mermaids after what happened.'

'There's good and bad people in the world,' Joe replied with a shrug. 'So it makes perfect sense that there'd be good and bad mermaids too. I judge you based on your own actions, nothing else, and in five years you've not said or done anything to make me think you're not a thoroughly good egg. But no one else can ever know about this. Understand?' He spoke gently but there was the same look of worry in his eyes that Ursula had seen earlier, back at the docks. 'Explorer types have some strange ideas. If they knew the truth about you, there's every chance they'd nail you up on one of their trophy walls too.'

Ursula shuddered, feeling the nails driving into her tail. She thought of the blue streak in her hair. It was small at the moment but she knew it might change as she got older, and eventually she could have full-blown multicoloured mermaid hair. Then people would be bound to know, whether she wanted them to or not. But there was no point going into that with Joe right now.

'Don't worry,' she said. 'I realise I can never tell.'

'Good,' said Joe. 'Your whole life depends on no explorer finding out. Ever. Now hurry up and drink your hot chocolate.'

Ursula looked down at the untouched drink in her lap and saw that Joe had put her favourite dolphin-shaped marshmallows on top. Wordlessly she drank up, feeling the chocolate melt into all those bits of her that had been cold and afraid.

'Come on, then,' Joe said, taking the mug from her. 'Let's get you back where you belong with Miss Soames.'

'She's going to be so cross,' Ursula said, picking up her bag. 'It's bad luck that someone decided to cook a fireworks crab and set off the alarm.'

Joe went suddenly still. 'Oh,' he said. 'I guess you were in the water so you don't know.'

'Don't know what?'

'Why the alarm went off. It wasn't a fireworks crab this time.'

'What was it then?'

'It was Scarlett Sauvage. She attacked the Sky Phoenix Explorers' Club this evening. All the other clubs evacuated as a precaution.'

Ursula felt a new coldness spread through her. 'Why did she attack the Sky Phoenix Explorers' Club?'

'Who knows? Maybe because Stella Starflake Pearl was visiting there? Maybe she's still angry with the girl for exposing her.'

'Was Stella hurt? Was anyone else?'

'I reckon not,' Joe said. 'President Verne said he received a telegram saying that the club's phoenixes chased Scarlett away. For now. But I wouldn't want to be in Stella's shoes at the minute.'

Ursula frowned. It was all very worrying. But she was prevented from discussing it with Joe any further because Miss Soames arrived then and began hammering on the door.

'I guess it turns out your ankle was all right after all,' Joe said as he went to answer it. Ursula sighed and trailed after him, preparing herself for a very big telling-off from the schoolmistress.

CHAPTER FIVE

The next day, it was almost lunchtime when Ursula finally escaped from Miss Soames's office. The schoolmistress was furious about her midnight swim and Ursula had to endure a lecture that went on for hours.

When she was finally free to go, she had only half an hour to spare before Joe would be expecting her at the docks for her shift. She hastily scooted over to the club to find out if there was any more news about what had happened last night. Quickly she found a newspaper, but it just confirmed what Joe had already told her.

Disappointed, she made her way back to the club's entrance hall. It was an impressive space with a chandelier made from coral, ocean-coloured tiles on the floor and a display of the club's most impressive specimens hung upon the walls. There was a great octopus, a sea monster with hundreds of teeth, a stuffed snow shark and even an entire tentacle from the fearsome screeching red devil squid – one of the most terrifying monsters in all the Seventeen Seas – brought back by the Rook family.

Ursula saw that there was someone standing before this tentacle now, and realised it was Ethan Edward Rook himself. He wore his black explorer's robe and stood with his arms crossed over his chest, glaring at the squid trophy.

Ursula had wanted to speak to him ever since he'd arrived at the club. She felt a bit nervous about it but there was currently no one else around and this chance might not come again. Ethan was friends with Stella, which meant he was bound to know more about what had happened last night.

At last she gathered up her courage, walked over to him and cleared her throat. 'Um ... excuse me?'

Ethan turned to look at her and she was surprised to see that his blond hair was dishevelled rather than being neatly combed back as usual, and there were circles under his eyes as if he hadn't slept a wink.

'Is the submarine ready?' he asked, taking in her engineer's uniform.

'I don't know. I'm not working on your submarine.'

'What do you want then?' he snapped.

He seemed so irate that Ursula almost made her

excuses and left, but she forced herself to stand her ground and meet his gaze.

'I wanted to ask about Stella,' she said. 'Is she all right?'

Ethan looked taken aback for a moment, then gave a short nod. 'Yes, she is,' he said. He looked at Ursula again. 'Nice to know someone around here cares.'

'You've been on several expeditions with Stella, haven't you?' Ursula pressed on.

'That's right.'

'So can I ask you something?'

Ethan shrugged, which Ursula took as permission.

'Do you think girls can be good explorers too?' she said.

'What?' Ethan scowled again. 'Yes, of course. What kind of question is that? Look, I'm not in the mood to hear any more nonsense today. I've had enough from President Verne already.'

'I asked the president for permission to join the Ocean Squid Explorers' Club, but he said no,' Ursula hurried on. 'He says he doesn't care what the other clubs decide, but that Ocean Squid will remain men only.'

'Well, I don't know what you expect me to do about it.'

'I wasn't expecting you to do any—'

'Verne is an imbecile,' Ethan said. 'I've just spent all morning trying to convince him that we need to do something to help protect Stella and take action against the Collector, but he thinks we should stay out of it and just dawdle about on the sidelines like cowards.'

'Oh. That's not good.'

'Well, I'm not standing for it,' Ethan said. 'The other explorers can do what they like, but as soon as our submarine is ready, Father and I are going to help.'

'Is there anything I can do?' Ursula asked hopefully. She so wanted to be involved and make herself useful.

But Ethan shook his head. 'It's too dangerous.'

Ursula felt a flare of irritation. 'It's not too dangerous for Stella,' she pointed out.

'That's different,' Ethan said. 'Stella is an ice princess.'

And I'm a mermaid, Ursula longed to say, but knew she couldn't.

'But more importantly,' Ethan went on, 'she has a team to back her up. Look, I don't know how much you know about exploring, kid, but having a team is the most vital thing there is. When you're out on an expedition, you have to know there are people who have your back. Stella and our other friends, Shay and Beanie, have saved my skin several times over.'

Ursula was surprised to hear him speak that way.

Normally his focus seemed to be more on his own feats of bravery. Now she felt a dull ache of longing deep in her belly. What she would give for a team of her own. But if Verne wouldn't let her join the club then that would never happen.

'You can't do anything by yourself,' Ethan went on. 'So my advice is to stay here and work on the submarines.'

Before Ursula could argue further, another engineer came into the hall and told Ethan that his submarine was ready to depart. The young explorer immediately hurried towards the exit with barely a glance at Ursula, but then he suddenly paused in the doorway and turned back.

'What's your name?' he asked.

'Ursula Jellyfin.'

'Well, Ursula, don't give up on the Ocean Squid Explorers' Club,' he said. 'Everyone told Stella that she couldn't be an explorer too, but she wouldn't accept it.'

Ursula felt a little surge of hope at his words. 'I won't,' she promised.

Ethan nodded, then turned around and disappeared through the door, his cloak flying behind him. And she felt more determined than ever that one day she would have an explorer's cloak of her own.

CHAPTER SIX

Ursula threw herself into her engineering duties over the next couple of weeks, working as hard as she could to take her mind off things. She'd been keeping her eye on the newspapers and knew that there was to be an emergency meeting at the Sky Phoenix Explorers' Club today to discuss what to do about Scarlett Sauvage. All the clubs were attending except Ocean Squid, although Ursula supposed Ethan was there with his father. She so wished she could be there too, actually helping and being useful in some way. It seemed a terrible shame that Ocean Squid was the only club not present and she found it made her feel a little ashamed on their behalf.

Clearly she wasn't alone in feeling that way. She was about to go to the engineering bay to report for duty that morning when she noticed a hubbub outside the clubhouse. Of course, hubbubs and hullabaloos were nothing unusual at the club and Ursula assumed that a group of explorers had gathered there because they were admiring a sea-monster carcass someone had brought back, or something. But then she realised that a junior explorer had climbed on to the top tentacle of the squid statue outside the club and seemed to be giving some kind of speech.

She wandered over to see what was happening and gasped when she realised the young explorer was none other than Jai Bartholomew Singh. His looks alone made him ideally suited to be the club's poster boy because he was extremely handsome with a long, straight nose, black hair and brown skin. But he didn't just look the part – he was also an extraordinary explorer who had achieved all kinds of amazing things. People said he was one of the most fearless and intrepid members the club had seen in decades, and he'd been awarded more medals for valour than anyone else his age in the history of the club. He seemed to be wearing every single one of those medals now – they were pinned to his chest in neat rows, gleaming in the sun.

He was formally dressed in his black explorer's cloak, which had been adapted by removing most of the left sleeve. Jai's left arm ended at the elbow and sometimes, like now, he wore a prosthetic arm instead.

'. . . wake up and see what's happening,' he was saying.

'I truly believe that the Ocean Squid Explorers' Club can be the most wonderful club in the world.'

There was a cheer from the gathered explorers.

'But it's not at the moment,' Jai went on. 'Not any more. Over the years we've earned a reputation for foul play and cheating, for being underhanded, sneaky, cowardly and greedy. The villainous club. We must do something to clean up our image. We must remind ourselves of the importance of following the rules and playing fair. We are far more technologically advanced than any of the other clubs, and yet we refuse to share that knowledge and expertise with them. Being the only club that's not present at the Sky Phoenix Explorers' Club today reflects very poorly on us. As does the shameful decision not to allow girls to join.'

Ursula gasped and there was a murmuring in the crowd around her but she couldn't quite tell if it was approving or disapproving or even a mixture of both. But her own heart soared to hear Jai say such a thing in front of everybody like that. Except for Ethan Edward Rook, no one else had been brave enough to speak out publicly against the no-girls policy. To have someone so influential do so now made hope bubble up inside her. Perhaps things would change sooner than she'd thought after all.

'Girls wouldn't last five minutes in a submarine,' one of the explorers called out.

'That is nonsense, sir,' Jai replied, looking cross. 'My twin sister has spent much of her life on submarines.'

The explorers were shaking their heads. 'Girls haven't got the right skills,' another one called out. 'They'd slow down expeditions, get in the way and put everyone at risk.'

Jai shook his head and there was a note of despair in his voice when he said, 'You're mistaken. Girls can be valuable members of the crew. My sister has been indispensable when travelling by submarine. She's a whisperer.'

Ursula had always felt rather envious of whisperers. They were special people who could speak to a certain type of animal inside their heads, and the animal could speak back to them. Ursula had seen turtle whisperers, jellyfish whisperers and even octopus whisperers pass through during her time at the club. They all had what was known as a shadow animal that went with them everywhere and took the form of whatever creature they were able to speak to. It looked perfectly solid, but in fact had no substance at all, so a person's hand would pass straight through if they tried to touch it. No one knew quite what shadow animals were, or where they came from, but many people believed they were a part of the whisperer's own soul given visual form.

'What kind of whisperer?' one of the explorers called out.

Jai hesitated for a moment, but then gave his reply. Unfortunately, the explorer next to Ursula chose that moment to noisily clear his throat, meaning that she didn't hear Jai's answer. The other explorers did though and reacted most surprisingly. They all began muttering and shaking their heads and fidgeting in a disconcerted sort of way.

'Not possible,' one of the explorers said, sounding quite outraged. 'There's not a person alive who can whisper to a creature such as that.'

'What kind of whisperer is she?' the throat-clearing explorer asked, turning to Ursula.

'I don't know,' she said, frowning at him. 'You were clearing your throat too loudly.'

'Mollusc whisperer, probably,' the explorer on the other side of her said. 'People used to think no one could talk to molluscs but one was verified by the Guild just last month. Would be rather a one-sided conversation though, what?'

'Ha ha! Quite so!' the other explorer replied.

'Shh!' Ursula hissed. 'I'm trying to hear what he's saying!'

'... she'd be an asset to any expedition,' Jai was insisting from the statue. 'She'd certainly be more useful than the expedition barber many submarines have taken to having. It's a disgrace that she's not allowed to join the club. The girls applying to join the other clubs have got all kinds of skills and specialities. There are medics, mechanics, scientists, geologists, whisperers and witches. There's a great wealth of talent and experience out there that would be so valuable to our club if only we weren't stupid enough to turn it away. I urge you all to reconsider your position and sign the petition I will be pinning up outside the dining room. Thank you.'

He started to climb down from the squid statue. Many of the explorers were still shaking their heads and muttering but Ursula was pleased to note that there was a scattering of applause. It was small and quickly faded, but at least it was something. It was a start.

People began to drift away and Ursula saw Jai striding into the club looking determined. He took a piece of paper from the pocket of his cloak and she realised this must be the petition he was going to put up. She hurried through the crowd after him, determined that her name should be the first signatory on it. If she could pluck up the courage she also very much wanted to speak to Jai – to thank him and explain that she dreamed of being an explorer herself.

But someone must have gone straight to the president to tell him what Jai had said, because when Ursula turned into the corridor she saw that President Verne was marching towards Jai with a thunderous expression on his red face.

'Stop!' his voice rang out. 'Don't even *think* about putting that petition on the noticeboard!'

Jai paused. 'As a junior explorer I have the right to put up any petition of my choosing,' he said calmly.

President Verne was before him now and Ursula winced as he snatched the paper from Jai.

'You forget yourself, Singh,' he snapped. 'How dare you presume to lecture me?' He tore the petition into little pieces then shook his head and went on, 'You've been a great asset to this club but if you carry on spouting such dangerous opinions then, well, let's just say I'm not afraid to take drastic action to protect our institution.'

'With respect, sir,' Jai said, 'if you weren't afraid that other explorers might agree with me then you would let me put the petition on the wall.'

'We will continue this discussion in my office,' President Verne said.

'Might I ask my sister to join us?' Jai asked. 'She's travelled with me in the hope of gaining an audience with you. I'm certain that if you only met and spoke with her, you'd—'

'My office.' President Verne growled out the words. 'Now.'

He clamped a hand on Jai's shoulder and steered him away. Ursula watched them go, feeling helpless and frustrated. But there was nothing she could do and she was already late reporting for duty so she made her way to the engineering bay to find Joe.

'I'm sorry I'm late,' she began. 'It's just that Jai Bartholomew Singh was giving a speech and—'

'Never mind about that.' Joe waved her explanation away. 'Explorers are always giving speeches about one thing or another but that's nothing to do with us. We've got lots of work on today. Quite a few submarines in. Most of the fleet, actually.'

'Good,' Ursula said. She was keen to busy herself with the submarines to take her mind off President Verne, and the Collector, and the reputation of the Ocean Squid Club.

'Your friend's finally gone too far, by the way,' Joe said, handing Ursula her toolkit.

'What friend?'

For a moment she thought he was talking about Minty, but then he said, 'That explorer boy with the robots.'

'You mean Max?' Ursula started to grin. 'What's he done now?'

Ursula was always very careful never to break the rules as she didn't want to draw any unnecessary attention to herself and have anyone discover her secret. But she very much enjoyed hearing about all the ways Max found to get into trouble.

Joe shook his head though, and said, 'It ain't no laughing matter this time. He's really gone and done it. In fact, he's been thrown out of the club and is waiting in one of the subs to be taken back to the mainland. From there he'll be packed off home.'

'But what did he do?' Ursula asked, suddenly feeling concerned rather than amused.

'Conspired with pirates.'

'*What*?' Conspiring with pirates was one of the most serious charges that could be brought against an Ocean Squid explorer. It wasn't the kind of thing that merely got you a rap on the knuckles and a stern talking to. Pirates were a menace to Ocean Squid explorers and there had been worrying reports that their attacks on explorer ships had increased in recent months.

'But that can't be right!' Ursula said. 'Max wouldn't do a thing like that!'

Joe glanced at her. 'The truth is, you don't really know him, missy,' he said. 'So you don't know what he's capable of. Some of the explorers are decent enough but some of 'em are rotten.'

'Not Max,' Ursula said stubbornly. 'Someone must have made a mistake.'

'There ain't no mistake,' Joe said.

'How can you know?'

'Because he's admitted to it,' Joe replied.

Ursula could hardly believe it. She knew Max had a disregard for rules and authority, but he would never do something truly bad. Would he? Ursula couldn't think of a single reason why anyone would say they'd conspired with pirates if they hadn't. She recalled how Max had looked a little downcast last time she'd seen him and thought that there must be more to this than met the eye.

Ursula went through her work that morning with a bad taste in her mouth. She was worried about Max and thought maybe she should try to find him and hear his side of things. She decided to wait until lunch when there'd be fewer people around.

In the meantime, she worked so hard on the

submarines that she even got to one that wasn't scheduled for maintenance until tomorrow. Deciding she would get a head start, Ursula climbed on board only to hear the scuttling of hasty footsteps behind the walls and then a scraping sound coming from within the pipes. There was an interesting assortment of bogies stuck to the portholes too.

'Sea gremlins!' she exclaimed.

The little creatures had long been a problem on submarines, sneaking aboard and meddling with the machinery, biting through pipes and sticking objects into the propellers. The scourge of the Ocean Squid Explorers' Club, they had been responsible for countless explorer deaths over the years. No one had been able to explain why they did it but Ursula knew that recently Stella Starflake Pearl had claimed that the gremlins were in league with Scarlett Sauvage and acted on her orders. The Ocean Squid Club had denounced these claims as nonsense, but Ursula suspected that was simply because they didn't want to get involved in stopping the Collector.

'Get lost!' a croaky voice hissed through the air duct. 'Or I'll pelt you with bogies!'

Ursula glared up at the grate. It was definitely a sea gremlin. But what this one didn't know was that Ursula had been dealing with gremlins in submarines since she was seven years old. She rolled up her sleeves and put on her safety goggles so the gremlin couldn't use its favourite move of poking at her eyes with its long, dirty fingers. Then she dragged over a crate of Captain Ishmael's expedition-flavour smoked caviar and used it as a stool to reach the vent, which she quickly took off with a screwdriver. She heard the sea gremlin squeal as she launched herself into the vent and there was the sound of running footsteps as the creature fled.

They were extremely fast but, fortunately, Ursula knew the layout of all the submarines like the back of her hand and forced the gremlin back to the engine room where she knew it would be trapped. She dropped down into the room with a metallic clang as her boots hit the runway. Bulky machinery filled most of the space and Ursula quickly located the gremlin's nest, fashioned out of a cardboard box, in the corner.

She reached in and dragged the squirming gremlin out into the light. 'Gotcha!' she said triumphantly.

The little creature had pale blue skin, bulging bug eyes and big, bat-like ears.

'You're too late!' it shrieked as it twisted in her grasp.

'Too late for what?' Ursula demanded. 'I hope you haven't been biting through the pipes down here?'

'Not that!' the sea gremlin giggled. 'Something much, much worse!'

Ursula frowned. She'd never known a gremlin to wear clothes before but this one wore a green jacket with some kind of crest stamped on the lapel. She lifted the creature higher to peer at it and then gasped. It was the crest of the Phantom Atlas Society.

'You really are working for the Collector!' she exclaimed. 'What have you been up to?'

'Too late, too late!' the gremlin said gleefully. 'You'll never stop it now! She's coming! Hee hee hee!'

Ursula bent to peer into the nest. Sea gremlins were scavengers and she'd normally expect a nest to be full of bits and pieces they'd stolen from the crew: perhaps a marble, a few coins, a family photo, stuff like that. But this nest contained a radio and was full of papers.

While her attention was distracted, the gremlin suddenly bit her hard on the hand.

'Ouch!' Ursula dropped him and he fell to the ground before shooting off back into the pipe. She let him go and got down on her knees to drag out the papers. There was a whole load of them, covered in the gremlin's untidy scrawl. Ursula cast her eyes over them, and to her horror realised they were reports. The gremlin had obviously been hiding out here for several days and had been writing notes about the club's security. He'd confirmed that there were no phoenixes here, but sea cannons instead. He'd identified where they were positioned around the club, how they worked. Ursula looked back at the radio. The gremlin was obviously a spy and the emblem on his jacket made it quite clear who he was working for. He'd been secretly reporting to Scarlett Sauvage. Which meant that the entire club was in danger. The gremlin's words sounded over and over again in her head.

'*She's coming!*'

The papers fell through Ursula's fingers as she scrambled back to her feet. She had to get back to the club and warn everyone as quickly as possible. She pulled the submarine's keys from her pocket and ran to the door, but just as she slipped the key into the lock, there was a great rumble of an explosion from outside, ten times louder than thunder. Ursula was thrown back as shockwaves rocked the submarine in the water. And from outside came the sound of voices raised in fear and panic.

CHAPTER SEVEN

Ursula ran back through the submarine as fast as she could. She knew something terrible was happening above because the sub continued to roll and shudder in the water, despite the fact that it was moored in the shelter of the harbour.

Finally, she reached the top, threw back the hatch and climbed out on deck. Another explosion lit up the sky in a cloud of red-and-orange flames, throwing debris into the ocean. Ursula staggered to the rails and gripped them hard, trying to make sense of what she was seeing. Two of the sea cannons outside the club lay in piles of smoking rubble. The boardwalk was crawling with sea gremlins, hundreds and hundreds of them. Ursula couldn't believe it. The submarines were regularly checked for gremlins. How could so many possibly have gone undetected?

Then she realised they hadn't been hiding – they were only just arriving. The sky above the club was full of parachutes, each bearing a grinning gremlin. The second they touched down they ran straight for a cannon. Ursula saw two of them stuff something inside one before throwing a lit match in after it that blew the whole thing to bits, starting several small fires around the dock.

Explorers ran about, trying to put out the fires and see off the gremlins, but they were outnumbered. Several of the expedition ships were on fire, their scorched sails in tatters. The explorers pointed up at the sky yelling and Ursula thought they were indicating the parachuting sea gremlins at first, but then she realised they were actually pointing to the thing that was dropping them.

Ursula gaped as a flying machine passed straight over her head. It was an amazing winged thing that travelled much faster than any hot-air balloon or dirigible. It zoomed across the sky leaving a trail of smoke in its wake. Ursula caught a glimpse of its pilot – a young woman with a mass of dark hair trailing from beneath her leather aviator's cap and a pair of goggles over her eyes. The flying machine bore the symbol of the Phantom Atlas Society and an iron cage dangled beneath it from a chain. This cage had obviously once been full of sea gremlins but as Ursula watched, the final ones leaped from between the bars to create havoc in the club below.

She scrambled from the submarine, slipping and sliding her way down the ladder, and began to run along the pier. If only someone could get to one of the remaining sea cannons before the gremlins destroyed it, then perhaps they could use it to chase Scarlett away . . .

But as her eyes swept down the length of the boardwalk, she saw that there didn't seem to be a single cannon left. And that meant the club was defenceless against an airborne attack. Everyone was running around, shouting, and there were some explorers crumpled on the floor who'd clearly been hurt in the explosions. But when Ursula looked back up at the flying machine she saw the glint of a snow globe and realised there was no more time. The sea gremlins were diving back into the ocean and swimming away.

The club was about to be taken and if she wasn't careful then she'd be snatched away too, a prisoner inside the globe. There was nothing she could do to stop it but perhaps she could save one small piece of the club.

Acting on autopilot, she untied the ropes of the nearest submarine – a long, sleek one called the

Blowfish – and then threw herself into the water. Her legs immediately turned into a mermaid's fin, ripping through her coveralls. Ursula struggled out of them and, wearing only her vest top, grabbed the submarine's rope and pulled as hard as she could, desperately trying to tug it to safety. It was so heavy, though, and she began to despair of moving it by herself. She looked back at the submarine and thought she saw faces peering out of the porthole. In that moment, she didn't even feel horrified that explorers might have discovered her secret. All she could think about was saving the Ocean Squid members on board. Then Minty appeared at her side, grabbed hold of another rope, and together they were able to move the submarine through the water, away from the club.

And not a moment too soon.

Ursula knew that the club had been snatched away. The waves and ripples it made in the water pushed the submarine out even further. Keeping hold of the rope, Ursula swam up to the surface and looked back towards where the club should have been.

It had completely vanished. There was absolutely nothing there. The boardwalks were gone, along with the submarines that had been docked beside them. The starfish building had gone, along with the sea-flower garden and jellyfish nursery, and even the white sandy beach, leaving only piles of crumbly dirt. It was like the Ocean Squid Explorers' Club had never existed at all.

'No!' Ursula said, tightening her grip on the rope.

With a loud revving of its engine, the flying machine above turned in a big arc and then shot out over the sea, taking its new prize with it. Tears filled Ursula's eyes as she thought of Joe and Mutt locked away inside the snow globe, along with the president and everyone else.

Her hands trembled and she took a deep breath as she tried to work out what to do. The nearest island was miles away. Perhaps she should go straight there and raise the alarm? But there were people inside the submarine, so surely they would spread the word on their radio? The crew must have flooded the ballast tanks with water, because already the submarine's nose was sinking into the water, preparing to dive beneath the surface. The submarine was all that remained of the Ocean Squid Explorers' Club and Ursula longed to go on board, but if they'd seen her through the portholes then they would know she was a mermaid. They'd probably shoot her with a harpoon gun if they got half the chance.

A sudden surge of fear flooded through her as she realised what danger she was in. She would have to flee – she didn't have any choice. She was just casting one last despairing look back at the empty island, when something bit her hard on the tail.

Ursula cried out and dived underwater only to find herself surrounded by sea gremlins. It seemed some of them hadn't swum away after all, and now they fell on her at once. Ursula could deal with one or two of them by herself, but there must have been almost fifty of them in the water with her now, each one scratching and biting.

Minty tried to come to her aid by charging, but they were completely outnumbered. One gremlin bit Ursula on her neck, another scratched her arm and a third sank its teeth into the fin of her tail. She could feel a hopeless blind panic rising up as she struggled amongst them. Suddenly, the ocean lit up with a bright white light.

The sea gremlins were extremely sensitive to light and released her immediately, letting out streams of bubbles as they shrieked and clapped their hands over their large eyes. Ursula turned and saw that there was a diver in the water. The propulsion technology in his suit kept him from sinking to the seabed and he was attached to a chain that led back to the submarine. She couldn't make out much of his appearance as he was encased in the suit with a big helmet fastened on top, but she saw that he held a flare gun, which he used to fire another flare into the water.

The gremlins scattered, and seeing that Ursula had back-up, Minty vanished too. The diver clamped his hand around her wrist and gestured back to the submarine. The next moment the chain was being reeled in, taking them both with it. Ursula could hardly believe it. It seemed that the explorer was actually rescuing her. She thought of Joe's unexpected reaction to her being a mermaid and wondered whether she'd been wrong to keep it a secret all these years. Perhaps people would understand after all.

She quickly found herself drawn into the swim-out chamber, the hatch slammed shut and the water began to race towards the corners as it ran back out into the sea. It had soon drained away completely and oxygen flooded back into the room from the air vents.

As soon as it did so, the hatch burst open and a girl with brown skin and glossy black hair rushed into the room. She must have been right outside at the control panel and Ursula guessed she was the one who'd reeled them back in. She looked the same age as Ursula and was, rather startlingly, dressed in sparkly pink cowgirl boots, a blue and green striped top with a seahorse on it and an elaborate knitted hat in the shape of a pink octopus, whose tentacles trailed down her back.

The diver struggled out of his helmet and, to Ursula's surprise, he wasn't an adult either. He was an explorer she recognised instantly – Jai Bartholomew Singh.

Ursula felt relief flood through her. Of all the people who might have come to her rescue, Jai was probably the best possible person. Surely he would know what to do about the Collector and how to put things right. Suddenly she had the most wonderful vision of them becoming a team and doing it together, and the idea pushed some of her worry and fear about the Collector's attack to one side. Instead there was excitement and happiness at the idea of going on a rescue expedition with Jai Bartholomew Singh himself!

But all of that vanished when Jai snatched up a harpoon that had been clipped to the wall and pointed it directly at her.

'Don't even think of attacking us!' he warned.

'*Attacking* you?' Ursula repeated, frowning in sudden confusion.

'Now,' Jai said, his eyes bright with fear, 'you're going to tell us everything you know about how you and the Collector managed to steal the club.'

CHAPTER EIGHT

The bright lights overhead shone down, making Ursula feel very exposed where she sprawled on the wet floor. She had nothing to dry her tail with so she couldn't turn back into a human. The inside of her head seemed to ring with dismay as she realised that they hadn't rescued her after all – they had *captured* her! And they believed that she was working with the Collector; that somehow she had helped steal the club. Jai was still staring suspiciously down the length of the harpoon at her, and behind him the girl looked just as shocked. Both of them were staring at Ursula as if she was a villain.

'Oh!' Ursula exclaimed. 'Oh no, listen, I'm not working *with* the Collector! I'm as horrified about what's happened as you are!'

Before Jai could reply, the hatch leading to the rest of the submarine burst open again and a second boy ran in with a robot penguin tucked under his arm. He wore a pair of black jeans and a white T-shirt which had a picture of a robot duck on it, complete with laser-beam eyes.

'What did I miss?' he gasped.

It was Maxwell Xavier Clark. Ursula recalled what Joe had told her earlier about Max being on board one of the submarines, ready to be taken back to the mainland.

'Max!' she gasped, pleased to see a familiar face.

He stared at her. '*Ursula?*'

'Do you two know each other?' Jai said. He kept the harpoon trained on Ursula but was looking at Max. 'And why have you got that robot penguin?'

Max set the penguin down. 'It's the only one of my robots that hasn't been confiscated, so I decided to come to your aid since you were mad enough to bring a mermaid on board our submarine,' he said. 'I thought for sure she'd be singing you to an early grave by now.'

'You can't seriously expect us to believe that you meant to rescue us with a robot penguin?' Jai said, looking disbelieving.

'Believe what you like, but it's the truth,' Max replied. 'That penguin can flay a person alive with its laser-beam eyes.'

Ursula frowned. She recognised the penguin because

it was one of Max's own inventions and he had shown it to her on one of his previous visits to the club. 'No it can't,' she said. 'It's a popcorn maker.'

'Ah.' Max looked sheepish. 'So it is. But it *could* have had laser-beam eyes. And it is extremely strong – this penguin could pick up a carriage if it had to. In my defence, I wasn't expecting the mermaid to be a friend of mine who'd already seen the robot.'

'Perhaps you should stop pointing that harpoon at her,' the girl said to Jai. 'It's very rude. And she'd probably be more willing to answer your questions if you asked them nicely.'

Ursula shot the girl a grateful look. 'My name's Ursula Jellyfin,' she said. 'I'm an engineer at the club. I'm also half mermaid but I had nothing to do with what just happened, I swear! The Ocean Squid Explorers' Club has been my home for the last five years and I love it. I hope more than anything that I can join it as an explorer one day. I was raised by humans. I can't speak for other mermaids but *I* would never drown anyone. Ever.'

'She's telling the truth, at least about the engineer bit,' Max said. 'I'll vouch for her. She's been at the club for years. She—'

'You don't get to vouch for anyone!' Jai snapped. 'Why do you think we're going to set any store by what *you* say? A known pirate conspirer. If anything, your recommendation counts against her. You're both in this together for all we know. We've already got the Phantom Atlas Society and sea gremlins in the mix – why not just throw in pirates and disgraced explorers and mermaids as well?'

'It sounds like a rip-roaring time, that's for sure,' Max replied.

'Do you think this is a *joke*?' Jai demanded. 'It's a total disaster!'

'It's not a *total* disaster,' the girl said. 'If it was a total disaster, then we would have been stolen away along with our submarine and now be in a snow globe. If you look at it like that we've actually been tremendously lucky—'

'Genie, for heaven's sake, now is not the time for your optimism!' Jai snapped. 'We've just witnessed a horrific attack on the Ocean Squid Explorers' Club, the likes of which has never been heard of before!'

'That's too bad,' Max replied. 'What will we do without a bunch of old men telling us off all the time?'

At that, Jai moved the harpoon away from Ursula to point it at Max instead. '*Are* you involved in this? It wouldn't surprise me one bit to discover that you've been in cahoots with the Collector all along.'

Max raised his eyebrows. 'I've never heard anyone use the word "cahoots" in normal conversation before,' he said. 'Are you for real, or did the club make you in some sort of petri dish?'

The girl cleared her throat. 'He was definitely born in the normal way,' she said. 'I know because we're twins. My name is Genie Delilah Singh.' She moved around her brother to stand in front of Ursula. 'So let's get this straight. Are you saying you had nothing to do with the Collector's attack and that you don't mean us any harm?'

'Yes!' Ursula said. 'That's exactly what I'm saying. The Collector sent her sea gremlins to spy on the club and disarm the cannons. It was nothing to do with me.'

'Why did you draw our submarine away then?' Genie asked.

'I was trying to save you,' Ursula replied. 'As you said yourself, it would have been sucked up inside the snow globe otherwise and stolen away with everything else.'

'How can we know you're telling the truth?' Jai said. 'How do we know you didn't move the submarine for some other reason?'

'Well … I guess you can't,' Ursula said. 'But what other reason could I have?'

'Perhaps you mean to hijack the submarine and join the Collector?' Jai said. 'I've never heard of a mermaid rescuing an explorer before.'

'Well, I have,' Genie said. 'Stella Starflake Pearl wrote about it in her Flag Report, remember? Some mermaids helped her and her team when they found themselves stranded in the ocean on that inflatable hippo.'

'Mermaids are responsible for more deaths in the Ocean Squid Explorers' Club than kraken, squid and sharks combined!' Jai said.

Genie crossed her arms over her chest. 'Well, I think we should judge this one for how she's treated us, not for rumours about her people. Remember what Papa said about how explorer disappearances were automatically blamed on mermaids and that we don't really know how dangerous they are?'

A dark look came over Jai's face. 'Why would we listen to anything our father said? We may as well start taking advice from Clark over there.' He jerked his head towards Max.

'I'm more than happy to give you the benefit of my advice,' Max said. 'For starters, don't wear every single one of your medals all the time, everywhere you go. It makes you look like a chump.'

'Papa might not have been a very good man,' Genie

said quietly to Jai. 'But he was a good explorer.' She gestured back at Ursula and said, 'She's got bites all over her tail from the sea gremlins and if she's telling the truth, then she just saved all of our lives and we've done a pretty poor job of thanking her.'

Ursula felt so grateful to the other girl for sticking up for her that she could almost have cried.

'The most important thing to do right now is get to the bridge and message for help,' Genie went on 'We need to let the other clubs know what's happened.'

'You're right,' Jai agreed. He looked at Ursula and said, 'Look, if I've misjudged you then I'm sorry, but you can't blame me for being cautious. The rest of our team were in the club when the Collector attacked, meaning that responsibility for this submarine and everyone on it now falls to me.'

'It's fine,' Ursula said. 'Have you got a towel or something? I need to dry my tail to get my legs back.'

'There are some towels and robes in the next room,' Max said. 'I'll fetch them.'

Jai propped the harpoon up against the wall and struggled out of his diving suit until he stood in just his trunks. Max came back with towels and robes, and Ursula slipped gratefully into hers, which was a dark blue colour and stamped with the Ocean Squid crest.

'Could someone help me over to the doorway?' she asked.

'I will.' Max came over to crouch in front of her. 'Put your arms around my neck,' he said.

Ursula did as he said and he lifted her up and took her over to the doorway, where he set her down carefully.

'How do you manage to make yourself look like a human anyway?' Max asked curiously.

'My mum is a mermaid, but my dad was human,' Ursula said. 'So I'm both.'

'How extraordinary!' Max marvelled.

Ursula towelled off her tail, noticing that the bite and scratch marks from the gremlins became identical marks on her legs when she was finally dry. She tied the robe around her waist and stood up, glad she could finally face the others eye to eye.

'We'll decide what to do about you later,' Jai said, clearly still not convinced. 'But first we have to signal for help.'

CHAPTER NINE

Ursula followed the other children down several corridors with gleaming wooden floors and shiny brass fittings. They made their way to the bridge, which was full of machinery, all covered in different dials and buttons and lights. There was a periscope in the middle, allowing them to see above the surface, and a big wheel for steering the submarine. Several large portholes looked out at the ocean and Ursula was glad there was no sign of any sea gremlins.

Jai went straight to the radio and picked it up, but then hesitated.

'What are you waiting for?' Max demanded.

'I'm just thinking about who to call,' Jai said. 'Normally I'd send out a distress signal to the club but I don't suppose we'll be able to reach them inside the snow globe.'

'Give it a try anyway!' Genie said immediately. 'Maybe it will work and we'll be able to speak to someone and see if they're all OK.'

Ursula felt a flash of hope at the thought of being able to check on Joe, but when Jai adjusted the signals, nothing came back to them but static.

'Well, it was worth a go,' Genie said, looking deflated.

'Call the Sky Phoenix Explorers' Club,' Ursula suggested. 'They're having an emergency meeting there today, aren't they? I think representatives from all the clubs are supposed to be there. Except Ocean Squid, of course.'

'Good idea.' Jai flicked through the radio signals book until he found the newly added wavelength for the Sky Phoenix Club. He fiddled with the dials again and they all listened as he rang through to the other end. 'Mayday, mayday, mayday,' he said. 'Come in.'

There was a crackle of static, and then to their relief a somewhat peeved voice came through.

'Is that you again, Rudyard?' the man snapped. 'If you've got another phoenix stuck in the fire maze then I really am going to be very cross.'

Max sniggered. 'You do sound like a Rudyard,' he said.

Jai scowled. 'This isn't Rudyard,' he said. He puffed out his chest slightly and said in an important voice, 'My name is Jai Bartholomew Singh.'

'Never heard of him,' the man replied.

Jai looked aghast. 'Never heard of me?' he exclaimed.
'I like that! I'm only the first junior explorer to ever
face a deep-cave shark and live to tell the tale. To say
nothing of the fact that I saved the yodelling turtle
from extinction, discovered an entirely new type of
plankton and single-handedly rescued a scientific
expedition that was swept up in a whirlpool in the
Frozen North Sea and—'

'Jai, don't be a silly billy,' Genie said. 'The Sky
Phoenix Club has been stuck inside a snow globe for
the last hundred years. Of course they have no idea
who you are.'

'I can't believe you saved the yodelling turtle from
extinction,' Max said, looking amazed. 'Surely if any
animal ever should have been allowed to slide quietly
into extinction it's the yodelling turtle.'

'I don't think it would have been quiet,' Ursula
couldn't resist saying. 'They probably would have been
yodelling all the way.'

Genie snatched the radio and elbowed Jai aside.
'Hello. My name is Genie Delilah Singh. I'm calling
from the *Blowfish* submarine, of the Ocean Squid
Explorers' Club.'

'What?' the voice exclaimed. 'You've misdialled.
This is the Sky Phoenix Explorers' Club. If you need

help, then you should phone your own club. We're miles and miles away from your location. Besides which, we haven't the time to be rescuing every Ocean Squid explorer who finds himself tangled up in a lobster net.'

'We're not tangled up in a lobster net,' Jai said, leaning over his sister to speak into the radio. 'And the Ocean Squid Explorers' Club is gone.'

'Gone?' the voice barked. 'Nonsense.'

'It really has!' Genie said. 'We saw it happen. The Collector came in a flying machine and stole it away in one of her snow globes.'

There was a long pause. Then the voice said, 'Wait a second. I'm going to patch you through to the meeting room.'

They waited several minutes before a fruity voice came through. 'This is Alistair Fox Jacob, the president of the Sky Phoenix Explorers' Club. Now what's all this about the Ocean Squid Explorers' Club disappearing?'

Genie repeated the story and they heard a great gasp at the other end from more than one person.

Then a girl's voice rang out. 'I *told* you this was Scarlett's plan! Maybe now you'll take me seriously!'

They heard several people all speaking at once in a great cacophony. Ursula realised they must have been patched through to the meeting. Which surely meant that the girl's voice had belonged to Stella Starflake Pearl herself!

'What the blazes?' President Jacob said. 'Look here, who am I talking to?'

'I'm Genie Delilah Singh. I'm here with my brother, Jai.'

'Surely you're not the only two on board?'

Genie glanced at Max and Ursula but before she could reply, Jai took the receiver from her and said, 'Sir, the *Blowfish* is also carrying an expelled explorer named Maxwell Xavier Clark and a half mermaid called Ursula Jellyfin.'

Ursula bit back a groan. She'd hoped that he wouldn't give her away but now it seemed her secret was really out for good.

'Expelled explorer?' the president spluttered. 'Half mermaid? Good Lord!'

'We're all that's left,' Jai went on. 'The rest of our crew was inside the club when it happened.'

'How old are you?'

'Twelve.'

'Good Lord!' the president said again. 'Isn't there an adult with you?'

'No, it's just us.'

'Good Lord!'

There was a slight commotion on the other end of the line and they heard President Jacob exclaim, 'There's no need to snatch!'

Then a new male voice spoke. 'Did you say your submarine is the *Blowfish*?'

'That's right.'

'Wasn't the *Blowfish* supposed to be taking the Sunken City of Pacifica back to its coordinates?'

'Yes,' Jai confirmed. 'After we'd stopped off at the mainland to drop off Clark and my sister. The snow globe is in the submarine's safe.'

'You have it?' the voice said eagerly. 'Listen, that globe may well be one of the most important weapons we have in the fight against Scarlett Sauvage. The inhabitants of Pacifica are said to be blessed with psychic abilities. If we help free them, then the hope is that they will assist us to track down Sauvage's whereabouts. As it stands, she's always one step ahead of us, always giving us the slip.'

Ursula felt a great surge of excitement rise up in her chest. Here, at last, was a chance to be useful and to do something that mattered.

'We can do it,' Jai said at once. 'We'll take the lost island back. The submarine is already stocked with all the supplies we might need for the expedition, including eleven thousand tea bags, two thousand ship's biscuits and eight hundred toilet rolls. Just give us the coordinates and we can—'

'Don't be absurd, boy!' President Jacob came back on the line. 'One explorer can't possibly assume responsibility for this mission. It's far too important. Far too dangerous.'

'We'd really like to help, though—' Genie began.

'Absolutely out of the question,' President Jacob said. 'It's a journey of several hundred nautical miles, there aren't enough of you to man the submarine and you don't even have a crewman who can maintain it—'

'Yes, we do. I'm a mechanic,' Ursula said. 'I earned my first dolphin recently. I can keep the submarine running all right.'

'And I'm a robot inventor,' Max said, leaning in. 'I have some engineering knowledge as well.'

'Good Lord, is that the disgraced explorer and the mermaid speaking?' President Jacob said. 'Put Jai back on the line at once.'

Jai held the receiver closer to his face and said, 'Hello, sir, it's me.'

'See here, boy, the expelled lad and the mermaid ought to be in the brig. I don't know what you were thinking of, letting them up on the bridge!'

'Well, I ought to say that the mermaid may not be a threat to us,' Jai said, looking uncomfortable. 'There's a chance she saved our submarine from the Collector.'

'Don't be absurd, she's a *mermaid*. You must make your way to the nearest island and dock the submarine there. Then you will hand your mermaid over to the authorities and the disgraced explorer will be sent home. In the meantime, an adult explorer party will be sent to take over the submarine and its mission. Are my instructions quite clear?'

For a moment Ursula thought Jai was going to argue further, but then his shoulders seemed to slump and he simply said, 'Yes, sir. Quite clear.'

'Good. You and your sister will return to your family too, of course, assuming they weren't all in the club?'

'Our father left our family some time ago,' Jai said. 'He has no contact with us. And our mother is working abroad.'

'Well, don't worry. We will discuss the matter here and I'm sure one of the other clubs can take you in until your own is recovered, or your mother returns. Certainly the Sky Phoenix Explorers' Club would be more than happy to have you as our guests. But, for now, all you have to do is concentrate on getting to the nearest island. Take heart, my boy, help is on the way.'

'What a load of old baloney,' Genie said as they ended the call and hung up the radio. 'Those silly old duffers! We're going to waste so much time waiting for them to come and fetch the submarine. It'll take them two weeks at least, and that's if they leave straightaway.'

'Which they probably won't,' Ursula sighed. Explorers were quite notorious for fussing about, wasting time, packing and repacking all their bits and bobs. 'Stella Starflake Pearl and her friends are our age and they've done all kinds of amazing things. They ought to have trusted us to deliver the snow globe.'

'You could always ignore them and set off anyway,' Max suggested. 'If you could bring yourself to break a rule for once.'

'We would all need to go,' Ursula said. 'This type of submarine is meant to have a twenty-man crew but it requires four crew members minimum. And you're not likely to find anyone else who can do it since most of the Ocean Squid Explorers' Club has just been snatched away.'

It was a good point. There might be a few submarines out on expeditions that had avoided the attack but they could be anywhere and it would take an age to hunt them down.

'Well, it's irrelevant anyway,' Jai said. 'We can't

return the snow globe because we haven't got the coordinates for the Sunken City of Pacifica. We can't take it back where it came from without them because we wouldn't know where to go.'

Ursula felt her hopes deflating. It seemed like Jai was right and their adventure was doomed to be over before it had even begun.

But then the light on the radio station started flashing again and a girl's voice came through.

'Are you four still there?'

Jai snatched up the receiver. 'Yes, this is the *Blowfish*, Jai speaking. Who's that?'

'I'm Stella Starflake Pearl. I'd like to speak to Ursula, please.'

Ursula gasped. Jai paused a moment, then shrugged and handed the receiver over to her. Ursula clutched it tightly. She could hardly believe she was going to speak to the first female explorer herself.

'Hello?' she said, her voice coming out a bit of a squeak.

'Are you the Ursula that Ethan told me about?' Stella asked. 'The one who wants to be an explorer?'

'Yes, that's me!'

'Well, this might be your chance. Look, the adult explorers will spend ages dithering over who to send after you, and then it'll take them weeks to get there and we don't have time to waste. Scarlett Sauvage is very dangerous and if we don't stop her she's sure to turn on the other clubs next. I have the coordinates for the Sunken City of Pacifica. It comes from deep in the Bubble Ocean so President Jacob was right when he said it was hundreds of nautical miles away.'

Ursula's breath caught in her throat at Stella's mention of the Bubble Ocean – the very place where her mother lived.

'Much of that sea hasn't been properly explored,' the ice princess went on, 'so I daresay you might face all kinds of terrible peril. But if you're willing to take on these hazards, and if you're prepared to get in trouble with the other clubs, then I think you ought to carry out the mission yourselves.'

'You haven't asked me if I'm dangerous or if I mean to drown the crew,' Ursula blurted.

There was a pause. Then Stella said, 'Why would I? I haven't asked the rest of your team that question either. I'm afraid I'm going to have to hang up now or else they'll realise I'm gone and might get suspicious. Let me give you those coordinates and then you can talk it over with the others and decide what you're going to do.'

In her excitement, Ursula could barely breathe. Suddenly it seemed as though submarine voyages, daring rescue missions and a brand-new crew to have adventures with might be on the cards after all. And, most thrillingly of all, if she ventured out further into the ocean, then she might, after all this time, finally get to see a water horse.

CHAPTER TEN

'I say we do it,' Max said as soon as they'd ended the call with Stella.

'Me too,' Ursula and Genie both said at the same time and then smiled at each other.

Everyone looked at Jai, who was silent for a long moment, apparently wrestling with some inner dilemma. Ursula really hoped he wasn't about to spoil everything.

'Typical,' Max said. 'You never met a rule you didn't like. I suppose you wouldn't even contemplate breaking one as big as this.'

'Rules are important,' Jai snapped. 'They're there for a reason. But the president of the Sky Phoenix Explorers' Club isn't *my* president. He's got no authority over me. My responsibility is to the Ocean Squid Explorers' Club and it can't be right that we abandon them to their fate at the hands of the Collector.'

Ursula felt a surge of hope rise in her chest. Perhaps Jai's affinity for rules wasn't going to get in the way after all.

'I want to go on the mission to return the Sunken City,' he went on. 'But not with you two! I need a team I can trust.'

'You can trust me,' Ursula hurried to say.

'You absolutely can't trust me,' Max said. 'I'm completely untrustworthy. And I don't particularly care about saving the club either. I just want to go because it sounds fun.'

'Shut up!' Ursula said, jabbing him in the ribs. Usually she enjoyed how flippant Max could be but, right now, she was afraid he was going to ruin it for both of them.

'You know you can trust me,' Genie said cheerfully to her brother. 'The rest we'll just have to figure out as we go.'

Jai took a deep breath. 'Very well,' he said. 'We need four people and we're the only four available.' He eyed the other two warily and said, 'I guess we'll have to put our personal differences aside and call a truce for the duration of this rescue mission.'

Ursula could feel a huge grin spreading over her face. 'You won't regret this,' she promised.

Genie was grinning too. 'I know we can do it.'

'That's all very well,' Max said. 'But you haven't heard my demands yet.'

Everyone stared at him.

'*Demands?*' Jai choked.

'Certainly. If you're expecting me to go tearing off into treacherous, dangerous, uncharted waters, all to save a club I don't care about – that's just expelled me, no less – then you've been drinking too much of Captain Ishmael's expedition-strength salted rum.'

'This is an outrage!' Jai exclaimed.

'For starters,' Max said, 'I want all of my confiscated robots returned to me.'

'Absolutely not,' Jai replied.

'Quiet, please, I'm not finished.' Max help up his hand. 'I also want to wear the captain's hat.'

He gestured to where the said hat hung from a hook beside the captain's chair.

'*I'm* the highest-ranking explorer on board!' Jai exclaimed. 'In fact, I'm the only explorer on board full stop, since you've been expelled from the club, so if anyone's going to wear that hat it ought to be me.'

'And finally,' Max went on, as if Jai hadn't spoken. 'I want one of your medals. I don't mind which one. You can pick.'

Jai stared at him for a moment, looking utterly horrified.

'Why?' he finally said. 'My medals don't mean anything to you.'

'But they mean something to *you*,' Max replied. 'And that's the point.'

Jai shook his head. 'Not a chance.'

Max shrugged, then walked over to sit in the captain's seat. 'Robots, hat, medal,' he said, counting them off on his fingers. 'If you want me to join this mission, then that's my price.'

Ursula frowned. It seemed fair enough to her that he should have his robots back, but the captain's hat and the medal were pushing it a bit.

Jai looked like he might be sick, but after his various suggestions, threats and cajolements were ineffective, he gritted his teeth and said, 'Fine.'

He grabbed the captain's hat and threw it across the room to him.

'Thanks a million, old chum,' Max said, putting it straight on his head with a smug expression.

'Don't call me your chum,' Jai practically snarled. 'We are not friends. We'll sort the robots and medal out later. First we have to see to some things that are actually important.'

Genie was already at the navigating station and the other three joined her to spread out an assortment of maps alongside a battered copy of *Captain Filibuster's Guide to Sea Monsters*.

'Has anyone ever plotted a route before?' Ursula asked.

'I have,' Jai replied, dumping an assortment of compasses and sextants on the table. He drew one of the maps closer. 'Right now we're in the Jelly Ocean, but that's next to the Voltic, and we'll have to pass through part of that in order to reach the Bubble Ocean.' He pointed at another spot on the map. 'As long as there are no mishaps, I calculate that the trip will take about two weeks.'

Since Stella was right about much of the Bubble Ocean being unexplored, Ursula couldn't help thinking it was highly unlikely there would be no mishaps. They were pretty much inevitable when exploring new places.

'We've got plenty of rations and fuel,' Jai went on, 'but the water tanks haven't been topped up. That was due to happen this afternoon, I think. There's only a small amount of water left in the tanks so we'll have to replenish our supplies somewhere.'

'Ooh, can we stop at the Island of Fairy Giraffes?' Genie said, pointing at the map. 'I've always wanted to see them!'

'This isn't a tourist trip, Genie,' Jai replied.

'Actually,' Ursula said, 'the Island of Fairy Giraffes is quite a good choice because it's right on the edge of the Jelly Ocean. If we stop there, then hopefully we won't need to stop in the Voltic.'

She opened up *Captain Filibusters' Guide to Sea Monsters* to the Voltic section, where its subheading read: *A Vast Sea Where There Is Nothing But the Abode of Sea Monsters.*

'How encouraging,' Max remarked, peering over Ursula's shoulder as she flicked through several pages detailing the multiple scary monsters they might find.

'It's all right,' Jai said. 'We have the emergency trumpet.' He indicated the glass case on the wall of the bridge. Inside it was a trumpet, and a sign on the wall above instructed them to use the attached hammer to break the glass in an emergency. 'Captain Filibuster says that most attacking whales will be frightened off if someone goes out on deck and plays the trumpet at them.'

Ursula frowned. 'I don't know all that much about whales but that doesn't seem very likely,' she said.

'Good grief, you're not questioning the sacred wisdom of Captain Filibuster, are you?' Max exclaimed in mock horror. 'He's revered in the explorers' world, you know, so we all have to go along with whatever he says, no matter how ludicrously daft. If you ask me, Captain Filibuster is probably responsible for far more explorer deaths than mermaids.'

'No one is asking you,' Jai snapped. 'Can't you show a little respect? Captain Filibuster is one of the greatest explorers our world has ever known. The literature he's produced is the most comprehensive guide to exploring we have. I've got all the guides. *To Expeditions and Exploration*, obviously, but also the ones about *Forbidden Islands*, *Yetis and Snow Monsters*, *Raft Adventures*, *Mountain Adventures* and—'

'What a hopeless nerd,' Max said.

'Some of them are signed first editions!' Jai said defiantly.

'That just makes it worse.'

'Well, I'm glad we have the *Sea Monsters* guide,' Genie said, looking at the book on the table. 'Although I'm sure that most sea monsters are very misunderstood. *They* don't think they're monsters, after all. They're just going about their ordinary business and then some ship comes across them and starts panicking and shooting cannons and harpoons at them. It's no wonder they fight back.'

'Well, I still hope we don't come across the head-crunching terror whale,' Max said, pointing at a rather horrifying, and unnecessarily graphic, drawing in the book.

'Or the juggling purple clown octopuses,' Jai said, frowning. 'I can't stand juggling.'

'I can juggle,' Max said.

'I'm not surprised,' Jai replied.

'At least they haven't got mime squids,' Ursula said. 'But it looks like there are spiky eels.' She sighed. 'I don't suppose it says anything in there about water horses, does it?'

Genie shook her head. 'Afraid not.'

'Well, we knew this was going to be dangerous,' Jai pointed out. 'The submarine is equipped with harpoon guns and a sea cannon. And the emergency trumpet of course. We should be able to frighten away most of these monsters if we're unlucky enough to come across them, or at least outrun them. The submarine can reach top speeds of fifty knots.'

The expedition was bound to be frightening at times, and part of Ursula wished they had more experienced adult explorers on board to help, but the rest of her was secretly thrilled that they got to be in charge of the whole submarine and mission by themselves. The adults would never have allowed her to come anyway. And, most importantly of all, there was Joe and Mutt to think of, and the club itself.

'We'll chart a course for the Island of Fairy Giraffes first,' Jai said. He glanced at Ursula and said, 'Do you know how to start up the engine? I suppose you must do if you're an engineer?'

Ursula nodded, feeling extremely grateful for her training.

'It'll take two of us so I'll need someone to help me.'

She'd been telling the truth to President Jacob – she knew every inch of these submarines and could clean, maintain, repair and operate them effortlessly. But there was something she wanted to do before they set off.

'I need to go back into the sea for a few minutes first,' she said.

Jai immediately looked suspicious. 'Why?' he asked.

'To pick up some of my belongings.'

'Belongings?' Max raised an eyebrow. 'But the whole club's been stolen away. Are you planning on doing a runner? That's probably what I'd do in your situation.'

'I'm not going to do a runner,' Ursula said, rolling her eyes. 'I have a cave under the sea. My ... my mermaid mother visits me there once a year on my birthday. It has all my presents from her in it. I don't want to leave them behind.'

'Absolutely!' Genie exclaimed. 'You must fetch them.'

'I don't know,' Jai said, looking unsure. 'You could just swim off and we'd never see you again.'

'Am I a prisoner on this submarine?' Ursula asked.

'Of course not!' Jai replied, looking shocked.

'Then I'm going to get my things. Besides, one of the presents my mother gave me is a map of the Bubble Ocean.'

'But how can you have a map?' Jai asked. 'No one's explored there before.'

'No *human* has explored there before,' Ursula corrected. 'My mother lives there in a mermaid city. The map could come in useful to us. I also want to check on my friends. The turtles and the sea fairies and everyone. It won't take long. I'd like to send a message to my mother too.' She held up her hand before Jai could protest and said, 'It's not foul play. If she hears about what's happened to the club she'll be worried. I need to let her know I'm OK. That's all.'

'How are you going to send this message?' Jai asked, looking suspicious.

'Using the bubble tide. It's like the postal service for mermaids. It carries our messages through the ocean.'

'All right,' Jai said reluctantly. 'I suppose that's OK. We'll wait for you.'

The others accompanied her down below and waited outside the swim-out chamber. Ursula went back into the sea in her mermaid form and quickly swam through the coral garden, the caves and the wrecks, checking that everyone was unhurt.

Apart from being scared by all the commotion, her friends thankfully appeared to be fine. Ursula explained to the sea fairies what had happened and that she was going to have to go away for a while. She also said a proper goodbye to Minty before collecting her treasure chest from her cave. Finally, she snatched up the first shell she found on the seabed and whispered a hasty message to her mother. She released the shell into the ocean current, and in less than five minutes was back on the submarine.

'You returned,' Max said, looking surprised. 'I guess that either makes you very brave or very dumb.'

'The club is my home,' Ursula replied. 'I have nowhere else to go. Besides, *someone* has to save it from the Collector.'

They returned to the bridge and while Jai was putting the coordinates of the Island of Fairy Giraffes into the navigation system, Ursula showed Genie how to start up the submarine's propeller. Soon there were tiny little bubbles whooshing past the portholes as the submarine surged forward. Ursula said a silent goodbye to Minty and her other underwater friends, hoping she would see them again soon.

'I've set up the automatic navigation systems,' Jai said. 'So an alarm should go off if anything large appears on the radar. If we carry on at full steam ahead then it will probably take around two days to reach the Island of Fairy Giraffes. Later on, I'll draw up a list of everyone's duties and responsibilities and hand them out. Ursula and I should go and put some clothes on first.'

Ursula was glad to hear him suggest this because she was starting to feel a little chilly in her robe.

'Not so fast,' Max said. 'You owe me some robots and a medal.'

'You go and do that, and I'll find some clothes for Ursula,' Genie suggested.

Jai hesitated so Genie said, 'Look, we're all going to have to start trusting each other to *some* extent or we'll never get anything done. I don't think Ursula is going to attack me, but if she does then Bess will fetch you for help.'

So Jai and Max left, although Jai looked thoroughly miserable about it all.

'Who's Bess?' Ursula asked, wondering if there was someone else on board she didn't know about.

'She's my shadow animal,' Genie said. 'She's very nosy so I'm sure you'll meet her soon.'

Ursula recalled what Jai had said at the club about his sister being a whisperer. She was about to ask what kind of animal Genie could speak to when the other girl said, 'Boys are silly sometimes, aren't they? But just so you know, *I* believe that you saved us and that you have nothing to do with the Collector. So thank you. I guess no one else has said it, but we owe you our freedom.'

Then, without warning, Genie threw her arms around Ursula in a hug. Ursula felt a jolt of shock. She couldn't remember how long it had been since anyone had hugged her apart from her mother, but it must have been several years at least. Miss Soames certainly never touched her unless it was to rap her knuckles, and even Joe only ever gave her a pat on the shoulder. It felt nice to have someone's arms wrapped around her like that and Ursula found herself awkwardly returning the embrace.

'Thanks,' she said. 'I hope I can prove myself to your brother eventually too.'

'Oh, don't worry about Jai,' Genie said, drawing back. 'He's always been the serious type but it got worse after our father left. He just walked out on us, you see, a couple of years ago. He wasn't a very good dad, really.

It was pretty sad when he left but it could have been worse. At least we've still got Mum. And each other.'

'You're good at looking on the bright side, aren't you?' Ursula said.

Genie nodded vigorously. 'Definitely,' she said. 'It's better to feel happy about the things you've got rather than being sad about what's missing. My dad taught me that, although he didn't mean to. He was always making himself so unhappy thinking about the things he thought he was missing out on that he missed out on what he actually had. Which seems like the silliest thing in the world to me.'

'It does seem pretty silly,' Ursula agreed.

'I knew you'd understand,' Genie said brightly. 'I hope we're going to be best friends. I've never had a best friend before. Except for Bess of course.' She linked arms with Ursula and said, 'It will be so nice having another girl on board. I love Jai but he can be terribly boring about his medals and plankton sometimes. You're not interested in plankton, are you?'

'I don't know,' Ursula replied. 'I guess I've never paid much attention to plankton. I've spent more time with dolphins and sea fairies and turtles.'

'That makes far more sense,' Genie said. 'Those animals make much better friends. Come on, let's get those gremlin bites washed up and then I'll find you some clothes.'

Ursula picked up her treasure chest and followed Genie to the sick bay. They cleaned the bites, which weren't as bad as Ursula had first feared, and after sticking some dolphin plasters over them, they made their way to Genie's bedroom.

To Ursula's delight, the sleeping quarters were located in little glass bubbles attached to the side of the submarine, meaning you could look out at the ocean surrounding you as you travelled. Each bubble had a glass floor and was big enough to contain a set of bunk beds.

'You can sleep in my room if you like,' Genie offered, as she led the way inside. 'It'd be lonely for you otherwise and I've got a spare bunk. Jai sleeps in the bubble next door.'

Ursula thought the room was wonderful and couldn't have been more different to the soulless dormitory she slept in back at the club. She was just about to say so when the most gigantic, nightmarish silver-blue tentacle suddenly coiled into the room and wrapped itself around Genie!

Ursula cried out in dismay. She couldn't understand how or why, but an awful sea monster must somehow

have got on board and was now surely about to whip Genie away to be gobbled up in its crushing maw. Ursula dropped her treasure chest and lunged forward with some vague, hopeless idea of grabbing Genie and making a run for it. But to her surprise, the other girl held up her hand.

'It's all right,' she said quite calmly. 'Please don't be scared. This is Bess.'

'Bess?' Ursula gaped at her. 'Your ... your shadow animal? But ... but ... how ... what ...?'

Genie lifted her head to meet Ursula's gaze. 'It's like this,' she said calmly. 'I'm a kraken whisperer.'

Ursula was completely dumbstruck. She'd never heard of such a thing and could now understand that strange reaction from the assembled explorers outside the club when Jai had given his speech. There were turtle whisperers and dolphin whisperers and the like but she had never, ever heard of a kraken whisperer.

There was rumoured to be one yeti whisperer in the Polar Bear Explorers' Club, but other than him, people weren't usually able to talk to monsters. And from the sounds of it even the yeti whisperer was mostly shunned. After all, if a person's shadow animal was meant to represent a piece of their own soul, then what did it say about a person if their shadow animal was a monster?

'I know she looks monstrous,' Genie said quietly, as if reading Ursula's thoughts. 'But I promise she isn't. She's strange, and beautiful, and mysterious – but she's not evil.'

There was a sort of sad resignation in Genie's brown eyes as she waited for Ursula's reaction. Presumably most people showed fear, or shock, or horror. Certainly, Ursula's own heart was beating quite fast and her limbs trembled a little with the effort of not running away.

And yet ... standing there in her sparkly cowgirl boots and ridiculous knitted octopus hat, Genie herself didn't seem at all dangerous. And Ursula could see now that the tentacle curled around her wasn't clenching in a death grip to whisk her off to her doom but looked more like an affectionate embrace.

'Sorry,' she finally said, willing her heart to slow down. 'She just ... startled me, that's all. I hope I haven't offended her?'

'Not at all,' Genie said, grinning. 'She *is* a bit startling on account of how big she is. And most people have never seen a kraken close up before.'

The thought flashed into Ursula's head that most people prayed they never would either. Kraken were generally thought to be some of the most dangerous monsters that roamed the Seventeen Seas.

'Where's the rest of her?' Ursula asked, trying to work out where the tentacle entered the room.

'Outside.' Genie gestured towards the glass walls of the bubble.

Ursula turned her head to look, and this time found herself trembling so severely that she was obliged to sit down on a nearby chair.

'Oh.' The word escaped her lips in a little gasp as she stared through the glass walls at the kraken.

It was just like the ones she'd seen in books, or immortalised in terrifying paintings on the walls of the Ocean Squid Explorers' Club. The paintings normally showed the kraken with its great tentacles wrapped around a doomed galleon, preparing to drag it down beneath the surface, and Genie's kraken was easily big enough to do precisely that.

She was silver-blue in colour, quite similar to Minty. Only the very tip of one tentacle reached into the submarine, the rest of them drifted silently in the ocean beyond. The kraken had a large head with two huge eyes that stared in at them curiously. Each eye was larger than Ursula herself. Even though she knew it was a shadow animal with no substance and that it couldn't touch her, much less hurt her, it was hard not to feel scared when faced with a sea monster the size of a house.

In the paintings you normally got a confused impression of flailing tentacles and didn't see the creature in its entirety, but like this, Ursula had a clear view of the kraken and she was a terrifying beast.

'You and Max are the first kids who haven't run away from her screaming,' Genie said, sounding both surprised and pleased. She tilted her head as if listening to something, then said, 'She'd like to take a closer look at you. Is that OK?'

Ursula knew that whisperers could speak to their shadow animals silently inside their heads without anyone else being able to hear, but it was strange to think that this was what Bess must just have done. She swallowed hard but nodded slowly.

The silver tentacle slowly uncoiled from around Genie and began to reach towards Ursula. Despite herself, she couldn't help flinching. The tentacle immediately stopped, frozen in mid-air, as if it had noticed her reaction. The idea of the kraken being able to see her well enough through the bubble to clock this, somehow made it even more frightening, but Ursula hadn't meant to flinch. She forced herself to stand up and tentatively reached out her hand.

At this encouragement, Bess's tentacle crept closer towards her again, curling around her hand, up her arm and over her shoulders. It was terrifying, but it was amazing too, and Ursula found herself grinning at Genie.

'She's incredible,' she said.

'She likes you,' Genie said, beaming. 'Bess is an excellent judge of character.'

The kraken slowly withdrew her tentacle from the bubble until all of her floated in the sea beyond the submarine.

'Do you think we can still be friends, even though part of my soul is a kraken?' Genie asked.

'Of course,' Ursula replied.

'The kids at school are terrified of her,' Genie said. 'In fact, it looks like I might not be able to go back to school at all. They say it's too much of a distraction when Bess sunbathes on the sports field or pokes her tentacles into the classroom windows.' She looked sad. 'I've tried asking her to stay away when I'm there but shadow animals need to be close to their whisperer. She's got a shy, gentle temperament so it's too bad that the other kids scream at her. She doesn't want to hurt anybody. She's really good and doesn't react when the kids throw stones at her, but she gets cross if they throw them at me.'

'They throw *stones* at you?' Ursula exclaimed. 'But that's awful.'

Genie shrugged. 'They pass through Bess, but they hit me so I guess it's more satisfying.'

Ursula felt a big bubble of anger rising up in her on Genie's behalf. 'Can't the teachers do anything?' she asked.

'They've tried,' Genie said. 'But the problem is no one knows what to do with a kraken whisperer. The Guild thinks I'm the first one there's ever been in the world. They had to get my kraken pendant specially made.'

She reached beneath her jumper and pulled a silver chain free. On the end dangled a little silver clockwork kraken. Ursula knew that these pendants were given out by the Royal Guild of Whisperers to people who had been vetted and proved themselves to be genuine whisperers. You could always tell when a whisperer was talking inside their heads to their shadow animals because their pendant would open its eyes.

'Even Dad didn't like it,' Genie said quietly. 'You're born a whisperer so Bess has been there right from when I was a baby. She was only small to begin with and everyone thought she was an octopus. That would have been OK. But as I got older she grew bigger and bigger until she was the size she is now. Dad was embarrassed about it. Thought it would reflect badly on him if people knew his daughter was a kraken whisperer.

He and Mum used to argue about it and if Bess tried to poke her tentacles into the house he'd yell at her. I think it's one of the reasons he left in the end. He just couldn't cope with Bess.'

A look of sadness passed over her face but it was only there for a moment before she straightened her shoulders and said brightly, 'But there's not much use dwelling on gloomy things you've got no control over, is there? So, do you still want to share a room with me now that you know about my shadow kraken? I should warn you that she usually pokes one of her tentacles in here at night. And sometimes she hums to herself a bit too. I find it quite relaxing but I won't be offended if you'd prefer to sleep somewhere else.'

Ursula shook her head. 'I'd love to share with you,' she said. 'I've been sleeping in a dormitory by myself back at the club and it's quite lonely. It'll be nice to have you and Bess for company.'

Genie grinned. 'Great,' she said. 'Which bunk would you like?'

Ursula could tell straightaway that Genie slept in the bottom one because there was a bedspread covered in dozens of blue octopuses and a soft toy octopus nestled against her pillow. She also had an octopus-shaped hairbrush on her dressing table.

'Octopuses are the nearest thing you can get to kraken,' Genie explained, seeing her looking.

'Well, if you're already in the bottom bunk then shall I take the top?' Ursula asked.

'OK. Let me know if you want to swap, though. I don't mind.'

Genie set about clearing some space on the dresser for Ursula to put her treasure chest.

'Would you show me what's inside?' Genie asked. 'I'd love to see real-life mermaid gifts!'

So Ursula opened the lid and brought out the contents. Genie was extremely impressed and Ursula enjoyed showing off her treasures, which she'd always had to keep secret before.

'And what does this do?' Genie asked, pointing at the clam necklace.

Ursula hesitated. Her first instinct was to lie and say it was just a necklace, that it didn't have any magical significance. She wanted to be friends with Genie and was afraid that admitting her potential powers would make the other girl more likely to be afraid of her, even if she was a kraken whisperer. But she didn't want to start their friendship off with a lie either, so she took a deep breath and told her the truth.

'It's to help channel and control my mermaid magic,'

she said. 'It might not happen to me because I'm only half mermaid,' she hurried to add. 'But Mum said if I were an ordinary mermaid girl then I'd start to get my magic around now.'

To her relief, Genie didn't look horrified. Instead she smiled, touched her whisperer's pendant and said, 'That's cool! We have matching magical necklaces!'

Ursula hadn't planned to put her clam necklace on – she'd only ever worn it for a few minutes at a time in her cave under the sea. But she liked the idea of matching with Genie, so she draped the necklace over her head, enjoying the cool, solid feel of the silver clam against her collarbone.

She and Genie examined their reflections in the mirror above the dresser, each touching their necklace. Ursula felt a sudden glow of happiness at the thought that she might actually have made a real friend. She grinned at Genie, who smiled back at her. They were both different from most other girls their age, but maybe that made them exactly right for each other?

'Now we just need to find you something to wear.' Genie opened her wardrobe. 'We're about the same size, I think. You can pick anything you like.'

Ursula looked at the clothes on the rails and realised that Genie's current outfit was representative of the rest of her wardrobe. Everything seemed to be brightly coloured or sequinned, and there were a lot of stripy scarves and strange headgear.

'I always wear a hat,' Genie said, seeing Ursula looking. 'I even make some of them myself. The hats they sell in shops are always so boring, don't you think?'

'I haven't ever thought about it,' Ursula admitted. 'I've never really worn hats. Normally I just wear a scarf headband with dolphins on it to keep my hair out of my face, but I think it must have come off when I jumped into the sea.'

'Oh, I think I've got one somewhere,' Genie said, starting to rifle through drawers. 'Here it is!' She pressed a dolphin scarf into Ursula's hands. 'I never wear it so you can keep it if you like.'

Ursula quickly fashioned the scarf into a headband and tied it over her hair. 'That's better. I feel more like myself already.'

Genie snapped her fingers. 'Of course!' she exclaimed. 'Clothes are great for expressing your personality, aren't they? That's why it feels weird wearing someone else's. There might be some engineering kit down below. Would you prefer to wear that?'

'Oh. Actually, yes,' Ursula said. 'That would be wonderful.'

Genie took her to the engineering bay where they did indeed find a white T-shirt, a spare set of coveralls and some work boots that were the perfect size for Ursula. She slipped into them gratefully, buckling up the straps over her shoulders.

'Perfect,' she said, grinning.

She'd always liked how comfortable the coveralls were and, more importantly, how many pockets they came with for storing spanners, screwdrivers, sticky tape, flashlights and all manner of other useful bits and pieces. She felt a surge of gratitude to Genie for understanding about finding the right clothes and smiled at her.

'Thanks a lot,' she said.

'No problem,' Genie replied. 'Just let me know if you want to borrow any of my hats or head boppers. Now, shall I give you a tour of the rest of the submarine?'

Ursula was already very familiar with the layout, but she had spent most of her time on subs in the engine room or crawling around in the air vents and salt pipes. She'd never been taken through the interior as a guest before and it was thrilling to breathe in the scent of wood and brass polish and to see all the rooms the explorers used.

They were spread over several floors and included the

dining room, which had jewelled green walls, a coral chandelier and cabinets full of china stamped with the Ocean Squid Explorers' Club crest. There was a viewing gallery with several large portholes for peering out at spectacular finds. A library fully stocked with travel diaries, atlases, almanacs and scientific journals. And a soda fountain that really was a fountain and had different jets for cola, cherryade or cream soda. Ursula was quite thrilled since cream soda was her favourite drink.

'They give the submarines a soda fountain and an ice-cream maker to help compensate for the fact that the actual food isn't great,' Genie said. 'It's mostly tins of Spam, mint cake, instant chicken dinners, things like that. Oh, and there's a candyfloss maker too,' Genie went on. 'But the ice cream one is my favourite. It can do a mermaid sundae. Look.'

She went over to the ice-cream machine and pressed a few buttons. Soon they both held bowls of ice cream that was a mix of green, blue and purple swirls with silver sprinkles and a chocolate mermaid's tail sticking out of the top.

They ate these as Genie showed Ursula through the rest of the submarine, taking in a monster-stuffing room, as well as a rock-climbing wall, a skating rink and a small cinema with its own popcorn machine.

Best of all, though, was the saltwater swimming pool, which even had flumes, whirlpools and a whole load of inflatable seahorses bobbing around on the surface. It would be perfect whenever Ursula needed to change into a mermaid for a bit.

Finally, they stopped off at the robotics lab where they found Max checking over his robots, which had obviously been returned to him. He also had a medal in the shape of a turtle pinned to his T-shirt, which Ursula guessed had come from Jai.

'Howdy,' he said, looking up at them.

'Hi,' Genie said. 'Where's my brother?'

Max shrugged. 'He seemed quite stressed by the time he'd sorted out my demands, so I guess he's gone off to do whatever he does to relax. Polish his medals, probably. The ones he has left, at least. I've got the yodelling turtle one now.' He pointed at the medal pinned to his T-shirt and shook his head. 'Isn't it amazing what the club will give out medals for?'

'What's that smell?' Ursula asked, sniffing the air.

'Robot grease, probably,' Max said, waving towards a nearby canister. 'I've been oiling their joints to stop them getting rusty.'

'No, it smells like smoke,' Ursula said. 'Like something burning.'

'I hope not!' Max said, leaning over the nearest robot. 'Fires are very dangerous on submarines.' As he spoke, he kicked at a bright orange feather that lay on the floor, pushing it out of sight beneath the table.

Ursula frowned and was about to say something more when Max suddenly looked up at Genie and said, 'Listen, I know your brother and I can't stand each other, but I just want you to know that I have no beef with you. I've a lot of respect for whisperers. I hope we can be friends rather than nemeses?'

'Oh, I don't ever want to have a nemesis,' Genie replied. 'Friends are much better and I'm glad that you didn't scream or try to throw anything at Bess.' She paused and said, 'You have to trust someone to really call them a friend, though, and I'm not sure if I can trust you if you've been conspiring with pirates.'

'Well, that's fair enough,' Max replied. 'I hope you'll like me, but it's probably for the best that you don't trust me. I'm only going along with this mission as far as it suits me.'

Ursula still wanted to get to the bottom of what had happened with the pirates, but before she could ask any questions, Max looked over and said, 'Well, and aren't you full of surprises, Jellyfin? I never would have dreamed you had such an interesting secret! What a thrill. So, would the two of you like to see my robot fleet? Jai turned his nose up at them, but let me show you the midget submarines at least.'

Max proceeded to present them with the tiny robot submarines he'd invented. There were ten of them, each painted a bright yellow colour and tiny enough to fit in the palm of the hand. They all had their very own waterproof Ocean Squid Explorers' Club flag too.

'They've got little cameras in them,' Max explained. 'So I thought they could be used to gather more information about places, like a deep-sea cave or something, before the human divers go in. They've got mechanical arms, look. I've started to make different attachments for them so that they can be used to clean the main submarine, or sent on rescue missions.'

'Ingenious!' Ursula said, admiring the little subs.

She'd always loved it when Max showed her his robot inventions and enjoyed the passionate way he talked about them. She couldn't help thinking that this side of him seemed in conflict with the rule-breaking side.

'I know you love being a robot inventor with the club,' she said now. 'So why did you conspire with those pirates? I don't understand it. Surely there must have been extenuating circumstances or something? Perhaps they were *good* pirates?' After all, Ursula thought, if there were good ice princesses and good mermaids, then perhaps there were good pirates too?

But Max shook his head. A distant look had come into his eyes, as if shutters had closed behind them. 'Nope,' he said. 'They were your standard pirates. Sailing around looking for other ships to attack and steal from, scoping out port towns to plunder, that sort of thing.'

Ursula frowned. Now was a very bad time to be helping pirates, when they'd started attacking explorers' ships more and more, for reasons no one could understand.

'But why, Max?' she asked. 'They'll never let you put on an explorer's cloak again and even if you don't have much respect for the club, you love exploring. Why would you throw it all away?'

'Don't worry about it, Jellyfin,' Max replied. 'Exploring's fun and all, but there's other things that are even more important.'

'Like what?' Ursula pressed.

Max hesitated for just a moment and she hoped he might give her a genuine answer, but then he adjusted his hat to a jauntier angle and said, 'Like wearing the captain's hat.'

Ursula tried to contain her disappointment. She'd been sure that Max must have had some reason for conspiring with pirates and it was painful to realise that maybe he didn't. It made her feel the same flicker of distrust for him that the other two felt. She'd always found him funny and she loved his robots but, like Joe had said, she didn't really know him all that well, or what he was capable of.

'Well, thanks for showing us the robots,' she said as she and Genie left the lab.

'Any time,' Max replied, already bending over a new invention he was tinkering with on the workbench.

'Did you see that orange feather?' Ursula asked Genie as they stepped out into the corridor.

'Where?'

'In the robotics lab just now. Max kicked it under the table, as if he didn't want anyone to see it.'

Genie shrugged. 'It's probably mine,' she said. 'Some of my hats have feathers on them. Jai's always telling me off for leaving feathers and sequins and googly eyes about the place.'

'Oh.' Ursula was relieved to hear that there was an innocent explanation for the feather at least. 'Where is Jai, do you think? I'd like to talk to him. Try to reassure him that I'm not a threat.'

'We can ask the submarine computer,' Genie said, walking over to the nearest control panel in the corridor. 'Although Max was probably right about him polishing his medals. He *does* rather like to do that, especially when he's stressed. He usually polishes them in the library.'

The computer confirmed that Jai was indeed in the library.

'Do you know the way by yourself?' Genie asked. 'I'd like to head back to the bridge for a bit to take another look at that sea monster book. Gosh, I do hope we see some of those glorious creatures! It's terrible that the club has been stolen away, but I'm excited to be going on an expedition at last. I feel guilty, but I *am* excited!'

'I know what you mean,' Ursula replied.

The two girls parted ways and Ursula walked alone down the corridor, catching the odd glimpse of a big swordfish or shimmering shoal of tuna through the portholes.

She walked back into the library where she found Jai sitting at one of the tables. Ursula was surprised to see that he was wearing his full Ocean Squid uniform, which consisted of dark trousers and a green jacket with gold braid and the Ocean Squid crest stamped on the lapel. It was the rules that you had to wear your cloak during an expedition and the full uniform for a formal occasion like a club dinner, but other than that most explorers wore casual clothes. Ursula liked Jai very much, especially after what he'd said at the club about girl explorers, but she couldn't help wondering why he felt the need to be so formal all the time.

He had a grand total of fourteen medals, five of which were pinned to his jacket, while the other nine were lined up on the table in front of him. Ursula saw that he'd attached a prosthetic arm that allowed him to hold the medal in one hand and polish it with the other hand.

She cleared her throat. 'Hello,' she said, suddenly feeling a little shy.

Jai looked up at her. 'Don't tell me you have a list of demands too,' he said.

'No, of course not,' Ursula replied. 'I just wanted to say thank you for letting me stay. I know we're not your ideal team but I really love the Ocean Squid Explorers' Club and I'd do anything to save it. I heard the speech you gave earlier today and I thought it was wonderful!'

Jai paused his polishing and looked up at her. 'I've been thinking about what Genie said earlier and she was right,' he said. 'Stella Starflake Pearl's report did say that mermaids helped them. And some explorers have suggested that perhaps the clubs are just as responsible for whatever animosity there is between us. I want you to know that I don't approve of the mermaid tail that hangs on the wall of the club's trophy room. I've told the president I think it should be removed. It's barbaric and I feel ashamed of the club every time I see it. But the president doesn't listen to me about anything.'

'Well, thank you for asking him anyway,' Ursula replied.

'I hope to be a good and fair commander one day but I'm more nervous about getting it wrong when Genie is on the submarine,' Jai went on. 'She's my twin and the most important person in the world to me, you see.'

Ursula was surprised but pleased by his honesty. 'I understand,' she said. 'I know I have to earn your trust and respect, but I'm going to try really hard to do that.'

'In that case,' Jai said, 'welcome on board. I'm glad to have you.'

Ursula smiled and felt a flicker of excitement deep in her tummy. It may not have been the most auspicious start, and there was more distrust and animosity in the group than any of them would have liked, but at least they were a team now, with an important mission, and they were on their way. Apart from the island where she'd been born, Ursula had never really seen anything much beyond the Ocean Squid Explorers' Club. There was a great big world out there, with a great big ocean, and she was finally going to have adventures in it.

CHAPTER ELEVEN

That night, Ursula lay in the top bunk and looked up through the glass roof of the bubble at the ocean rushing past. She could feel excitement thrumming in her veins along with the gentle vibration of the sub's engines. The ocean was very dark but she could still make out occasional large shapes gliding past that she guessed were whales.

At one point Bess appeared on the other side of the bubble and wound one of her tentacles into the room. It seemed to fill up the entire space but Ursula was less afraid of the kraken this time. She didn't even mind that one of the gigantic eyes was right there behind the glass, peering in at her. When Bess started to hum, Ursula agreed with Genie that it was actually quite a relaxing sound. It was deep and low and strange, a bit like whale song. Ursula had thought she was too excited to sleep but eventually she drifted off to the low rumble of the kraken's humming.

It felt like she'd only been asleep for about five minutes when an alarm rang through the whole submarine causing her to jerk upright in her bunk. Bess had gone, but below, she heard Genie give a groan and stuff her head beneath the pillow.

'What's going on?' Ursula said, as she scrambled down the ladder to the floor. She had terrible visions of a pirate attack or jellyfish ambush or some such, but Genie pushed the pillow aside and said, 'It's just my brother being a big pain in the butt.'

She pointed at the clock by her bedside and Ursula saw that it wasn't yet six o'clock in the morning.

'He's making us keep to regulation time,' Genie explained, dragging herself out of bed. 'I saw it on the duty list he gave us both yesterday evening but thought it was a typo. We'll have to go up to the bridge to perform the safety checks and fire drill. The alarm won't stop otherwise.'

The girls went to the bridge in their pyjamas to find the other two already there. Max was also in his pyjamas and looking rather sleep-dishevelled and grouchy about the early start. Jai, on the other hand, was fully dressed in his Ocean Squid uniform, all fourteen of his medals pinned to his chest.

The four children ran through the different

146

systems as quickly as they could, and finally the bell stopped ringing.

'Was that *completely* necessary?' Max asked. 'I almost had a heart attack when the alarm went off. It's not the most relaxing way to be woken up.'

'Well, that's your fault for still being a lazybones in bed,' Jai replied. 'It said quite clearly on the list I gave you that you'd be expected on the bridge at 6 a.m. I've been up for hours. I've already been for a run around the observation deck, had breakfast *and* completed most of my duties. Now I have the rest of the morning free to work on my book.'

'It's some sort of rule book, I suppose?' Max said glumly.

'Not at all,' Jai replied. 'It's to be called *A Biographical Tribute to the Memory of Biscuit* and will detail the life and achievements of my seafaring cat of that name, who accompanied me on all my expeditions before dying of old age last year.'

Max raised an eyebrow. 'Will that take up many volumes, do you think?'

'Hard to say,' Jai replied. 'But the manuscript stands at over three hundred pages already.'

'Sounds like an important book for posterity,' Max said. 'Biscuit must have been quite a hero.'

'He was the best and most illustrious of his kind,' Jai replied solemnly. For a moment, Ursula thought she saw the glimmer of tears in his eyes before he quickly blinked them away.

She felt a surge of liking for him. Anyone who loved their pet that much had to be a good egg, as far as she was concerned.

'The book sounds wonderful,' she said, frowning at Max in an attempt to ward off any more sarcastic remarks.

While Jai worked on his book, the others spent their time going through the remaining jobs on their list. To their dismay, they found that they had rather a lot of cleaning and swabbing of the corridors to do.

It seemed like it was going to be a long morning until Max managed to hijack the announcement system to blare loud music throughout the entire submarine. Fortunately, it took Jai an hour to work out how to turn it off.

They made good time and arrived at the Island of Fairy Giraffes the following day. It was a bright and sunny afternoon when the four of them gathered together on the bridge and brought the submarine up to the surface. After two nights and almost two days spent travelling underwater, they all enjoyed seeing the sun sparkling off the waves and the island's green palm trees swaying in the breeze.

Genie was immediately glued to her binoculars in an attempt to make out a fairy giraffe. She'd put on her sparkly pink cowgirl boots, a bright green dress and an interesting knitted hat in the shape of a squid that seemed to cling to the side of her head with a faintly surprised expression on its face.

They'd only been on the surface a few minutes when the light on the radio began flashing urgently to indicate that they had an incoming call. Ursula knew it could be difficult for radio waves to reach them when they were deep under the water, but they could come through a lot more easily on the surface.

When Jai answered it, they were dismayed to hear the voice of an official from the Sky Phoenix Explorers' Club demanding that they hold the line while he fetched the president. Wordlessly, Max took the receiver from Jai and ended the call.

'No sense going through all that again,' he said cheerfully. 'We're doing this now and they'll just have to put up with it.'

The others agreed that they didn't have time to waste being told off again and they ignored the radio's insistently flashing light. The submarine was too large to take into the shallow waters surrounding the island so the four children made their way to the submarine's top fin where there was an access hatch that led outside on to the roof, or hull, as it was called. The air was pleasantly warm and smelled of sea spray and coconuts.

Jai pressed a button and part of the roof slid back to allow a small motorboat to rise up. It had a little sail with the Ocean Squid crest stamped on it, along with some back-up oars. Much of the space was occupied with an empty water drum and a wooden stretcher, so it was only just about large enough for the four of them.

'We'll save the motor's fuel for the way back when the water drum is full,' Jai said, screwing on one of his prosthetic arms. 'It's not too far to row on the way out.'

They all climbed into the boat, Jai pressed another button and then the craft was lowered over the side of the submarine on a series of ropes and pulleys. They landed in the sea with a soft splash. The explorers then released the boat's ropes, and the four of them picked up oars and rowed for the island. The journey wasn't far but Ursula's shoulders still ached by the end of it and she was glad they were using the motor to get back.

They pulled up on a white sandy beach scattered with pretty pink shells and dragged the boat up out of the water. Jai took a map of the island from his bag and rolled it out on the sand.

'I haven't stopped here before but it looks safe enough,' he said. 'I don't think anything dangerous lives on this island and it says there's an Ocean Squid outpost next to the waterfall where we'll fill up the drum.'

They rolled the drum from the boat and tied it to the wooden stretcher. Genie and Jai took the two handles at the front, while Max and Ursula each took one of the handles at the back. They then set off towards the waterfall, but very quickly realised something was wrong on the island.

For one thing, the miniature apricot groves were deserted. Previous Ocean Squid explorers had built raised boardwalks around the tiny trees, which were only half a foot high, so as to avoid stepping on the fairy giraffes usually found in herds here. But they couldn't see so much as a single orange spot.

'That's weird,' Genie said, frowning. 'There ought to be dozens of them.'

The children set down the water drum so that they could look at the grove more closely.

'I can see a couple of piles of giraffe poo,' Ursula said, pointing at the little lumps no bigger than raisins. 'So they *were* here.'

'Have you noticed how quiet it is?' Max suddenly said.

He was right. The only sound was the crashing of waves on the nearby beach.

'Fairy giraffes are supposed to hum,' Genie said. 'This seems wrong.'

'Let's leave the water drum here while we find out what's going on,' Jai suggested. 'If everything is OK then we can come back for it later, but we'd better check it's safe first.'

They followed the boardwalk that led them up the mountain towards the waterfall.

'What's that smell?' Genie asked, wrinkling her nose.

'It's fuel,' Ursula replied. She was very familiar with it from all her time spent in the engineering bay.

She was proved right when they reached the waterfall about twenty minutes later. The smell of fuel and engine oil was even more overpowering here, and to their dismay they saw that the water had been contaminated. The waterfall tumbled over the edge of a cliff to land in a large pool, but instead of being blue and fresh and clean, there were swirls of greasy petrol gleaming on the surface and clinging in shiny droplets to the rocks. And they could immediately see the cause.

A flying machine had crash-landed at the top of the waterfall and the wreckage was wedged between a couple of rocks.

'The fuel tank must still be leaking into the water,' Jai said.

'There's only one person in the world who has a flying machine,' Ursula replied.

And indeed they could make out the remains of the Phantom Atlas Society's flag fluttering from the wreckage.

Genie gasped. 'Did the Collector crash here after stealing the club? Perhaps she's still here. We might be able to find some way of taking her prisoner and getting the club's snow globe off her!'

Ursula shook her head. 'I don't think she's here any more,' she said. 'That plane isn't the same one she came to the club in. It looks like it's been here for a while; there's algae growing on the frame. She must have crashed on this island some time ago.'

'But then how did she get another flying machine?' Genie wondered.

'Let's take a look around,' Jai said. 'Perhaps we'll work out what happened. Everyone be on your guard.'

'Let's start with the Ocean Squid outpost,' Genie suggested, gesturing over to the log cabin perched beside the pool. It was meant to have an Ocean Squid flag flying from the mast but they noticed that this too had been replaced with one for the Phantom Atlas Society.

The young explorers crept quietly up to peer in at the windows, just in case Scarlett Sauvage herself was inside, but they could see that the cabin was empty so they let themselves in. Explorer outposts tended to be small spaces with a table, chair, perhaps a bed and some emergency supplies of dried meat or canned fuel. Usually they were left neat and tidy, but when they walked in they found this one was a mess, littered with pieces of paper.

Ursula picked up the nearest sheet and saw that it contained a sketch for a flying machine.

'Scarlett must have designed a new flying machine while she was here,' she said, showing the others.

There were many similar sketches on the desk and scattered on the floor around them. It seemed Scarlett had gone through several versions before she'd been able to perfect her design.

'It looks like she took bits off her old plane and created the rest with materials she found on the island,'

Jai said. 'She must have taken the food and fuel from the cabin too.'

They went over to the logbook, which still sat open on the desk. Explorers sometimes filled in details of their stay in these books, or listed supplies they'd taken and left, but the last entry wasn't from an explorer – it was from Scarlett Sauvage herself.

Her small, spidery handwriting crawled across the page, describing how a storm had caused her to crash-land on the island and destroy her flying machine, but she'd managed to create a new one.

Unfortunately, the island's water supply was polluted in the process – an accident for which Stella Starflake Pearl is solely to blame. Had she not forced me to flee my old headquarters, I never would have crashed here in the first place. But if any explorers are reading this, then have no fear! I will rebuild my headquarters, just like I rebuilt my flying machine. This time it will be somewhere no explorer will be able to reach, even if they are an ice princess.

In the meantime, I have taken the fairy giraffes with me since this island is no longer habitable for them thanks to Stella.

'That's not fair!' Ursula exclaimed. 'She can't blame Stella for this when she's the one who crashed her flying machine here and ruined the water supply.'

'I don't think she has any scruples,' Jai replied. 'But I guess there's no point hanging around if there's no water. We'll have to find it elsewhere.'

'But won't that mean stopping off somewhere dangerous in the Voltic?' Genie asked, looking worried.

'Probably, but we don't have a choice,' Jai said. 'We won't last long on the submarine without water.'

They all knew he was right, so they headed back, collecting the empty water drum along the way. When they returned to the beach they loaded the drum on to the motorboat.

'We'll have to be very careful with the water we've got left,' Max remarked. 'No long leisurely bubble baths for anyone.'

'Given how low our water is, we should probably avoid washing altogether for now,' Jai said. 'We've got to preserve our drinking water.'

No one much liked the idea of that, but as Genie

pointed out, explorers in the other clubs pretty much always went unwashed when travelling through snowy landscapes or strange deserts or unexplored jungles. The Ocean Squid Club were the only ones who explored in submarines with all the conveniences they provided.

'If those other explorers can do it, I'm sure we can too,' Genie said cheerfully.

At any rate, it didn't look as if they would have much choice, so they got back into the boat, started up the motor and set off towards the submarine.

CHAPTER TWELVE

'This is desperate,' Jai said, frowning down at the maps. 'Even if we ration it, we're going to run out of water about eight or nine days before we reach the next island.'

The four children looked grim. They all knew how dangerous it was to be stuck on a submarine with no water. Ursula had spent some time back at the club tinkering with different systems, trying to come up with a way for submarines to create their own fresh drinking water from the sea, but hadn't been successful yet. Many Ocean Squid explorers had come a cropper by running out of supplies over the years. An explorer could last without food for quite a long time but no one would survive without water for more than a few days. Even Genie was unable to come up with a positive side.

'As I see it, we've got two choices,' Jai said, pointing at the map spread out before them. 'We can travel the safest known route through the Voltic and aim for Peppercorn Island, but that will take us at least another five days beyond the time when we run out of water and we'll very likely die of dehydration. Or we could take a shortcut through the Bottomless Canyon.' He pointed at another spot on the map. 'It's not actually bottomless but it is very deep, narrow and treacherous, so it's quite difficult trying to navigate a submarine through it. But if we manage to get to the other side then we should get to Gilly's Island just a day after our water runs out. I don't think anyone's ever been there, but it's quite big so the chances are that it'll have some kind of water supply.' He looked up at the others. 'What do you think?'

Neither of them were good options but Ursula pointed at the canyon and said, 'I think we'd better take the shortcut. It's a gamble but if we run out of water for five days then we're done for. At least we've got a chance this way.'

'I agree,' Genie said, although she looked worried. 'Let's go through the canyon.'

'Definitely the canyon,' Max agreed. 'If we're going to go out, then better to go with a bang, I always say.'

*

Later that afternoon, the four children gathered on the bridge with an air of trepidation as they began their journey into the Voltic Sea. Steep sides of rock loomed up ahead through the portholes and Ursula could see why it was called the Bottomless Canyon. It looked like it went on forever and the bottom was completely lost in the deep dark depths of the ocean.

'I don't think anyone's travelled through here since Dr Winston Wallaby Scott,' Genie said, poring over a pile of travel diaries she'd brought up from the library. 'And that was about forty years ago. In here it says that they lowered a bathysphere down on a cable to measure the depth and that the canyon is more than eight thousand feet deep! That can't be right, can it? Even the Great Canyon on land is only about six thousand feet and that's considered one of the wonders of the world.'

'They say that the ocean is home to the tallest mountains and the deepest canyons on the planet,' Jai said. 'Yet another reason to be a member of the Ocean Squid Explorers' Club. Deserts and jungles and ice lands are nowhere near as interesting or spectacular as the wonders of the sea.'

'The squid cupcakes the chef makes aren't bad either,' Max said.

Ursula thought Jai was exactly right about the club.

Besides which, there was so much more ocean yet to discover than there was land. By modern calculations, only a mere five per cent of the sea had been explored so far. The rest of it was a mystery. There could be anything waiting out there for them. Ursula couldn't understand why everyone didn't want to be an Ocean Squid explorer. Ursula knew the Bottomless Canyon was potentially dangerous, but she was still thrilled at the idea of seeing it for herself.

'I think we'd better take the automatic navigation systems off and steer the submarine manually,' she said. 'Even at this slow speed, we can't risk hitting the rock wall and damaging the submarine.'

'You're right,' Jai replied. He hesitated, then looked at Ursula and said, 'Do you think you could do it? You've got more experience of handling submarines than the rest of us.'

Ursula was pleased that Jai had trusted her enough to ask, but she still felt nervous at the idea.

'I've done a lot of work repairing submarines but I've never actually piloted one before,' she said. 'I'm very familiar with the dimensions, though, so I'm happy to try.'

She took the helm and was pleased to find that the wheel felt right in her hands. As she stood on the bridge gripping it she felt a sudden sense of calm flood all the way down to her boots.

'Right,' Ursula said, taking a deep breath. 'Perhaps you three could keep watch out of the portholes and let me know if you see any juggling octopuses or spiky eels?'

'Aye aye, Cap'n,' Genie said, hurrying over to one side.

Max and Jai took up position on the opposite end and Ursula nosed the submarine gently into the canyon, biting her lip as the sides got taller and made the sea even darker. She switched on the submarine's headlights, which sent a powerful beam slicing through the water ahead of them. Everything depended on her steering the submarine at exactly the right moment to avoid the steep sides. Unfortunately, the canyon wasn't long and straight, but twisty and crooked with deep shelves of rock jutting out into the middle, which meant there was no way of knowing what was around the corner until they'd actually turned it.

'I can see some transparent spookfish here on the starboard side,' Genie said. 'But they're not any danger to us.'

'There are some flower-hat jellies just below us too,' Max said.

They weren't a problem either and Ursula prayed their luck would hold and they'd come across nothing more dangerous in the canyon. With some careful navigating, perhaps they'd soon be safely out the other side after all.

'There's a blue light up ahead,' Genie suddenly said.

'Isn't it just the submarine's lights reflecting back at us?' Ursula asked.

'No, she's right,' Jai said. 'It's a blue glow that's coming from something around the next bend.'

Ursula could see it now too – a soft blue haze that spilled out from the other side of the rocky shelf and lit up the sea around them.

'What could it be?' she wondered.

'Some plankton give out their own light,' Jai said. 'It's called bioluminescence.'

'Surely whatever that is, it's too big to be plankton?' Max asked.

But Jai shook his head. 'Most plankton are tiny, but not all of them.'

'Perhaps we should wait for a minute and go through the journals to find out what it might be?' Genie suggested.

'We can't,' Ursula said. 'Even if I cut the engines now, it would take us a while to come to a stop.'

She turned off the engines anyway, but as she had said, the submarine kept moving ahead through the water, driven forward by the force of its own momentum.

'Whatever that thing is,' Ursula went on, 'we're heading straight for it. Maybe one of you should man the sea cannons?'

Jai left his watch station and hurried over to the nearest cannon, gripping the handles in readiness.

'Best turn the sub's lights off too,' Max suggested. 'We're begging to be eaten if we go in with all our lamps blazing.'

Ursula flicked a switch and the lights went off. Without them, the ghostly blue glow immediately seemed to become much brighter, filling up the ocean around them. Ursula's palms turned slippery as she began to carefully ease the submarine around the corner, the blue light getting brighter and brighter all the while.

'Watch out!' Max said suddenly. 'There's bubblegum coral growing on the walls of the canyon!'

Ursula saw he was right. Bright pink pom-poms of coral covered the canyon wall. It was well known for being one of the stickiest substances in existence and was quite impossible to remove from surfaces once it had fastened on. She turned the submarine slightly to the starboard side to avoid it but then Genie yelped from the porthole, 'You're too close to the other side now! It's growing on both walls!'

'There's nothing I can do,' Ursula gasped. 'The submarine is too big and the gap is too small.'

Sure enough, as they went around the corner, the submarine brushed up against the bubblegum coral on the starboard side. They felt the sticky snag as the *Blowfish* tilted over slightly, causing them all to grab on to the nearest surface for balance. There was a squelchy *thump* as the submarine stuck to the side of the canyon, like a fly in a spider's web. But that was the least of their problems. Now that they'd passed the corner, they could see what was making the blue light, and the children all stared dumbstruck.

Before them was a monstrous jellyfish, easily the size of a house. In fact, it looked as though it was even bigger than a yeti, and those reached heights of sixty feet. This jellyfish was double that, its glowing tentacles stretched a shockingly long way down into the depths of the canyon, while its billowing gelatinous body completely blocked the route forwards.

It was a nefarious sea monster and every Ocean Squid explorer in the world knew its name.

'The colossal sneezing jellyfish,' all four children whispered at exactly the same time.

CHAPTER THIRTEEN

Aside from the blue glow emitted by the giant jellyfish, the sea around them was lit up with thousands of pinprick lights in a host of jewel colours, from pink to green to orange, like a rainbow of stars in the night sky.

'Plankton,' Jai said, peering out through the porthole. 'They're attracted by the colossal sneezing jellyfish's light.'

Ursula left her position to join Jai.

'I'm really sorry,' she said. 'This is all my fault.'

'It's not.' Jai waved her apology away. 'There's no way anyone could have got the submarine through that gap. This was always going to happen.'

Ursula was grateful that Jai's sense of fairness made him see it this way, but she still felt as if she'd let everyone down.

'What are we going to do?' Genie asked.

'The good news is that the jellyfish probably won't

come after us,' Jai said. 'The fact it's giving off a blue light means it's well fed so it'll be happy to sit there and let the plankton come to it. It would be much more dangerous if it was orange because that would mean it was hungry and would actively hunt bigger prey. But the bad news is that the colossal sneezing jellyfish is one of the most deadly jellies in the Seventeen Seas. Their sting is supposed to be so painful that the agony will kill you before the poison does.'

'How do you know so much about colossal sneezing jellyfish?' Max asked, looking almost impressed.

'Jellyfish are a type of plankton, even a very large one like this. Of course most plankton are tiny – some are even microscopic – but I try to include all of them in my plankton studies,' Jai said.

Max stared at him. '*Plankton* studies? Why would anyone study plankton when there are so many more interesting things in the sea?'

'Plankton are my favourite sea creature,' Jai said defensively.

Max looked horrified. 'But they're just blobs!' he protested. 'They don't do anything!'

'They do all kinds of things,' Jai replied, looking cross. 'And they're very important for the health of the ocean. They're the foundation of the marine food web. They help keep the air clean too. We owe a lot to plankton.'

'I can't *believe* that plankton is your favourite animal,' Max said, shaking his head. 'It shouldn't be allowed.'

'Well, what's yours?' Jai said, sounding irritated.

'Sharks,' Max replied. 'Obviously.'

'You're right,' Jai sniffed. 'It is an obvious choice. Probably shared by every other boy our age at the club.'

Genie rolled her eyes. She pointed at herself and then the two boys, 'Kraken, plankton, sharks.' Then she pointed at Ursula. 'What's your favourite sea animal?'

'Water horses,' Ursula said.

'Right, now that we all know what each other's favourite is, perhaps we can get back to business? Even if the jellyfish doesn't come after us, we still need to find some way to free the submarine from the bubblegum coral. And once we've done that we need to work out how we're going to get past the jellyfish. It's filling the whole gap.'

'We'll have to take the submarine into a dive and go under it,' Ursula said.

Jai looked worried. 'We're already pretty deep.' He glanced at her. 'How deep can this type of submarine go before the pressure is too much?'

'It'll be close,' Ursula said grimly. 'Very close. But what other choice do we have?'

To make matters worse, she felt desperately thirsty but didn't dare have anything to drink when they were trying to conserve their rations. Even so, her throat started to burn as she searched her mind for a solution.

'Couldn't you just turn the submarine's engines back on and put all the power into a dive?' Genie asked. 'Wouldn't that be strong enough to break the bubblegum coral?'

Ursula shook her head. She and Joe had spent many an hour scraping bubblegum coral off submarines in the past and she'd seen the damage that was done when a foolhardy captain tried to escape it using the power of the sub's engines.

'It won't work,' Ursula said. 'Bubblegum coral is really stretchy, like an elastic band. It would stretch out so far but then it would snap us back against the cliff and we'd be smashed against the rocks, incurring significant damage. The coral has to be cut off manually.'

'You mean . . . go out into the sea?' Max asked. 'With that monster right there?'

'Afraid so.'

'Perhaps we don't have to go ourselves,' Max said. 'We could send the robot mini subs instead.'

A few minutes later, the children were gathered in the robotics lab where Max's ten midget submarines gleamed on their racks.

'I've been working on this knife attachment,' he said, showing the others. 'For the miniature subs' mechanical arms. I thought it might come in handy in case the mother submarine got itself stuck in seaweed while out on a mission and needed to cut its way to freedom. But it should work for cutting through the bubblegum coral too. I just have to program them.'

When Max had finished, he pressed a button and the robot submarines were all shot out into the water via a tube.

The children returned to the bridge feeling hopeful, but quarter of an hour later the robot submarines had made very little progress, and several of them had got caught up in the bubblegum coral themselves. Even the ones that weren't had to saw back and forth with their knives for ages before they cut through the sticky pink strands.

'They're only a prototype,' Max said gloomily. 'I still have a lot of work to do on them.'

'It was worth a try,' Jai said.

Max changed the programming to recall the robot subs and those that weren't stuck in the coral returned to the chutes, where they were sent back to their racks in the lab.

'So it looks like we're going to have to do this ourselves,' Genie said, rolling up her sleeves.

'I'll go,' Ursula said, although the thought of venturing into the ocean with such a formidable sea monster made her palms sweat. 'I'll be a lot more mobile and faster in the water since I won't need a diving suit.'

'Well, we can't allow you to go out on your own,' Jai said. 'Explorers always work in pairs outside the submarine.'

'I'll do it,' Max said.

'You will?' Jai narrowed his eyes at him. 'Why?'

'Why not?' Max replied. 'Someone's got to. Besides, I've never been in the water with a colossal sneezing jellyfish before.'

Genie shook her head. 'No, I'll do it. Whoever stays behind needs to man the sea cannons in case the jellyfish attacks and I might end up feeling too guilty to shoot it. I like sea monsters. I know I'm not supposed to, but I do. So I should be the one to go out to the jellyfish.'

Jai was shaking his head before she even finished speaking. 'Absolutely not,' he said.

Genie paused. Then she said, quite calmly, 'It's not up to you, Jai. We're on an unauthorised expedition so I have just as much right to go out there as you do.'

'It's dangerous, Genie,' Jai said.

'Obviously. But it makes sense for me to go because I've got Bess.' She gestured through the porthole to where the blue-grey kraken had appeared in the sea. Massive as she was, she was still nowhere near as large as the jellyfish.

'She won't be able to help you,' Jai said. 'She can't fight off the jellyfish if it decides to attack and she won't be able to fool it into believing she's a real kraken either. Jellyfish don't have the same senses as us, or the same type of brain. It won't be afraid of Bess.'

'Maybe not, but Bess can still keep an eye on the jelly while I'm working on the coral and she can warn me if it starts to move. She can help me find the bubblegum coral too. This might be the only expedition I ever get to join if the club don't change their mind about girl members. I'm not sitting on the sidelines. You've always claimed you support my application to join the club. Did you really mean all those things you said about girls being explorers?'

'You know I did,' Jai replied.

Genie straightened her squid hat and said, 'Well,

here's your chance to prove it and show you weren't just lying, safe in the knowledge that the club would never accept me.'

'I'd never lie to you!' Jai looked offended. 'And I do think you'd make an excellent explorer. Just ... please be careful, OK?'

So they went down to the diving chamber. Genie changed into a swimming costume and climbed into the cumbersome diving suit. She attached the helmet, then she and Ursula each took a knife from the underwater exploring bags hanging from the hooks on the wall. Once they were equipped, Ursula and Genie went next door to the swim-out chamber, while Jai and Max returned to the bridge to man the sea cannons.

Genie attached her suit to the rope and then they pressed the button to flood the chamber. Foaming seawater rushed up through the floor. Ursula's legs immediately transformed into a blue tail and the cool ocean felt delicious against her skin and scales. Once the chamber was full they unlocked the hatch and opened it to reveal a great blue expanse of ocean.

Also directly in front of them was the colossal sneezing jellyfish and, somehow, it seemed even more gigantic now that they were in the water with it. Ursula could see the top umbrella part undulating slightly and the stingers sparkling in the long tentacles. It looked almost pretty with its bright blue glow surrounded by specks of brightly coloured plankton. But of course it was deadly too, and Ursula didn't blame Genie for hesitating at the hatch. They were both scared but there would be no escaping from the jellyfish if they didn't free the submarine first.

Ursula swam straight out but it took Genie a little longer in her awkward diving suit. They emerged on the roof, just in front of the top fin. Bess was immediately there, floating directly above them in the water. Even though she was getting a bit more used to the kraken, Ursula still felt a surge of adrenaline at being in the water with her. You couldn't tell by looking at Bess that she had no physical substance and it really seemed as if they were in the sea with a colossal sneezing jellyfish *and* a kraken.

Still, at least the sea monster was on their side. Ursula swam towards the coral and Genie followed behind, walking on top of the roof with Bess drifting along in her wake. The bubblegum coral was even worse than they'd thought, attaching to the submarine in several different places. They could see the robot subs stuck in the gum and cut those out first so they could return to the mother submarine.

Then they got straight to work on the *Blowfish*, taking care to keep as far away from the coral as possible. To Ursula's relief, the diver's knives were quite effective at cutting through the sticky stuff and they only had to saw a few times before each strand broke free. By the time they'd reached the back of the submarine, Ursula could feel a sense of triumph rising in her chest and she looked over at Genie to see the kraken whisperer grinning back at her through her mask. They were doing it! Just a few more strands to go and then they'd be free!

But then Ursula felt a sudden movement in the water and she looked over at the jellyfish to see that its bell had started to pulsate, faster and faster.

'Oh no!' Ursula gasped. She gestured wildly to Genie, waving her arms to get the other girl's attention. 'The jellyfish!' she exclaimed, knowing that Genie couldn't hear her, but hoping she could lip read. 'I think it's going to—'

Before she could finish the sentence, the worst thing that could possibly happen actually happened – the colossal sneezing jellyfish gave a great, colossal sneeze.

Shockwaves blasted through the ocean, turning it into a whirlpool around them. Fortunately, Genie had already activated the magnetic grip on her diving boots, which were so strong that she remained glued to the roof. Bess wasn't affected by the currents, but Ursula found herself picked up and turned over and over so that she couldn't work out which direction she was going. Genie dropped her knife and ran down the submarine roof to grab hold of her just before she could go flying into the sticky arms of the bubblegum coral – or the stinging tentacles of the jellyfish.

The water around them was suddenly full of swirling plankton, from tiny plants and algae, to crabs and shrimps and snails. Most alarmingly of all, the colossal sneezing jellyfish had changed colour and was now giving off a bright orange glow, like a small underwater sun. Ursula realised it must have sneezed out all its food, meaning that it would now be ravenous. She remembered what Jai had said about how it would actively hunt bigger prey and she realised that there was no larger prey around than the submarine itself . . .

No sooner did the thought pass through her mind than the colossal sneezing jellyfish was reaching its long tentacles towards them, flying out so fast that Ursula and Genie both had to duck to avoid being knocked down, although of course they passed straight through Bess.

'Quick!' Ursula gasped, racing back to the coral.

Some of it had become reattached when the jellyfish sneezed and Ursula took her knife to it in a frenzy while also trying to avoid the jellyfish tentacles, which were slipping and sliding over the submarine in a horribly eager, greedy sort of way. Genie looked around for her own knife but it had been lost when she'd run to help Ursula. Bess thrashed her tentacles menacingly, but Jai had been right about the jellyfish not being fooled. If it was aware of the kraken at all, it clearly knew that she had no form, and didn't react to her in the slightest.

Before the jelly could get a proper purchase on the submarine, a deep, rumbling *boom* from down below told them that Jai and Max had taken to the sea cannons. The metal ball tore through the air, and although it didn't hit the jellyfish, it did cause it to flinch back. This gave Ursula the few precious moments she needed to saw through the last of the coral.

The submarine was finally free and Genie must have communicated this to the bridge through the radio because the sub angled its nose and dived down a few metres. Ursula quickly swam after it and Genie ran along the roof towards the swim-out hatch, with Bess hovering close behind her. They were almost back when the tentacle raced through the water towards them, passed straight through Bess, curled around Genie and ripped her magnetic boots right off the deck. There was a flash of light as it tried to sting, and Ursula prayed it wasn't able to pass through the metal diving suit.

Ursula and Bess both lunged after the tentacle, but the jellyfish was desperately hungry and whipped Genie back towards its body so fast that the surrounding ocean became full of streams and streams of bubbles, white and round as pearls. Panic flooded through Ursula as she realised her new friend was already in the centre of the long glowing tentacles. Bess tore after her and her own tentacles mixed confusingly with the jellyfish's so that they started to look like one awful monster combined. But of course Bess had no way of making any physical impact on the jellyfish no matter how ferociously she flailed in the water.

Ursula recalled what Jai had said about their sting – not only deadly but so painful the agony would kill you before the poison did. And Ursula didn't even have a diving suit to protect her. The only clothing she wore was her bikini top – the rest of her was just skin and scales. But Genie needed help and as she'd dropped her knife in order to help Ursula earlier, she had no means of defending herself. There was no way that Ursula was going to let her down now.

She beat her tail to swim forwards as fast as she

could. When she'd had races back home with Minty she'd found that she could swim even faster than the dolphin if she really tried, and now she put every last drop of energy into racing towards the monster, using all her mermaid's grace to twist and weave between the tentacles, both kraken and jelly. She could see little lightning flashes in the water where the jellyfish tried to sting her, but she was too fast as she zigzagged her way through.

She raced up to Genie, who was kicking awkwardly, but unable to free herself from the tentacle's grip. They were right underneath the jellyfish now and Ursula could see the terrible mouth opening wide in the centre of the undulating umbrella.

She gripped the knife tightly, reached back her arm and slashed straight through the tentacle in one blow. A thick, inky substance spurted into the water around them as Ursula grabbed hold of Genie. She was horrendously heavy in her metal diving suit and Ursula's arms burned with the weight. She realised the suit's propulsion technology must have been damaged in the attack. One of the tentacles brushed so close to her that she felt the static from the sting, which made her hair stand on end but thankfully just missed touching her.

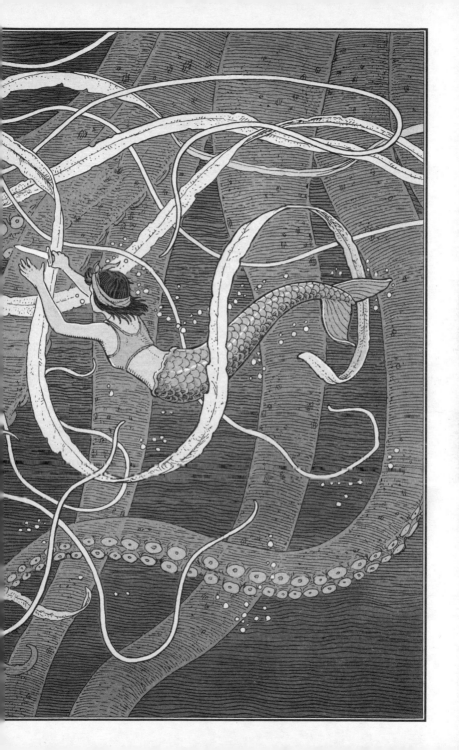

Keeping a firm hold on Genie, Ursula beat her tail as fast as she could to get them back to the hatch, all the while having to duck, weave, twist and roll around the enraged jellyfish's thrashing tentacles. Bess followed them to the submarine and saw them safely inside.

They tumbled into the hatch and Ursula reached around to slam the door shut only just in the nick of time. They could see the jellyfish's tentacles flying after them and then heard the thud as they passed through Bess and hit the closed metal door. Inside her helmet, Genie activated her radio straight to the bridge.

'Dive!' she gasped. 'We're both on board. Dive, dive, dive!'

They did as she'd said and the submarine tilted down so sharply that Genie and Ursula both fell over each other and slammed into the wall as the water drained from the room around them.

CHAPTER FOURTEEN

Finally the submarine ceased to descend and came to a stop in the water. The moment the green light went on to indicate that the swim-out chamber had drained, the hatch flew open and Jai and Max burst into the room. Jai was wild-eyed as he raced to his twin's side, falling to his knees on the wet floor and helping her to take off her helmet.

'Are you all right?' he asked.

Genie was very pale but she nodded and said, 'Yes. The suit protected me against the sting.'

'And you?' Max said sharply to Ursula, who was coughing jellyfish ink up on to the floor. 'Are you hurt?'

'No,' she said, once she'd finally stopped coughing. 'Just covered in this gross stuff.'

The ink was so sticky that it remained all over her tail and hair. It stank like fish guts, but miraculously she'd managed to miss the tentacles. She felt a sudden surge of satisfaction rush through her. 'That was some pretty good mermaid swimming,' she said. 'Even if I say so my— Oof!'

She broke off because Jai had scrambled over to wrap his arm around her and was squeezing her tight in a suffocating hug.

'Oh!' Ursula exclaimed. 'Oh no, you're getting yourself covered in jellyfish slime!'

'I don't care,' he replied. 'Thank you. Oh, thank you! That was ... I've never seen that kind of bravery before on all my expeditions.'

Ursula felt a pink blush warming her cheeks. 'But ... that's what being an explorer is all about, isn't it?' she said. 'I'm always hearing the explorers back at the club talking about their daring rescue missions.'

Max grunted. 'Normally they do their daring rescues from the safety of a submarine,' he said. 'That was quite something, Jellyfin.'

'We saw everything from the portholes,' Jai said. 'When that jellyfish took Genie, I thought ... well, I feared the worst. I never dreamed you'd go after her.'

'You can stop squeezing me so hard now,' Ursula said. 'Listen, Genie would have been able to save herself if it hadn't been for me. She dropped her knife to catch me when the jellyfish sneezed. So we rescued each other.'

She looked over at the kraken whisperer, who grinned back at her. 'We're a good team,' Genie said.

'Excellent work,' Max agreed. 'Especially since, of course, you know a jellyfish's mouth is also its bum, so that would have been a pretty nasty way to go.'

Suddenly there was the sound of a shuddering groan all around them.

'What's that?' Genie exclaimed, hurrying to struggle out of her suit. 'Surely not another sea monster?'

Jai shook his head. 'It's the submarine,' he said. 'We had to dive deep enough to get below the jellyfish and it doesn't like the pressure. We're not out of danger yet.'

They helped Genie scramble from her diving suit, then she and Ursula both threw on robes, Ursula dried off her tail to change it back into legs, and then the four of them raced to the bridge. Ursula pushed her inky hair from her eyes to peer out of the portholes. The only creature she could see drifting outside was Bess.

'Have we got away from the jellyfish?' she asked.

'Yes, it's right above us,' Jai replied, pointing to one of the radars. 'We've just got to navigate a little further along the canyon and then we can go back up once we're clear of it.'

Ursula took the steering wheel again. The canyon

was just as narrow further down so it was still difficult trying to guide the submarine through.

'This is the deepest any expedition has ever gone in this canyon,' Max said, looking at the depth reader. He glanced at the nearest porthole. 'They say the deeper you go in the sea, the weirder the sea creatures become. There could be anything out there. Vampire squid, deep-sea devil shrimp, rage sharks, those ugly fish with really big eyes and all those teeth bursting out of their mouths, which look a bit like aliens—'

'It's best not to speculate,' Jai said sharply. Then he swallowed and said, 'Still, I suppose it doesn't hurt for us to man the cannons. Just in case.'

The boys went to the cannons while Genie and Bess kept watch to port and starboard. Ursula didn't think she'd ever been more desperate for a shower in her life but she tried not to think about the ink drying all over her and just concentrate on manoeuvring the submarine.

Further and further they nosed into the canyon, which was so deep that the water was almost completely black. They couldn't even see Bess beyond the portholes. They may as well have been in outer space. A tense silence descended on them with the only sound being the occasional ominous groan of the sub itself as it strained to withstand the immense pressure of the ocean weighing down on it. Several warnings flashed up on the control panel and Ursula knew the submarine wasn't designed to go this deep, but what choice did they have? No one wanted to get swallowed up by a colossal sneezing jellyfish especially when, as Max had said, its mouth was also its bum.

'I can hear something,' Max said.

'It's just the submarine groaning,' Jai replied.

'No,' Max said. 'It's something else. Listen. It sounds . . . it almost sounds like music.'

Ursula frowned. It didn't seem likely that they would hear music miles and miles below the surface of the sea, deep in this underwater canyon. But then, all of a sudden, she heard it too.

'He's right!' she said. 'I think it's . . . disco music!'

'There are lights up ahead too. Look.' Genie pointed.

'We'll be sunk if it's something dangerous,' Jai said. 'We can't go back up because of the jellyfish and we can't go further down because the *Blowfish* can't take it.'

'Discos aren't usually dangerous, are they?' Max said.

Jai frowned. 'They can be. They put on a disco at the club once and someone got so over-excited that they ended up running stark naked through the sea-flower garden.'

'Oh yes, I remember that,' Max said. 'I wasn't over-excited, though. It was a dare.'

'That was *you*?' Jai exclaimed.

Max shrugged. 'You should never dare me to do a thing,' he said, 'because I'll do it. Anyway, it's not dangerous – it's called having fun. You should try it some time.'

'Look!' Genie exclaimed. 'There're lights flashing in the water ahead too!'

'I hope it's not another jellyfish,' Ursula said.

'You're the plankton expert,' Max said, looking at Jai. 'Is there any such thing as a disco jellyfish?'

'No,' Jai replied. 'Not that we've discovered anyway. Although there is a lesser-known warbling opera crab that dwells in the underwater caves of Emerald Cove. And a sing-along swordfish that likes to escort boats to join in with the crew's sea shanties.'

'And there are singing cucumbers, of course,' Genie said. 'But they don't have discos, do they?'

Ursula glanced at the monitors in front of her. 'There's nothing big showing on the screen ahead. Anyway, we can't go back up yet so we're going to have to risk it.'

Everyone held their breath as she steered the submarine around the next bend in the rock. Their minds were all filled with visions of deep-sea devil shrimps and rage sharks and juggling octopuses, so it was a relief when they turned the corner and saw through the portholes what appeared to be a starfish disco in full swing.

The music was so loud now that the beat thudded through the walls of the submarine and they felt it in the soles of their boots. A great, glittering disco ball hung suspended between the walls of the canyon, shedding sparkling light – that turned multicoloured where it hit the starfish – over everything.

Ursula had never seen anything like these starfish. They were completely covered in sequins and were all different colours, from ruby-red to sky-blue to candyfloss-pink. They were spread all over the canyon walls in a great patchwork of sparkles. Many of the starfish were launching themselves from one wall to the other and Ursula supposed this was their form of dancing. They spun through the dark waters so fast that they left vivid trails of their neon colours in the water behind them.

The music itself seemed to be coming from a little stage cut into one of the canyon walls where an octopus DJ was shuffling records around on a turntable.

'Amazing!' Max yelled. 'This is the best thing I've ever seen!'

The music was so catchy that Ursula, Max and Genie all started to dance a little bit where they stood, and even Jai was tapping his foot in time with the beat. They could see Bess through the portholes joining in by waving her tentacles around.

Ursula slowed the submarine to a crawl so as not to smash into the dancing starfish. Carefully she eased the *Blowfish* forwards until they were right in the middle of the disco, passing beneath the sparkling ball overhead. The bridge became flooded with rainbow colours.

'What's the name for a group of starfish?' Max yelled, raising his voice to be heard over the music.

'A galaxy!' Genie shouted back. 'Or a constellation of sea stars!'

Ursula thought that was a perfect description. Apart from the giant disco ball and the octopus DJ, it did feel a bit like being in outer space surrounded by stars.

The starfish didn't seem to mind them interrupting their disco. The octopus even put on a disco version of the Ocean Squid Explorers' Club anthem to serenade them as they went past. A few of the starfish flew on to the submarine and attached themselves to the portholes, but it was hard to tell if they were doing this by accident or whether they were just being nosy and wanted to peer inside. Ursula remembered reading in a book back at the club that a starfish's eyes were located at the tips of their five arms.

After a little while, they flew off back to their disco and soon enough the submarine was out the other side. The music grew fainter and the lights faded as they travelled further from it. Finally, Ursula checked the screen and saw they'd passed the colossal sneezing jellyfish too, so she started to raise the submarine back up towards the surface. The sides stopped shaking and then all became peaceful and quiet once again, with the canyon behind them and nothing but blue water stretching out beyond the portholes.

Once they'd established that there were no more monsters or sparkly starfish, Ursula transformed back into a mermaid in order to wash herself off in the sea. A shower would have been better, but since they still had to conserve their water supply, the ocean was the next best thing. At least she managed to get all the ink out of her hair and no longer smelt like fish guts.

Bess drifted over and Ursula made a special point of thanking the kraken for her help. After washing off the ink, she swam back to the edge of the canyon and plucked a few blue sea flowers from the walls to thread into Bess's necklace. The kraken waved her tentacles around in excitement the whole time Ursula was putting them in, so she assumed she was pleased.

When she came back on board, Jai was waiting in the corridor with some clothes for her, but it wasn't another one of Genie's seahorse jumpers as she'd expected – it was the dark cloth of the Ocean Squid Explorers' Club cloak.

'What's that?' she asked, staring.

'It's for you,' Jai replied. 'I just looked it up and rule number two hundred and thirty-nine in the captain's rule book says that the acting captain of a submarine has the power to temporarily induct someone into the Ocean Squid Explorers' Club if they've shown great valour or committed a particularly impressive act of derring-do. I think what you did earlier ticks both those boxes. I've already given Genie her cloak. You said you wanted to be an explorer. I can't promise what will happen once we save the club; the president would then have to confirm you as permanent or else strip the membership away. But if you'd like to join the expedition as a formal member of the team for now, then I'd be glad to have you.'

'That's great!' Ursula exclaimed. 'And what about Max?'

A shadow passed over Jai's face. 'Even if I wanted

to – and I don't, especially – I haven't got the authority to reinstate an expelled member. I can offer it to you, though. If you want it.'

Ursula was disappointed to hear that Max wasn't going to get his membership back, but she was delighted to receive her own uniform. 'Thank you,' she said, taking it. The material felt heavy and expensive in her hands. 'I'll be proud to wear it for however long I can.'

CHAPTER FIFTEEN

They ran out of water and soda after two more days. Ursula had never been so thirsty before in her life. Jai even agreed they could suspend their daily duty of polishing all the brass and buffing the wooden floors, since it seemed more important for them to conserve their energy. The constant thirst put everyone in a bad mood, though, and they found themselves snapping at each other, when they could be bothered to speak at all. Talking made their dry throats burn even worse and their parched lips crack, so they all became very quiet.

The explorers had hoped they'd only have to hold on for a little while longer because Gilly's Island was just one day away, but as they got closer, they noticed something disturbing through the portholes – the seabed around them was littered with shipwrecks. There were dozens of them: explorer ships and merchant vessels, fishing boats and pirate galleons.

There was even a great battleship slowly rotting away with its cannons rusting and its sails in tatters.

'I don't like this,' Max muttered, staring out at the skeletal boats. 'What's responsible for sinking them all? There are no treacherous rocks or coastlines around here.'

Nobody had an answer, although they agreed a schedule between them for keeping watch for sea monsters, and they all secretly dreaded the juddering impact of huge tentacles suddenly wrapping around the submarine.

It was therefore a great relief to finally reach Gilly's Island later that morning. They raised the submarine to the surface and went out on deck. The girls had donned their cloaks for the first time and Ursula loved the weight of it on her shoulders and the way it billowed out in the breeze. It made her feel like a real explorer. She'd kept her dolphin headband, though, to keep her hair out of her eyes. And Genie wore one of her hats. This one was made from papier mâché and took the form of a pirate galleon, complete with white sails, miniature cannons and a matchstick pirate captain on the bridge.

'What an extraordinary hat!' Max exclaimed.

'I made it,' Genie said, with pride.

'I love the attention to detail.' Ursula pointed at the

pirate captain and said, 'He's even wearing his own little hat!'

'There used to be an entire crew,' Genie said. 'They all had hats and cutlasses. And the captain had a parrot. But I wore it to school once and the other kids took it off me at break time and ripped some of it up. I managed to save the ship, but the crew all got stamped on.'

An angry look flashed over Jai's face. He sighed and said, 'I told you not to wear it to school, Genie. I knew they'd make fun of you.'

Genie shrugged. 'They'd pick on me anyway, so I might as well wear my hats.'

'You know why they pick on you, of course?' Max asked.

'It's because they think I'm weird,' Genie replied. 'And they're frightened of Bess.'

'No, it's because they're unbearably jealous,' Max said. 'I bet none of them could imagine being friends with a kraken in their wildest dreams, or owning a hat as cool as that.'

Genie brightened, and even Jai gave Max an approving look.

'Do you really think it's cool?' Genie asked.

'Obviously,' Max replied. 'Almost as cool as my

robot T-shirts.' Today he had one with a robot penguin which, like the duck, had laser-beam eyes.

'Maybe you shouldn't wear the hat on an expedition, though, Genie,' Jai said. 'It might get ruined. Plus it looks like it's going to rain.'

They all looked up. They'd expected it to be bright and sunny once again, but in fact the sky was choked with clouds.

'That's odd,' Ursula said. 'I thought it hardly ever rained in this part of the world.'

'It would be good if it did,' Genie said. 'We could fill up our reserve water barrels then too. And I'm still going to wear my hat. I didn't make it to sit in the cupboard. I'd rather it got ruined than not worn.'

'Well, we can't just hang around waiting for it to rain,' Jai said. 'We're going to have to go on land and try to find some water. Just remember to keep your wits about you. No one's ever explored this island before so we don't know how safe it is.'

Ursula didn't think it looked very appealing. Instead of the golden sand and waving palm trees of the Island of Fairy Giraffes, this one was all grey slate and jagged rock and towering cliffs.

'It must be inhabited,' Genie said. 'There's a lighthouse on the cliff there, look!'

She pointed and Ursula saw she was right. A towering lighthouse stretched up into the sky like a finger, right on the edge of the cliff.

'That's good,' Jai said, hoisting his bag on to his back. 'If it's inhabited then there must be water there.'

Ursula frowned. There was something about the lighthouse she didn't like. It looked creepy to her, all alone on the cliff like that. And its red-and-white stripes were peeling and dirty, as though it hadn't been painted in a long time.

'Its light is on,' she pointed out. 'That's odd. I thought lighthouses only shone their lights at night?'

The lighthouse did indeed have its lantern burning, but instead of the usual golden light, it was giving off a green one.

'More importantly,' Genie said, 'how are we going to get on to the island? I can't see any beaches to pull in to.'

'Oh.' Jai's face fell. 'You're right.'

They all looked at the island. Its cliffs rose up many feet from the water and were far too steep to climb.

'I know a way,' Max said, sounding smug. 'We'll get as close to the cliff as we can in the motorboat and take a rope ladder with us. Then my robot dragon can fly the ladder to the top of the cliff and attach it to something at the top.'

The others agreed that this seemed like the best solution, so they waited while Max disappeared to fetch the robot. He came back a few minutes later with a mechanical dragon in his arms. It was about the size of a sheepdog, with metal wings, a pointed, lizardy face and glowing red eyes.

'That's so cool!' Ursula said, peering at it. 'Does it have laser-beam eyes?'

'No. She can fly, though.'

'If she doesn't have laser-beam eyes then what's the heating element for?' Genie asked, pointing to a little box attached to the dragon's back.

'Oh, that's for the popcorn,' Max said. 'She's also a popcorn maker.'

'What is it with you and popcorn?' Jai asked.

'Popcorn is the second best food after pizza,' Max replied.

They piled into the motorboat and lowered it to the water before setting off towards Gilly's Island. The sea was quite choppy here, with white crests of foam on top, so it was a little tricky navigating the boat close to the mainland without dashing it on the cliffs. Finally, they managed to get it near enough and dropped the anchor. Ursula saw that the cliff face was covered in slippery-looking lichen, further ruling out any possibility of climbing it.

Then Max took a controller from his pocket and turned on the robot dragon, whose eyes glowed as it came to life.

'Right,' Max said, fiddling with the buttons on the controller. 'I haven't used this one in a while so I just have to remember how to do it. Oh no, that's the wrong button.'

There were a series of pops inside the dragon's metal belly and a delicious buttery smell filled the air.

'That's the popcorn button,' Max said.

Ursula thought it was a bit painful smelling popcorn knowing she couldn't eat it because it would make her even thirstier than she already was. The next moment, though, Max had pressed the right buttons and the robot dragon flapped its metal wings to fly up to the top of the cliff, trailing the rope ladder behind it. A few minutes later it had secured the ladder to something at the top and then flew back down to them.

'Good girl,' Max said, patting her on the head. 'Now, stay here and guard the boat.'

'How do we know she's properly secured the ladder?' Jai asked, staring up at the cliff. 'It's a long way to fall if she hasn't.'

'She'll have done it all right,' Max replied. 'Here, I'll go first if you're scared.'

'I'm not scared,' Jai said. He gestured at his chest and said, 'I have five medals for bravery.'

'Careful you don't lose one on your way up,' Max said. Then he reached forward to grip the ladder and hauled himself out of the boat to begin the climb. The others watched his progress with bated breath but soon he disappeared over the side of the cliff. He stuck his head back a moment later and waved them up.

'You can come together,' he called. 'The ladder is attached to a rock – it can easily take all your weight. Um . . . it's a bit strange up here, though.'

'Strange?' Jai called back. 'How do you mean?'

'You'd better come see for yourself.'

They did as he said and made their way up the rope ladder, leaving the robot dragon behind in the boat. The cliff seemed to get steeper the further they went and Ursula had to force herself not to look at the roiling grey waves below. It was a relief to reach the top of the cliff and be hauled over the side by Max. Finally, all four children were standing on Gilly's Island and could take it in for the first time.

'How peculiar,' Genie finally said.

Ursula had to agree. She'd expected a rugged landscape, maybe with some sea flowers or wild grass, but instead they were met with what appeared to be piles and piles of rope. Most of it was blue, but there were white coils in there too, and it stretched out over an area as big as a field. There were no trees or vegetation in sight apart from a small patch of grass in front of the lighthouse and, more importantly, there was no water. When the rope ran out, the land beyond was just slate with the odd cluster of barnacles stuck to it and some slippery-looking lichen. There was a funny metallic smell in the air and static made their hair stick on end.

Ursula knelt down to push aside some of the rope but found only more coils of it underneath. Her heart sank at the thought of leaving the island without water. She'd never been so thirsty before and couldn't have imagined how painful it was. Her entire throat burned and her tongue felt like a lump of wood inside her mouth.

'We should check the lighthouse,' Jai said. 'I don't think there can be anyone living there – it wouldn't be possible to survive on this island, but there might be some supplies.'

Not feeling too hopeful about it, the four children began making their way across the rope. It felt soft and spongy underfoot, causing them to wobble about a bit as they went.

'This is weird,' Max said. 'It doesn't feel like solid

ground. And why would anyone dump all this rope here anyway?'

None of them had an answer to that, but they were glad to get off the rope and finally set foot on the grass in front of the lighthouse. There was an old wooden sign in front of it which was quite difficult to read because the paint had faded, but they could just about make out the words: *Mango Island Lighthouse.*

'What idiot gave it that name?' Max wondered. 'There isn't a single mango tree here.'

They walked up to the lighthouse door and found it all boarded up, with more signs saying things like *Do Not Enter!* and *Permanently Closed* and *Beware of the Storm.*

'That's what the smell is!' Genie exclaimed, snapping her fingers. 'The air smells how it does when a storm is coming.'

Ursula realised she was right. It smelled of rain and lightning and it explained the static too. She looked up into the sky and saw that the clouds were still swirling around up there.

'It does look a bit like it might rain,' she said. 'Perhaps we should just go back to the submarine and wait for the rain to fill the barrels?'

'We might as well quickly check the lighthouse first,' Jai said. 'Since we're already here.'

They prised off the wooden boards, which were so old and rotten that they came away easily enough. Then they stepped inside the lighthouse expecting it to be dusty and dilapidated, but to their surprise it was spotlessly clean and smelled faintly of polish.

'That's strange,' Ursula said. She glanced at the others. 'You don't think there really can be anyone living here, do you?'

'Perhaps it's Gilly?' Genie suggested. 'It's their island, after all.'

There was a brief silence. None of them had stopped to think about where the island's name had come from and who Gilly might be.

Jai shook his head. 'There's nothing to eat or drink so no one could survive here for long,' he said. 'The lighthouse does seem very clean, though.'

A spiral staircase led to the upper floors and the explorers made their way up. None of them had ever been in a lighthouse before and they weren't sure what to expect. When they got to the second floor there was a small landing with a curved door set in the wall. It was closed but a bright yellow light shone through the gaps around and underneath so that the door was framed in a bright gold rectangle.

'What the heck's in there?' Max said.

'Maybe it's a spare lantern for the lighthouse?' Genie said. 'It would have to be very bright to shine out to sea.'

'This lighthouse's lantern has a green light, though,' Ursula said. 'And if it's a spare light then why would it be turned on inside a closed room?'

'Let's take a look,' Jai said. 'It could be an important discovery.'

Max gripped the handle and cautiously pushed the door open. Glittering yellow light spilled out of the door, sizzling in the air around them and tingling over their skin. The explorers' hair all stood on end as they stared inside.

It wasn't a spare lantern after all. Instead it was piles and piles of lightning bolts, leaned up against the wall or stacked on top of one another on the floor. Some of the bolts were taller than the explorers while others were no bigger than their forearms. They all crackled and fizzed with electrical energy, filling the air with sparks.

'Great Scott!' Jai said. 'How extraordinary! I thought lightning was supposed to be an electrostatic discharge in the atmosphere. How can they all just be piled up in a room like this?'

It was indeed a mystery. Max moved forwards and reached out towards one of the bolts.

'I wouldn't do that!' Jai said. 'You could electrocute yourself.'

But Max had already closed his fingers around one. The others cried out in alarm.

'It's fine,' Max said, grinning. 'It feels really weird and tingly, but it's OK.'

He held the bolt out to the others, who cautiously touched it and found he was right. It made strange little shivers go racing up Ursula's arm but it wasn't painful.

'I'm definitely taking this,' Max said, stuffing the bolt into his bag. 'Maybe I can make a lightning robot out of it.'

Max insisted on inspecting the bolts more closely before they finally left the room and went up to the next floor. They soon found that the rest of the lighthouse was just as peculiar. There was no kitchen, bedroom or generator. Instead, the next door they opened led to a room that was full of piles of hailstones, some of which were as large as their heads. The room after that contained weathervanes and roof tiles. And in the room on the fourth floor they found a whole bunch of weird silver cats prowling about on the ceiling, running up the walls and hissing mini tornadoes at them.

Jai hurriedly slammed the door closed. 'What the heck is this place?' he gasped.

There was one more room left to explore, right at the very top of the lighthouse. They paused to listen outside the door, but hearing no meowing or hissing, opened it slowly. Much of the room was taken up with the giant lantern that was beaming out the green light. Set up around this they finally found what looked like living quarters. There were shelves of food over in one corner, and a bed, a table, a stove and an armchair, but they were all so tiny that they looked like dolls' house furniture. Like the rest of the building, this room was completely clean and it even looked as if someone had been here recently. A tiny plate lay on the table, the little frying pan on the stove was still warm and there was a faint smell of bacon in the air.

'Are you the sacrificial offerings?' a voice suddenly asked, making them all jump. 'Normally they send pineapples.'

'What? Who said that?' Jai asked. 'And no, we're definitely not sacrificial offerings.'

'Outside,' the voice replied.

The four children looked to see that there was a door leading to the balcony that wrapped around the lighthouse. And sitting on the balcony was a tiny old man in a tiny rocking chair. They made their way out and gazed at him in astonishment. He had a bushy white beard and wore a bright yellow rain mac and hat with matching welly boots. There was a pipe clamped between his teeth, his eyes were blue and bright, and he was no larger than a thumb.

'You're not from Satsuma Island over there?' the old man said, pointing across the sea with his pipe at a neighbouring island a mile or so away. From this high up they had an excellent view of the surrounding ocean, as well as their docked submarine. Bess was stretched out on its roof to sunbathe, her long tentacles dangling contentedly over the side into the water.

'No,' Jai said. 'We're explorers from the Ocean Squid Explorers' Club.'

The man looked worried. 'So you don't want to be sacrificed then? It's just that it might be a bit late to change your mind now that you're here.'

'Of course we don't want to be sacrificed!' Max exclaimed. 'Sacrificed to what anyway? Is it the thing that sunk all those ships?'

'Oh, yes, she eats ships for breakfast,' the old man said.

'What does?' Ursula asked. 'Is it a kraken?'

They all looked round, expecting flailing tentacles to surge up out of the sea at any moment. It would be quite good if it *was* a kraken, actually, because then

Genie would be able to talk to it and calm it down and perhaps persuade it not to gobble them up too.

'Eh?' the old man blinked up at them. 'What are you talking about?'

'Barmy,' Max said beneath his breath to the others.

'I'm certainly not barmy, young man,' he said. 'And there's nothing wrong with my hearing either. Albert Thumb, at your service.'

'It's very nice to meet you,' Ursula said. 'Sorry to just walk in – we didn't realise anyone was living here. Would you mind telling us what kind of lighthouse this is? We've never seen one like it before. We were hoping to find water on the island.'

Albert Thumb's eyes widened at this. He set down his pipe and leaned forwards in his chair. 'Island?' he repeated. 'Is that what you think this is?'

The explorers looked at each other.

'Naturally,' Max said. 'It's a rock in the middle of the ocean, isn't it? What would you call it?'

'This ain't no rock,' Albert said, starting to grin. 'She's a storm maiden. And you're standing right on top of her.'

Chapter Sixteen

There was a momentary silence.

'There was an island here once, of course,' Albert went on. 'Mango Island, I think it was called. This bit of rock with the lighthouse on it is all that's left, though. Gilly threw the rest of it away to make room when she decided to settle here. I think it landed in the next ocean somewhere.'

'Are you saying that this entire island is actually a . . . a person?' Genie asked.

'Course it is.' The old man frowned at them. 'Don't you have storm maidens where you come from? Didn't you see the green light? It means there's a storm maiden here and you should stay away.'

'We didn't know,' Ursula said.

'I saw you arrive,' Albert went on. 'What did you think you were walking across?'

'We thought it was rope,' Jai said.

'Ha!' Albert shook his head. 'That ain't rope. It's her

hair. She doesn't like it being trampled over either. Very risky thing to do.'

Jai groaned. 'We had no idea,' he said.

The old man shrugged. 'That's what you get for blundering in someplace you've never been before,' he said. 'You're lucky it's a storm maiden and not a hurricane madam, to say nothing of the typhoon damsels and earthquake maids. But a storm maiden is still terribly dangerous. You might have been all right if you'd stumbled on to a whirlpool lass but any one of the others will eat you for breakfast! I've worked as a storm keeper for Gilly for years and I tell ya, she'll swallow up everything and anything in her path once she's woken up.'

'Is that what all the lightning bolts and things are for downstairs?' Ursula asked.

'Yep.' Albert nodded. 'She's got stores of her own, of course, but we keep the spares here. It's a mutually beneficial relationship, see? I keep her stocked up with storm supplies and she provides me with food and shelter and a front-row seat to the spectacle.'

'If the lighthouse is full of storm supplies then what the devil are those awful cats for?' Max demanded.

Albert raised an eyebrow. 'You don't have storm cats where you come from either?' He shook his head. 'Next thing, you'll expect me to believe that you don't have thunder ducks or hurricane platypuses neither.'

Max shook his head. 'All right, he's definitely making things up now,' he said. 'Only a complete moron would think there was such a thing as a hurricane platypus. I think this is just a normal island and not a storm maiden at all.'

'Why would I make it up?' Albert asked, narrowing his eyes.

'Maybe you've gone round the twist living here by yourself and actually believe it,' Max said with a shrug. 'Or maybe this is one of those practical-joke radio shows?' He looked at the others. 'Have you heard about them? There was a notice on the board at the club last week about this new trend in far-off parts for local people to play practical jokes on explorers by pretending there are all kinds of weird things there. I think the aim is to see who can get an explorer to believe the most outrageous claim. They win a lifetime's worth of ice cream or something.'

'Oh yeah, wasn't there an explorer who was ridiculed at the club because he wrote about an island in his Flag Report that had chocolate sand on its beaches but it turned out to be a hoax?' Genie said.

'And there was another explorer who claimed that there was an entire monkey city inside a coconut he brought back but when they opened it up it was just coconut,' Ursula said.

'It doesn't matter,' Jai said. 'The fact is, there's no water here so there's no need for us to linger.' He looked at Albert Thumb and said, 'It was a pleasure to make your acquaintance, Mr Thumb, but now we must be on our way.'

'Oh, you won't be able to leave the island,' he said. 'She won't let you. Especially if you try to take one of her lightning bolts.'

They all looked at Max.

'I haven't got one,' he lied.

'I can see it glowing inside your bag,' Albert replied, pointing. 'You ain't got much chance of slipping away as it is, but if you try to take that with you, you're toast.'

'Put it back where you found it,' Jai said with a sigh.

'No.' Max folded his arms over his chest. 'I'm not giving up on a lightning robot just because of some mad ramblings from this pixie.'

'I ain't no pixie!' Albert replied, looking indignant. 'I'm a storm keeper.'

'You're barking,' Max said. 'Come on, let's go.'

Before anyone could stop him, he'd turned and gone back inside.

'Good day to you, sir,' Jai said politely to Albert.

The girls said goodbye too and then they all went after Max.

'I'm not letting you take that lightning bolt,' Jai said as they all stepped outside the lighthouse. 'It's too dangerous.'

Max tightened his grip on the straps of his bag. 'It's mine,' he said. 'You've got no say in the matter.'

'Max, why are you being like this?' Ursula asked, frowning. 'Jai's right. If there's any chance that this really is a storm maiden, then it's not worth the risk.'

'It *is* worth the risk!' Max replied with sudden fierceness. 'A hundred times over!'

'What's this really about?' Ursula asked. 'Why do you need that lightning bolt?'

'I told you,' he said. 'For a robot.'

'This is ridiculous.' Jai strode forwards. 'Hand it over.'

'Don't even think about touching my bag,' Max replied in a quiet voice. 'You won't like what happens.'

Ignoring him, Jai reached for the bag but the second his hand touched it, Max grabbed his arm and in one movement flipped him over on to his back. Jai landed with a grunt and a thump. He quickly kicked Max's feet out from under him and the next moment they were scrabbling around in the grass together.

'For goodness' sake!' Ursula exclaimed. 'Cut it out!'

Genie looked around for something to chuck at them but there was nothing in sight. And that's when she realised that the ground beneath her feet was trembling. Ursula noticed at the same time and they both shouted out a warning, but it was too late. Ursula realised Albert had been telling the truth about the lighthouse being the only part of the island that was left. Before their eyes, the rest of it shuddered and then shifted, unfolding itself until it was no longer a lump of rock but a human figure.

Max and Jai stopped fighting before they could roll off the edge that had suddenly appeared. Their little patch of land with the lighthouse was all that remained. Before them loomed the giant that was the storm maiden. Her body was made of grey slate, she wore a lichen dress and had a huge mass of blue-and-white-rope hair that tumbled over her shoulders. She regarded them with bright green eyes that sparkled menacingly in her stone face.

'Great Scott!' Jai gasped. 'Albert was right!'

'What do we do?' Genie asked.

Without the rope ladder they had no way to climb back down the cliff. And already, the storm maiden had reached into the sky and plucked a lightning bolt from the clouds.

Max scrambled to his feet, pulled the lightning bolt from his bag and laid it down on the ground.

'I'm very sorry, madam,' he said. 'No harm meant.'

But Gilly didn't seem convinced by his apology. She drew back her arm and took aim with her lightning bolt.

'Perhaps we can reason with her.' Jai was on his feet too and had pulled his copy of *Captain Filibuster's Guide to Expeditions and Exploration* from his pocket. He thumbed through it frantically. 'There might be something in here.'

'She's a storm!' Max said. 'I think she's just going to do what storms do.'

Jai ignored him and located the right page. 'Greetings, madam,' he read. 'We are explorers from the Ocean Squid Explorers' Club and we have travelled a long way to—'

'Watch out!' Max yelled, bundling Jai to the floor just as the storm maiden cast her lightning bolt right where he'd stood.

It hit the ground with a deafening *CRACK*! Max and Jai scrambled to their feet and the explorers all raced for the lighthouse door but Albert must have locked it after them because it was shut fast. They could hear him cackling on the other side.

'I told yer!' he called. 'I told yer, but yer wouldn't listen!'

Ursula noticed that there was a tiny door cut into the big door, presumably for Albert to go in and out of, but there was no way any of the explorers were going to fit. To their horror, the storm maiden raised her arm again and the clouds all rushed to it like it was a magnet. She moved her hand in a circle, causing the clouds to whirl around her, growing bigger and angrier. The sky darkened and then seemed to break apart, letting loose a deluge of rain, hailstones and a few roof tiles. The explorers were all soaked within moments.

'We'll have to jump!' Genie yelled, raising her voice over the wind that had suddenly picked up and was tearing at their cloaks. 'And swim to the motorboat.'

Realising her hat wasn't going to make it after all, she took it off and set it down on the lighthouse steps.

Max glanced at Jai and said, '*Can* you swim without a prosthetic?'

Jai looked outraged. 'I'm Jai Bartholomew Singh!' he said. 'Of course I can swim, you dolt! I once swam five miles through the night to Plum Pudding Island while towing an injured team member by clamping their life jacket strap between my teeth, to say nothing of the time I—'

'All right, all right,' Max said, holding up his hands. 'Just checking.'

'It's a long way, though,' Ursula pointed out. 'I'll be OK, but will the three of you be able to—?'

Before she could finish, the storm maiden started grabbing handfuls of storm cats from the clouds and hurling them down. The silver creatures raced at the explorers, hissing out mini tornadoes that tore up the grass at the roots. At the same time, Gilly leaned forward, reaching out her gigantic hand towards them. Ursula had visions of being scooped up, ripped apart and thrown across the ocean like Mango Island.

There was nothing for it. The four explorers all turned and ran for the cliff edge. It looked terrifyingly high but it was their only chance. They took a flying leap off the side, their cloaks billowing out behind them, just as the storm maiden's fingers closed around the air where they'd been.

It seemed like an endless fall towards the roiling waves where Bess waited for them below. Ursula was too scared even to scream, although Max bellowed lustily all the way down. Ursula managed to lean forwards into a dive just as the ocean raced up to meet her. She plunged beneath the surface and her legs instantly changed into a mermaid's fin. The world went grey and quiet for a moment while she was tearing off her shredded trousers underwater, but then her head broke the surface and everything was chaos: huge waves and roaring wind and even a few storm cats, which unfortunately seemed to be able to swim extremely well.

Ursula struggled with a couple of them before a sharp whistle pierced the air, drawing them away from her. Blinking water from her eyes, she cast around desperately, searching for the others or clues as to where that whistle had come from. Genie had landed nearest the boat and had already dragged herself inside and started up the motor. A moment later she brought it up alongside Ursula. Bess's tentacles curled around the boat and went in and out of the surrounding water, while the robot dragon perched on the side.

'Where are the others?' Genie yelled.

Ursula shook her head. She'd lost sight of Max and Jai. Above them Gilly was gathering even more clouds, making the sky so dark that black explorer cloaks would be hard to spot in the water. Suddenly, there was a burst of spray at Ursula's side and Max came up to the surface spluttering.

'Have you got him?' he shouted.

'Who?'

'Jai! He was fighting with the storm cats, trying to take them all on by himself. Didn't you hear him whistle to get their attention? They dragged him down!'

'Oh no!' Genie cried. She lunged to the edge of the boat, clearly about to dive over the side, but Ursula stopped her.

'Don't!' she said. 'Someone needs to keep the motorboat steady. I'll go.'

She dived beneath the surface and quickly realised that Max had followed her and was swimming by her side. Ursula soon spotted Jai struggling with a bunch of storm cats quite close by.

She raced over to him and started grabbing the cats and thrusting them away. Max arrived soon after to help. The cats fought back at first, lashing out with their claws and churning up the water with their hisses, but finally they scattered and Ursula was able to get to Jai. To her horror, she saw that he'd gone limp in the water and was already starting to sink. She wrapped her arms around his chest and swam for the surface with Max right behind her. They came up close to the motorboat and Genie reached over to haul Jai inside. Ursula and Max scrabbled in after him.

The storm was still raging around them and Ursula was dimly aware of Gilly reaching her greedy hands out for the submarine. Bess had gone over to it and was trying to ward her off by flailing her tentacles, but the illusion couldn't last long. The storm maiden was bound to realise Bess was a shadow animal soon and then there'd be nothing to stop her grabbing the submarine. But they had more important things to worry about just then.

'He's not breathing!' Genie groaned, bending over her twin.

'Let me through.' Max nudged her aside and bent over Jai.

The first thing every junior explorer in the Ocean Squid Explorers' Club learned how to do was mouth to mouth resuscitation and Max went straight into rescue breaths before doing chest compressions. The boat rocked beneath them, and for a moment Ursula had awful visions of Jai dying. She knew explorers often died on expeditions – after all, her own father had died – but she'd always glossed over that in her mind when she'd dreamed about being an explorer, focusing instead on the fun, exciting parts. But this wasn't fun or exciting at all. It was terrifying and gut-wrenching and her whole body shivered with the shock of it.

But then Jai was suddenly coughing up seawater and gasping for breath on the floor of the boat. Genie wrapped her arms around him with a cry and Max fell back, wiping his forehead with trembling hands.

'Go!' he croaked, looking at Ursula, who was nearest the motor. 'We've got to get back to the submarine.'

It was awkward for her to move around in her mermaid form but she dragged herself over to the motor, revved it up and pointed the boat towards the submarine. The storm maiden was creating a whirlpool around it but Ursula managed to steer the boat past her gigantic fingers. It was impossible to approach slowly with the submarine being tossed about in the waves and they hit the side with a smash that sent them flying and almost tore the boat apart. But somehow Max and Ursula managed to grab hold of the ropes, attach them to the sides and then heaved with all their might to lift the boat up.

When they reached the deck, Max scooped Ursula out and Genie helped Jai to his feet. Together, they sprinted along the roof and tumbled into the hatch, slamming it closed just as the whirlpool dragged the submarine down beneath the surface.

CHAPTER SEVENTEEN

Ursula dried off her tail as quickly as she could to get her legs back, then raced to the bridge with the others. The submarine was being tossed about in the whirlpool, causing everything that wasn't nailed down to fall over and slide around. They could hear ominous crashes from other rooms and it was hard work keeping their footing. Jai, in particular, was still unsteady on his feet and there was an unhealthy pallor to his skin. As they reached the bridge he stumbled into the door and would have fallen down if Max hadn't caught him and helped him sit with his back against the wall.

Ursula and Genie ran to the engines and got them fired up. The first time they tried to escape the whirlpool it tossed them straight back down on to the ocean floor. A great *clang* went through the entire submarine and Ursula winced at the thought of all the sub's essential machinery being bashed around like that. Several warning lights flashed on the control panel and an alarm started wailing too.

'Again!' she gasped. 'Whirlpools have less strength in the middle so we'll have more power behind us from here.'

They charged up the engines, and this time the submarine managed to burst through the whirlpool and escape out the other side. They kept the engines at full power, putting as much distance as possible between themselves and the storm maiden. Thankfully, she didn't pursue them and the ocean became less turbulent the further away they got.

When there were several miles between them, Ursula turned off the engines and the submarine drifted to a stop.

'The ventilation systems are failing,' she said. 'We're going to have to resurface while I repair them.'

She brought the submarine up. Through the portholes they saw that although they'd passed through the storm, it was still raining heavily here so they pressed the buttons to get the rain barrels up on the deck.

'Can we help with the repairs?' Jai asked, struggling to his feet. 'Could you show us what to do?'

Ursula shook her head. 'You need to go and rest.'

'No, I don't—' Jai started to protest.

'Yes, you do,' Ursula said firmly. 'You stopped breathing. You drowned.'

Jai stared at her blankly. 'What?'

'The storm cats dragged you under. Max had to resuscitate you. Don't you remember?'

Jai frowned. 'Not properly,' he said. 'But I guess that explains why my ribs ache so much.'

'Sorry,' Max said, so quietly that they almost didn't hear him. There was a stricken expression on his face and for a moment Ursula wondered whether he was about to throw up. 'There's no way to do it without injuring the ribs.'

Jai glanced at him. 'I know that. Maybe I will go and lie down for a bit. If you're sure you don't need me, Ursula?'

'You go,' Ursula said. 'We'll let you know when the repairs are done.'

The work took Ursula most of the rest of the day. The air and water systems had been badly damaged in the whirlpool and although the others tried to help, Ursula was the only one who really had the skills to do the repairs. She changed back into her coveralls, and crawling around in one of the ducts, covered in grease with a spanner clasped in her hand, she felt even more at home on the submarine. Here was a job that she knew how to do and could do well. When the *Blowfish* was ready to set off again, she plotted a course for the unexplored Bubble Ocean, which she estimated they would reach sometime the next day.

Genie found her on the bridge as she was finishing and thanked her for her part in saving Jai.

Ursula waved her thanks away. 'He wouldn't have needed saving if he'd not taken on all the storm cats to try to help us,' she said.

'I know.' Genie chewed her lip, looking worried. 'He's always doing stuff like that. It's not the first time he's drowned, you know. I hate those medals of his,' she went on, with sudden feeling. 'They all represent times he put himself in danger, times he almost didn't come home. I think he does it because of our dad.'

'Your dad?' Ursula repeated, not understanding.

Genie nodded. 'Every time Jai's awarded another medal, it's reported in the Ocean Squid Explorers' Club *Gazette*. He thinks our father still reads it, and I guess part of him hopes that if he becomes the most amazing explorer ever, then maybe our dad will come back, but he won't. It doesn't matter what Jai does. It doesn't matter what he achieves. It won't change anything. Our dad just doesn't care about us.'

'I'm sorry,' Ursula said, feeling a bit helpless. 'That's really hard.'

Genie gave a small shrug and then returned to her usual optimism. 'At least the rain means our water supplies are completely refilled. You can have a bath now if you want to.'

Ursula couldn't think of anything better. She said goodbye to Genie and drank a pint of water in the galley before heading to one of the submarine's washrooms. It was a huge, beautiful space with elegant squid tentacles on the green tiles and a massive tub in the centre of the room in the shape of a clam shell. There was a control panel on the side with lots of buttons and Ursula experimented with pressing these. One of them caused a bubble-bath menu to appear, with scents ranging from blueberry pancakes to vanilla ice cream. Ursula chose coconut lime pie and the tub was soon filled with delicious-smelling bubbles.

The other buttons produced interesting results too. One of them caused a pile of rubber ducks wearing pirate hats to tumble into the water from a hidden chute. And another somehow made an entire silver platter of salted-fudge starfish appear beside the tub.

Ursula enjoyed her bath. As she was drying off, the

intercom crackled into life and Jai's voice rang through the submarine.

'All hands please report to the dining room,' he said. 'All hands to the dining room.'

Ursula was starving and very much hoped that whatever the summons to the dining room was about, it would involve food. The children hadn't eaten together on previous evenings – they had simply heated up their tray dinners whenever they felt like it. This time, however, when Ursula entered the dining room there was the delicious smell of roast chicken in the air and she saw that Jai had set four places at the table. He looked a bit better than the last time she'd seen him, although there were still dark circles under his eyes.

'I thought we ought to start eating our meals together,' Jai said when she came in. 'Like a proper crew.'

Ursula had found it rather lonely eating in the galley by herself so she nodded and said, 'Good idea.'

Max and Genie walked in right behind her and seemed pleased with Jai's idea too. They all took their seats at the end of the long table and Ursula enjoyed eating her chicken dinner off a proper china plate rather than from a plastic carton.

'I thought these would all have been smashed in the whirlpool,' she said.

'Many of them were,' Jai said. 'It took most of the afternoon to clear up this room.'

'You were supposed to be resting in bed,' Genie said with an accusing look.

'I don't like resting in bed,' Jai replied. 'Not when there are important things that need to be done.'

They bickered over this a little more, but finally everyone had finished eating and Jai pushed his plate to one side.

'You're very quiet this evening,' he said, looking right at Max.

In fact, Ursula realised that he hadn't said a word since entering the room and had barely touched his dinner either.

'I'm sorry,' he said now. 'Were you expecting a speech of some kind?'

'Actually, yes,' Jai said. 'I would like to know why we were fighting over a lightning bolt like a pair of complete twits.'

Max paused. Finally, he shrugged and said, 'I just like annoying you, that's all.'

'I don't believe you,' Jai said calmly.

'That's your problem.'

'Jai's right,' Ursula said. 'There's something you're not telling us, Max, it's obvious.'

'Why were you expelled from the Ocean Squid Explorers' Club?' Jai asked.

Genie frowned. 'We already know why.'

'We don't know the full story,' Jai said.

'There's more to it,' Ursula agreed. 'I know you like breaking rules, Max, but you've never broken a really serious one before. You've never put anyone else in danger.'

'I heard explorers talking about it at the club,' Jai said. 'Speculating about why you would conspire with pirates. Some said it was because you were stupid. Others thought you had no honour. I thought it was probably a bit of both.'

'How flattering,' Max replied.

'But now I realise I was wrong,' Jai said. 'You're obviously smart, or you wouldn't be able to invent those robots. And you clearly have a sense of honour or you wouldn't have put yourself at risk to come after me when the storm cats dragged me underwater. So what's going on?'

Max sighed. 'Listen,' he said. 'I'm really sorry about what happened with the storm maiden and the cats and the drowning and everything. But I needed that lightning bolt for something important.'

'We're all listening,' Jai said.

Max shrugged. 'I suppose you have a right to know since you basically drowned earlier today. You've all heard that the number of pirate attacks on explorer ships has increased recently?'

Everyone nodded.

'Well, a few weeks ago some pirates attacked a ship I was on and we repelled it with a robot dragon I'd made. It could shoot fire, you see, so all their sails were ablaze in no time. I guess word spread around the pirates about it. None of them had ever seen a robot dragon before. I don't think anyone else has ever been able to make one. About a week after that I got a letter from the Collector.'

Ursula gasped. 'The Collector!' she exclaimed. 'What did she want with you? How did she know where you were?'

'Well, she sent the letter by firebird.'

Firebirds looked a bit like phoenixes and everyone had thought they were extinct until Stella Starflake Pearl discovered some at the Collector's hideout in the Hanging Gardens of Amadon. They could disappear with a burst of fire and then reappear anywhere else they chose, whether in exactly the same place or a hundred miles away, all in the blink of an eye.

'The letter said she'd found out I was the inventor

of the robot dragon,' Max went on. 'And she wanted to offer me a reward.'

'A *reward*?' Genie stared at him. 'For doing what?'

'For making a weapon,' Max said with a sigh. 'To attack Stella Starflake Pearl.'

Ursula sucked in her breath. 'And you agreed?'

She regretted her words the next second when a flash of hurt crossed Max's face.

'No,' he said. 'I didn't. I tore up the letter and immediately reported it to President Verne.'

'And did he have anything remotely sensible to say?' Jai asked quietly.

Max shook his head. 'Actually, he didn't believe me. He accused me of lying to get attention.'

'He doesn't want the club to get involved with the hunt for the Collector,' Ursula said. 'He thinks the problem will just go away by itself.'

'Well, it won't,' Max said. 'The Collector is determined. Apparently her sorcerer's staff was damaged in the confrontation with Stella and she hasn't been able to fix it. That's why she needs something else. When I turned her down, Scarlett kidnapped my sister, Jada.'

Ursula gasped and Genie's hands flew to her mouth. Jai looked grim. 'I thought it must be something like that,' he said.

'You must be frantic with worry!' Genie exclaimed.

'I'm mainly concerned that she'll get bored of waiting for me and try to mount her own rescue, then find herself in even more trouble,' Max said, shaking his head. 'She's the most bull-headed person I know. And ...' He hesitated, then went on. 'And she's the most talented inventor in our family.'

Jai stared. 'What, better than you?'

Max offered a wry grin. 'Hard to believe, isn't it? But leave Jada with anything – I mean even a pair of shoelaces and a cup of water, for example – and she'll find a way to create some amazing invention from it. She's probably got the other children helping her get away already.'

'What other children?' Ursula asked.

'I'm not the only one the Collector has approached,' Max said. 'She really wants a new weapon and she's hedged her bets by going to a load of different inventors and magicians around the world. Some probably agreed to help willingly – the reward she offered was quite generous. But for those who said no, she's kidnapped a child from their family and stashed them away somewhere. Now she says it's a race. The first of us to give her what she wants will get our loved one back. She said all the other kids will be given the choice to join pirate crews, and if they refuse, will have to walk the plank.'

There was a stunned silence for a moment. Then Ursula said, 'Why haven't we heard about this? If the Collector has been going around kidnapping people, why hasn't there been an uproar?'

'She isn't kidnapping them herself,' Max replied. 'She's sending her pirates and sea gremlins to do it. And there hasn't been an uproar because she's told the inventors that if they say anything publicly then their loved one will be disposed of immediately. I told President Verne in confidence and requested permission to mount a rescue mission, but he refused. Said it was against the precious rules to launch a rescue mission for someone who wasn't actually a member of the club.'

'That's so unfair!' Ursula exclaimed. 'What did your parents say?'

'They don't know,' Max replied. 'They're both away. My dad's on an expedition in the Kelpie Sea. Completely unreachable and I'm not sure when he's coming home. And my mum is an aid worker; she's currently in the Ruby Desert helping to improve the water systems in a village there. She's not due back for weeks. Jada was staying with an elderly auntie of ours. Scarlett's sea gremlins just took her straight from the garden.'

'That's terrible, Max,' Ursula said. 'Why didn't you tell us before?'

'Because if I want to save Jada, I have to do something awful,' he said. 'And I've already done bad things. After Jada was taken, the next time pirates attacked our ship, I didn't send the dragon to attack them. I gave them the robot instead, for Scarlett to use as a weapon. That's why the club expelled me.' He looked at the others and Ursula clearly saw shame on his face. 'I know it was wrong,' he said, not meeting their eyes. 'But . . . tough as she is, Jada hasn't got any magical powers or anything. And she's only nine years old.'

There was a momentary silence. Finally, Ursula said, 'So did you get her back? Once you gave the Collector the dragon?'

Max shook his head. 'No. The Collector sent me a letter saying that the dragon's fire wasn't hot enough to defeat an ice princess's magic. So it was no good and I was expelled from the club for nothing. Then she demanded I try again. Only I don't know how. That's why I wanted the lightning bolt.'

'But it got left behind on Gilly's Island,' Genie said.

'Are we still calling it that?' Max asked, raising an

eyebrow. 'Personally, I think it should be renamed the Island of Storms and Mayhem. But actually, I only left one of the lightning bolts behind. The other I kept in my bag.'

'You mean you took two from the lighthouse?' Ursula asked.

'Yep. Just in case I needed a spare.'

'Where is it now?' Jai asked.

'In the lab,' Max said. 'I suppose you're going to demand I hand it over to be confiscated?'

Jai slowly shook his head. 'The first rule of command is never ask anyone to do what you wouldn't be willing to do yourself.' His eyes flicked towards his twin. 'If the Collector had Genie then I'd put her first too.'

Genie reached over the table to give him a fist bump and Bess, who had as much of her squeezed into the dining room as she could, reached up to curl a tentacle affectionately around Jai's shoulders.

'Well, that's just it,' Max said. 'I'm wondering if I should. Put her first, I mean. I love her, but ... I don't want the Collector to kill Stella. And you almost died today too,' he said, looking at Jai. 'In fact you *were* dead for a couple of minutes.'

'But I didn't stay that way, thanks to you,' Jai replied.

'When we were talking to Stella on the radio, I almost

told her,' Max said. 'I wanted to. Now I think maybe I should have. I don't know what to do. It seems like I'll hurt someone whichever way I go. And the worst part is that I never meant for my robots to be used as weapons, never! Deterrents against pirates and bandits, fair enough, but I never thought they'd be used against innocent people. It's the worst thing I could have imagined.'

'Where is Jada now?' Genie asked.

'I don't know. Scarlett says all the kidnapped children are at her headquarters, but obviously we have no clue where that is,' Max replied. 'She promised that Jada and the other children aren't being mistreated but I've only got her word to go on. And they're only kids. They must be terrified.'

'Well, the way I see it, our best chance is to continue with our mission to return the Sunken City of Pacifica,' Jai said. 'If the inhabitants can help us locate Scarlett's headquarters, then that will lead to your sister too.'

'Eventually, perhaps,' Max said. 'In the meantime, I just have to hope that no one else manages to come up with a suitable weapon and win the race.'

'Do you have a way to contact her?' Ursula asked.

Max hesitated, then nodded slowly. 'I have a firebird,' he admitted. 'I've been hiding it in my room. I'll go and fetch her.'

He walked out and came back a few moments later with the bird.

'She's beautiful!' Ursula exclaimed.

The little bird had orange-and-red feathers and bright, intelligent eyes. She seemed to enjoy being free because she fluttered joyfully around the room, poking into every corner and emitting delighted chirps. Ursula realised she must have been responsible for the smoky smell she'd detected in Max's robotics lab at the start of their voyage, as well as the orange feather he'd kicked under the table.

'Scarlett said that if I wanted to get in touch with her I could use the bird to send a message,' Max explained.

'Well, why don't you send her one about the lightning bolt?' Jai suggested. 'If she thinks you're on to something, maybe she'll keep hold of Jada even if someone else designs something for her first.'

Max looked shocked. 'I never thought I'd hear you suggest such a flagrant breach of the rules,' he said.

'That's because you don't know me as well as you think you do,' Jai replied. 'I'll gladly follow any rule that's fair but I have no time for nonsensical or arbitrary instructions.'

Ursula remembered what he'd said about the mermaid's tail hung in the trophy room back at the club, as well as the petition he'd tried to start for girl explorers, and she realised that he really wasn't as much of a stickler for the rules as she'd first thought. This fact made her like him even more.

'All right,' Max said. 'It's been a few days since she heard from me so she's probably getting quite impatient. I could do with buying some time.'

He took a scrap of paper from his pocket and they watched as he scribbled out a message explaining about the lightning bolt and promising to get to work creating a new robot with it. When he'd finished, he rolled the paper into a scroll and held it up to the firebird. She flew over to him immediately, took the scroll in her beak and then disappeared in a little puff of fire and smoke.

The message had only been gone a few minutes when the bird suddenly reappeared back in the room in another cloud of sparks.

'A firebird isn't exactly the safest thing to have on board a submarine,' Jai said, frowning. 'I hope she doesn't set anything alight. It could be disastrous.'

'I don't think she will,' Max said. 'She's been good so far.'

'She's got another message,' Genie pointed out.

Max reached for the scroll curled up in the firebird's

241

beak and they all gathered around as he unfurled it on the table. It was slightly scorched around the edges but contained just a single line in Scarlett's spidery scrawl.

Work quickly, Max. Others are getting close too.

Max sighed. 'A lot of her notes are like that.'

Ursula put a hand on his arm. 'We'll help you get Jada back,' she said.

Genie nodded. 'Bess and I will help too.'

'If there's anything that's in my power to aid your sister, then I promise I'll do it,' Jai agreed.

'Well, thanks,' Max said. 'Look, I feel a bit bad for taking your yodelling turtle medal now. Would you like it back?'

'Why *did* you make such a fuss about coming?' Ursula asked, as Max unpinned the medal from his T-shirt. 'When it was in your interests all along?'

Max grinned and gave a small shrug. 'Well, it got me what I wanted, didn't it?' He slid the medal across the table to Jai. 'And sometimes being a pain in the butt helps take my mind off Jada. Sorry,' he said, glancing at Jai. 'It is a ridiculous thing to get a medal for, though.'

'It's not his *most* ridiculous medal!' Genie piped up. 'His most ridiculous medal is for—'

'Don't,' Jai cut her off, looking suddenly flustered. 'There's no need to go into that.'

'Oh, come on!' Max said eagerly. 'You can't just leave us hanging! What's his most ridiculous medal for?'

Jai took a deep breath. 'We will endeavour to save your sister, and I'm grateful for your help today, but my medals are no business of yours.'

'So pompous!' Max replied, rolling his eyes. 'But while we're on the subject of Scarlett, I have some more bad news.'

'Go on,' Jai said, sighing.

'She knows that a submarine escaped the attack on the club. Maybe the sea gremlins told her. And she knows I'm on it because of the firebird. But you all ought to know . . . that she's made some threats.'

'Why don't you show us the letter,' Jai said.

Max fetched it from his room and handed the scroll to Jai. They could tell it had been sent by firebird because of the scorched bits at the edges. Scarlett's untidy scrawl filled the page and the Phantom Atlas Society emblem was clearly displayed at the bottom.

'I got this a few days ago,' he said.

Max,

Thanks to my firebird I've realised that you are one of the explorers on board the Blowfish. How fortuitous that you should have managed to escape being swept up in the snow globe. My dear boy, I had no idea you were going to be at the club, or else I would have ... well, I would have taken the club anyway, but then how sad for your sister to become so useless to me. I am truly glad that you have been gifted this second chance to create the robot for me after all.

In the meantime, perhaps you are already aware that the Sky Phoenix Explorers' Club has sent their phoenixes far and wide searching for you and alerting everyone to your perilous (and unauthorised) mission. So I know all about the Sunken City of Pacifica. How typical of explorers to meddle in things they do not understand! I have some important further instructions for you, Max - you are to steal that snow globe and hide it from the other explorers until it can be safely delivered to me. The city must not be returned. I promise that none of you will like what happens if you ignore my instruction - the consequences will be truly terrible.

With kind regards,
Scarlett Sauvage

P.S. Jada asks you to please hurry up with the robot, as she is eager to return home and misses you very much.

A glum silence descended on the explorers.

'I'm sorry you got a letter like that,' Jai said. 'What a terrible person she is.'

'I suppose she must know that Pacificans have psychic powers and will expose her hideout if we free them,' Ursula said. 'That's why she wants you to steal the snow globe. What did you tell her?'

Max glanced at her. 'The truth. That the snow globe is locked away in a safe and I can't access it. You should also know I told her that if I got the chance to steal it then I would. But that was a lie. I'd never forsake an entire city full of people. Not even to get my sister back.'

'We'll find another way,' Genie said.

'Agreed.' Jai glanced at Ursula. 'How long until we reach the Bubble Ocean?'

'We should be there by tomorrow.'

'In that case, I suggest everyone returns to their sleep bubbles and gets some rest,' Jai said. 'We venture into unknown seas tomorrow, and there might be anything up ahead.'

CHAPTER EIGHTEEN

The next morning, the explorers gathered on the bridge of the submarine, eager to get their first glimpse of the Bubble Ocean. They were all dressed for adventure – Jai in his cloak bearing all his medals, Max in his favourite robot duck T-shirt, Ursula in her engineer's coveralls and headband, and Genie in her pink cowgirl boots, a bright purple dress and a head bopper that had two coiled springs like little antennae with fat puffer fish wobbling about on the end of them.

There was an air of excitement on the bridge that morning. The Bubble Ocean was a completely unmarked place on explorers' maps, but of course Ursula had the mermaid map her mother had given her. She spread this out on the table, and was pleased when the others immediately *oohed* and *aahed* in appreciation.

All explorers were drawn to maps and the ones created by the clubs tended to be elaborate affairs with artistic renderings of ships and sea monsters scattered throughout. Indeed, the one on the wall in the Ocean Squid Club's Map Room was a gigantic twelve feet by twelve feet, and featured one hundred and sixty-five animals, twenty-five ships and galleys, seventy-two fishes, thirty-eight sea monsters, three hundred and forty flags on cities, ports and castles, and one hundred and forty trees. They'd even brought in a cartographic sea monster specialist to paint the sea monsters.

But even that extraordinary map was nothing compared to a mermaid map. Ursula had seen it many times and spent hours poring over it in her sea cave, imagining the magical place where her mother now lived, so she had grown somewhat accustomed to how special the map was, but now she saw it again through the others' eyes. It had the usual drawings of ships and sea monsters, but it also had pearls and shells set into the border, and bits that lit up when you touched them, like the Cove of Crystal Castles, and some locations were even scented.

'Ooh, the mermaid ice-cream parlour smells heavenly!' Genie exclaimed, leaning close to the paper to breathe in the creamy vanilla scent.

'I wouldn't sniff the whale graveyard, though,' Ursula warned. 'Some of the places have sounds too. Look.'

She touched a fingertip to the Grotto of Serenading Lobsters and a strange, gravelly music drifted from the map into the air.

'How lovely!' Genie exclaimed.

'Sounds like a duck in distress,' Max said. 'Whereabouts does your mother live?'

'Here.' Ursula pointed at a spot on the map. 'In the Sunken City of Mercadia. She says it's one of the largest mermaid cities in the world.'

'Perhaps you'll be able to see her after we return Pacifica,' Genie said.

'Maybe,' Ursula replied. She'd love to see her mother again more than anything, but didn't want to get her hopes up too much. 'I'd like to.'

'It's an amazing map,' Jai said. 'But we have no way of knowing where we are on it.'

'I guess we'll just have to look out for our first landmark,' Ursula said. 'Then we can orientate ourselves.'

She drew a cross on the map to mark the coordinates for the Sunken City of Pacifica and then they all set up watch on the bridge. Ursula had visions of anything looming up ahead of them, from fantastic underwater cities to dramatic sea-monster battles. She was therefore a little disappointed as time passed to see nothing but dark, empty ocean stretching out beyond the portholes.

'I'm sure something remarkable will come up on the monitoring screen soon,' Genie said optimistically.

But when they'd been travelling for most of the morning without seeing anything more interesting than a few specks of plankton, the young explorers had to admit that perhaps there simply wasn't anything to discover in this part of the Bubble Ocean.

'I suppose it's a good thing, really,' Genie said, 'seeing as we're on a rescue mission to return Pacifica. If there's nothing here then there's nothing to impede our progress, so we'll get there faster, won't we?'

'I suppose that's true,' Jai said. 'Still ... it would have been nice to make some remarkable discoveries along the way.'

'You're not still thinking of medals, are you?' Max asked. He'd positioned himself in a corner of the bridge and was practising his juggling using three seahorse toys Genie had loaned him.

'You talk about my medals more than I do,' Jai snapped. 'And would you stop that juggling? It's really annoying.'

Max shrugged. 'It's a big submarine,' he said. 'You can go somewhere else if it bothers you.'

'Fat chance of that,' Jai replied. 'The moment I leave the bridge we'll probably come across some extraordinary underwater volcano or sea-fairy fashion show or something.'

It was pretty boring sitting around on the bridge with nothing to do, though, so Jai eventually fetched a tank and began cleaning it out.

'What's in there?' Ursula asked, walking over.

She rather hoped it might be little terrapins or a pair of jousting crabs, or something similar, so she was disappointed when Jai said, 'They're my plankton. Let me introduce you. This is Brian, Jessop, Sofia and Clyde.' He looked very proud as he gazed into the tank.

'Gracious.' Ursula tried to look impressed. Two of the plankton were tiny shrimp, one was a miniature jellyfish the size of a penny and the last one just looked like a blob. 'So . . . what do they do?'

'That's about it,' Genie said.

'They do all kinds of things,' Jai insisted. 'They're quite fascinating. For example, ocean plankton produce as much oxygen as all the land forests and plants combined. They're the world's largest supplier of fossil fuels, which gives us electricity and the means to power our submarines. And they form the basis of the food chain, meaning we wouldn't enjoy fish and chips or ocean pie without them. We all owe a lot to plankton.'

'It does sound like they're important,' Ursula said. She had seen the tiny plants and animals drifting in the currents before, but had never really given them much thought.

'They're not as interesting as seahorses,' Genie said. 'Did you know that with seahorses it's the male who gets pregnant and has the babies?'

'Do they really?' Ursula asked.

'Yep. Seahorses are funny like that.'

'Can I see the plankton?' Max piped up, abandoning his juggling to wander over.

'No,' Jai snapped.

'Why not?'

'Because you're not really interested. You just want to make fun of me.'

Ignoring him, Max peered into the tank. 'I like the blob one the best,' he said, pointing. 'Which one is that? Clyde?'

'No, that's Sofia,' Jai said.

Max grinned. 'I bet these plankton are definitely something to do with your most ridiculous medal, aren't they?'

Before Jai could reply, a warning beep suddenly sounded from the control panel.

Ursula rushed over to it and said, 'There's something coming up ahead.'

They all crowded round the monitor and could immediately see that whatever it might be, it was very large indeed.

'I really hope it's not another colossal sneezing jellyfish,' Genie said, while Bess curled her tentacles around her reassuringly.

'It's too big for that,' Jai replied. He frowned and said, 'In fact, it's too big for any sea creature that I know of.'

'There's rumours of an absolutely gigantic shark in the sea somewhere,' Max said. 'A relic from the dinosaur age when there were actual proper dinosaurs around and not just the fairy ones. A few people claim to have glimpsed it over the years and they all reckon it's far bigger than anything anyone has ever imagined before.' He flicked through the pages of *Captain Filibuster's Guide to Sea Monsters* and said, 'He talks about them here. It says: "This deep, horrible and great sea nourishes a shark as huge as an island." He's not describing the Bubble Ocean, though. Apparently, the giant shark is one of the horrors in the Poison Tentacle Sea.'

The children glanced at one another. 'That's a relief,' Ursula said.

'It would be cool to see it, though,' Max said with a wistful expression.

'Look, there's a sign in the water up ahead!' Genie pointed.

'Does it say "Beware of Gigantic Sharks"?' Max asked, hopefully.

'No, it says, "Welcome to the superb splendour of the legendary Jaffles Hotel".'

'Jaffles Hotel?' Ursula said. 'That sounds familiar.'

'Does it?' Genie looked thoughtful. 'I don't think I've ever heard of it.'

'It was on the map,' Jai said. 'In the upper-right corner. Between the mermaid ice-cream parlour and the Garden of Sea Combs.'

'You were only looking at the map for a few minutes and it had dozens of places on it,' Max said. 'How can you remember it so exactly?'

'I have a photographic memory,' Jai said smugly. He tapped the side of his head. 'Just one glance at a map is all it takes for me to have it permanently saved up here in perfect detail.'

'That's very annoying,' Max said.

'I'm sure my mother mentioned Jaffles to me,' Ursula

said, unrolling the map. It was indeed right where Jai had said it would be. 'I remember sometimes if we had a really nice meal, or something like that, she would say it was almost as good as something she'd had at Jaffles.'

'Well, good,' Jai said. 'At least we can position ourselves on the map now. So to get to the coordinates for Pacifica we just have to go on past Jaffles, then head to the mermaid ice-cream parlour and— What was that?'

He broke off as the submarine juddered in the water slightly, as if it had suddenly come into impact with something. They all gazed out at the ocean through the portholes but couldn't see any explanation.

'That's weird!' Ursula exclaimed. 'We're changing course!'

The submarine should have been travelling straight ahead, but it had veered off sharply to starboard.

'Gosh!' Genie exclaimed. 'Look at that!'

The sub's new position meant they were now directly facing the Jaffles Hotel and it was quite unlike anything that any of them had laid eyes on before. Lit up by hundreds of glowing jellyfish that floated around it like lanterns, the underwater hotel was a beautiful building of several floors made entirely from green coral. Its façade was framed with elegant pillars and a large sign above the double doors spelled out its name in shining golden letters.

'Impressive, but we don't have time to stop at a hotel,' Jai said. He looked at Ursula. 'We must have been knocked off course by some kind of current but you can correct that, can't you?'

'I'm trying,' Ursula said, frowning down at the control panel. 'But the submarine isn't responding. Perhaps it needs more power.'

She pushed one of the levers forwards, but although the entire submarine shuddered again in the water, it remained fixed on its route towards the hotel.

'No current would be this strong and steady,' Ursula said. She looked up at the others. 'I think the hotel is responsible. It must have some kind of magnetic pull that's drawing us in. It's too strong to break free.'

She looked again at the hotel looming before them in the ocean.

'Like it or not,' she said, 'we're going to Jaffles.'

CHAPTER NINETEEN

The submarine was dragged slowly but surely through the sea towards the hotel and there was nothing they could do to stop it. The young explorers could only watch through the portholes as the palatial hotel grew closer and closer.

The magnetic pull drew them smoothly past the pillared front entrance and around to the back of the building, where they discovered a submarine dock. There were quite a few vessels there already, but they weren't submarines Ursula recognised and were quite different from the explorers' clubs' designs. Most of them were made to look like giant fish with great circular windows for eyes, or sleek swordfish with pointy tails for rudders. A couple of the vessels weren't subs at all, but were entirely spherical, like bathyspheres – the iron balls that brave people seal themselves up in while a steel cable lowers them deep into the sea.

The *Blowfish* was brought smoothly into one of the docks and, to their surprise, raised to the surface. Then they all felt a vibration as it locked firmly into place.

'Now what?' Max said.

'I suppose we'll have to somehow get into the hotel and find out who's responsible,' Jai said. 'We'll raise a complaint, explain we're on a very important mission and demand that they release us at once.'

'Perhaps we should take some weapons with us?' Max suggested. 'There's no guarantee they're going to be friendly. For all we know, this is a hotel for sea monsters and they've brought us in to be served up on the lunch buffet.'

'They wouldn't dare!' Jai exclaimed. 'Not members of the Ocean Squid Explorers' Club!'

'I don't think Jaffles is like that,' Ursula said, frowning. 'My mother always talked about it as though it were the most wonderful place in the world.'

'She is a mermaid, though,' Genie pointed out. 'Maybe they won't be so welcoming to humans.'

'It makes sense to be prepared,' Jai said. 'Especially as they've dragged the submarine into the dock against our will. They could have all kinds of nefarious motivations. Perhaps I should take my harpoon gun.'

'That's a bit aggressive, isn't it?' Max said doubtfully.

'Why don't I take my robot duck? He looks harmless enough but he actually shoots—'

'Don't say laser beams out of his eyes,' Jai said. 'Because we all know none of your robots can do that.'

'Not yet,' Max replied. 'I'll figure it out one day, though. But Ducky can shoot these little pellets of stink-berries. I got the idea from jungle fairies. Trust me, he's probably more effective at repelling people than harpoon guns, swords and rifles combined.'

'All right,' Jai said reluctantly. He glanced at Genie. 'You should get ready to call Bess too. At least that way we won't be a complete laughing stock.'

Ursula felt a little useless without a special weapon of her own, and for the first time wondered whether she should have made more of an effort to search inside herself for some scrap of mermaid magic rather than shying away from it these past few years. After all, being able to control a person with her voice would be very useful in a situation like this, even if the thought of doing so repulsed her.

The explorers made their way to the top fin's exit hatch. To their surprise, there was someone outside on the deck already, banging insistently on the hatch door. The sub's walls were so thick that they only heard it as a faint echo, but there was definitely a person out there getting impatient.

'Right, we don't know who or what's waiting for us, so everyone be on their guard,' Jai said. 'Ready?'

The others nodded. Max's robot duck was perched on his shoulder with its beak open wide in case it needed to shoot out a stinky pellet. Ursula gripped the spanner she'd taken from the engineering bay in case she needed to whack someone with it. Genie was ready to call Bess to their aid and Jai squared his shoulders before unlocking the hatch.

Everyone held their breath as the hatch swung outwards and sunlight spilled into the chamber. Ursula didn't know quite what she'd been expecting on the other side, but it certainly wasn't the sight of a squid the size of a man, dressed in a black tuxedo jacket, bow tie and bowler hat, holding a silver tray with some drinks on it. He'd moved back across the deck when the hatch started to open but now he advanced towards them again. Two of his tentacles went through his jacket sleeves, but the others trailed out beneath it. He had a single staring eye in his long head that, somehow, managed to convey his delight.

'Finally!' the squid said, causing all the children to yelp and leap back, as none of them had ever heard a squid speak before. 'I thought you were never going to come out. No need to be shy! Welcome to Jaffles!'

'You ... speak human?' Jai said.

'Naturally, young sir,' the squid replied with a bow. 'I am Gordon, your squid butler. I speak many languages and it is my special wish to serve your every whim during your stay here.'

'But we're not staying here,' Jai replied. 'And you had no business dragging our submarine in with that magnetic force field.'

'Dragging? Oh, but we were only trying to help, sir. We take the liberty of docking all our guests' submarines at the hotel,' the squid butler went on. 'Nothing is too much trouble. If you want to make a reservation in the Tiffin Room, or partake of the rubber-duck baths, or just enjoy some leisure time in the seaweed hammocks on the lido deck then do let me know and I will make all the arrangements.' He held out the silver tray. 'I brought you some welcome drinks. These are Jaffles' Ocean Potions, a speciality of the hotel.'

'Thanks, old chum,' Max said, stepping through the hatch and taking one of the drinks from the tray. He glanced at it, then said, 'Say, did you know these drinks have got little sharks in them?'

Ursula saw that he was right. The drinks were all

served in tall glasses, the liquid was bright blue and there were tiny sharks about the size of her thumb all swimming angrily up and down inside, gnashing their teeth and looking rather frightening.

'Those are candy sharks,' Gordon assured him. 'They can't hurt you.'

'OK.' Max stared into the glass doubtfully. 'Their teeth look pretty sharp, though.'

'I think there's been some kind of mistake,' Jai said, stepping out after Max. 'We're not here as guests.'

'Oh?' the squid looked confused. 'Then why did you approach the hotel?'

'We were just trying to pass by on our way somewhere else.'

Gordon looked appalled. 'Nobody simply *passes by* Jaffles!' he exclaimed. 'Nobody.'

Ursula and Genie climbed out of the chamber last and both gasped at the sight of the hotel. It rose right up out of the water, with half of it below the waves and the other half above. The top was every bit as stunning as the underwater section, made from the same green coral, with giant shells serving as balconies on the upper floors and pearl-studded tiles lining the turreted roof. A few seabirds wheeled in the bright blue sky overhead and the air was pleasantly warm.

'Smells like pineapples,' Genie remarked.

'That's Jaffles' signature scent, miss,' Gordon said.

'Never mind what it smells like,' Jai said impatiently. 'Listen, Gordon, thank you for the welcome and the, er . . . the shark drinks.'

Max was still looking dubiously at his and didn't resist when Jai reached out to take it from him and put it back on the tray.

'We're explorers from the Ocean Squid Explorers' Club,' Jai went on, 'and we need to—'

But that was as far as he got before Gordon dropped the entire drinks tray with a crash. The glasses smashed on the deck and the liquid and tiny sharks spilled out in a puddle. Max's robot duck immediately flapped down from his shoulder to poke at the thrashing sharks curiously.

'Good gracious!' Gordon exclaimed.

'Are you all right?' Ursula asked, concerned.

The squid butler's single eye had gone very wide and all his tentacles were waving around in consternation.

'Good gracious!' he exclaimed again. 'You're not *the* Ocean Squid explorers? The ones who stole the submarine to go on a mission to return the Sunken City of Pacifica?'

Jai frowned. 'I wouldn't say we *stole* it,' he said.

'We didn't exactly go through the proper channels to get permission, but rule thirty-seven says that in an emergency, and where the president is unavailable, it may be allowable to—'

'But this is wonderful!' the squid exclaimed. 'Wonderful! Come on, come on!' He began ushering them along the deck with his tentacles. 'Come inside!'

Max snatched up Ducky, who'd tried to pick up one of the sharks from the spilled Ocean Potion and found it clamped so firmly to his beak that it was making groove marks with its teeth in the metal. Max carefully gripped the shark by the tail and flung it away, feeling very glad that he hadn't tried to drink the sharks after all.

'What's all this about?' Jai asked as Gordon hurried them down the deck. 'Look, we really don't have time to come inside.'

'You shall be given a hero's welcome!' Gordon exclaimed happily.

That statement caused Jai to pause since he was quite partial to hero's welcomes.

'Well,' he said. 'Perhaps we could stop by. Just for a moment. But then we really do need to be on our way.'

'What are we being given a hero's welcome *for*, though?' Max asked as they stepped off the *Blowfish*'s deck and on to a boardwalk.

'For exposing the Collector, of course!' said Gordon.

'That wasn't us,' Genie said. 'It was Stella Starflake Pearl and her friends.'

'Quite so, but you're all explorers, aren't you?' Gordon replied. 'And you're all bravely fighting against the Phantom Atlas Society.'

'Actually, the Ocean Squid Explorers' Club is the only one that isn't actively—' Ursula began.

But Jai cut her off. 'It is now,' he said. 'With the *Blowfish*'s mission.'

Gordon led them beneath a striped canopy that went straight into the hotel.

'Yes, yes, through here,' he said. 'Into the Tiffin Room.'

The explorers' ears pricked up at that. Like the other clubs, food was of great importance at Ocean Squid and the headquarters served all the appropriate meals, from brunch and elevenses to afternoon tea and tiffin. Gordon threw open the door and the explorers were shown into a magnificent room.

Ursula was expecting a sort of restaurant with little round tables covered in crisp white tablecloths, rather like the dining room back at the Ocean Squid Explorers' Club, but in fact the Tiffin Room wasn't a room so much as a cave with beautiful sea-crystal walls and coral chandeliers. And it was completely underwater.

A few holes in the rock let in the sunshine, which caused a flickering light to wave through the water, dappling everything green and blue where it bounced off the crystal walls. Seated within were all kinds of sea creatures, from mermaids and sirens, to octopuses, molluscs and seahorses. There were also people who looked entirely human but for the fact that they were eating, talking and breathing underwater without apparent difficulty. A crab orchestra had set up various strange-looking instruments on a platform at the edge of the room and an elegant music filled the space.

Because everything was underwater, the tables and chairs floated about the room at random so that someone might find themselves sitting with a mermaid one minute and an octopus wearing a top hat the next. There was plenty of food for everyone, though, with each table holding a tiered silver cake plate full of exquisite-looking delicacies. A team of squid butlers drifted around keeping these replenished.

'How . . .?' Genie began, reaching her hand towards the entrance.

'The doorway is enchanted,' Gordon explained. 'So the water can't escape. The majority of our guests

are aquatic so you'll find the main rooms of the hotel are all submerged. You'll be able to enter quite safely, though. It's called breathing water. It's seawater that's been treated so you can breathe it as easily as if it were air, I assure you.'

'Is this like when you said the sharks were safe for drinking?' Max asked dubiously. 'Because one of them fair near chewed my robot duck's beak off.'

'Good heavens, what in the world do you have a robot duck for?' Gordon asked, looking rather put out. He peered at the clockwork creature in Max's arms and said, 'It won't savage any of our guests, will it? That wouldn't go down well at all. Might even lead to us receiving our first negative review in over a hundred years.'

'Of course he won't!' Max said, looking offended while discreetly switching off the stink-berry function.

'I'm very glad to hear it, sir. But please rest assured that you will certainly be able to breathe. In fact, we already have some human guests as you can see,' Gordon said, indicating the people Ursula had noticed earlier.

Since Jai was the most intrepid of the bunch, it was no surprise that he stepped through the doorway first.

'He's right!' he exclaimed, turning back round to look at the others. 'You can breathe the water.'

The others followed him into the cave. It was indeed quite possible for them to breathe the water, and of course Ursula turned into a mermaid and had no trouble either. She undid the buckles on her coveralls and stuffed them into her bag. The others all floated slightly, their cloaks drifting around them.

'Everyone, everyone!' Gordon called. 'Apologies for interrupting you, but I have a very important announcement!'

The crab orchestra paused their playing and the guests turned away from their cakes and sandwiches to stare at them curiously.

'These,' the squid butler said importantly, gesturing at Ursula and the others, 'are the explorers from the Ocean Squid Explorers' Club. The very same ones who have stolen a submarine and are even now on a daring mission to return the Sunken City of Pacifica!'

Jai tried again to explain that they hadn't stolen the submarine, but the squid's words created an immediate cacophony of cheers and whistles that drowned him out. The guests jumped down from their floating tables to swim over to the explorers, gathering around them in excitement. It seemed everybody wanted to congratulate them or shake them by the hands, even the mermaids. Noting the celebratory atmosphere, the squid butlers suddenly appeared with whistles, party hats and confetti for everyone.

'Thank you,' Jai managed, as one of the butlers insisted on putting a party hat on his head. 'But we haven't actually done anything yet.'

'How do you even know about the Collector?' Ursula asked.

'The sirens first heard the news,' one of the mermaids said. She had flowing blue hair and emerald eyes.

Ursula glanced at a nearby siren, who had the head of a woman and the body of a bird. She knew of them but had never seen one in real life before.

'You were human when you walked in,' the blue-haired mermaid said, looking at Ursula accusingly.

There seemed little point trying to lie about it so Ursula said, 'I'm half mermaid, half human.'

The mermaids looked uneasy. 'We've never heard of anything like that,' one of them said. She had green hair and wore a starfish necklace. 'Can such an abomination be possible?'

'Don't call her that!' Jai said, stepping forwards. 'She's a member of the Ocean Squid Explorers' Club and our friend.'

Ursula felt a flash of pleasure at hearing Jai describe her as a friend, even though the moment was spoilt slightly because of being called an abomination as well.

'Apologies,' the mermaid said. 'You just ... startled us, that's all.'

'If you want to see something really startling, you should take a look out that door,' Genie said sweetly, gesturing to where Bess's tentacles were just visible through the archway.

'No, really, please forgive me,' the mermaid with the starfish necklace said. 'We are grateful for what you're doing. Mermaids want to see the Collector captured as much as anyone.'

'She's been trying to recruit us,' the blue-haired mermaid said. 'She wanted us to join her pirate army.'

'Naturally we refused,' the other mermaid said. 'The ocean belongs to us all and is shared by the many creatures that live in it. The dolphins and turtles and seahorses and fish and crabs and—'

'And plankton,' Jai said. 'Don't forget them. They make up ninety-eight per cent of the ocean's living biomass and are very important for the health of our planet. We owe a lot to plankton.'

The mermaid looked taken aback for a moment. Then she said, 'Well, yes, the plankton too, I suppose. And the sea slugs and what have you. The point is, that stealing pieces of the ocean and tucking them away in some private collection is abhorrent to mermaids. We're against everything the Phantom Atlas Society stands for. So we want the explorer clubs to know that we will stand with you against her if you're willing to work together.'

The mermaid held out her hand to Ursula, who took it without hesitation.

'Thank you,' she said. 'I think I can speak for all of us when I say that we'd be glad to work with you.'

She glanced at her friends as they all nodded vehemently.

'I wish I could say the same for the other explorers' clubs,' Ursula went on. 'But the truth is, I don't know. Some of them might be sensible, but some might cling to old prejudices.'

The mermaid squeezed Ursula's hand briefly before letting it go. 'That's all right,' she said. 'There are merfolk who will be distrustful too, seeing the Collector as yet another destructive human. But if we can start to build alliances where we can, then that's a start.'

'Is there anything we can do to aid your mission?' another mermaid asked. 'The Collector was very angry when we refused to join forces with her. She made threats. Said she'd sent her pirates to attack our people.'

'We hope it was just empty words,' the first mermaid said. 'After all, most of our cities are too far underwater for pirates to reach. But still … people are scared. We know from Stella Starflake Pearl's report that the Collector has submarine technology. She might use it against us.'

'Hopefully she's too busy with other things right now,' Ursula said, although she was worried too, especially when she thought of her mother in Mercadia. 'I don't think there's anything you can do, but thank you for offering. We really appreciate it.'

'We should go,' Jai said, taking the hat from his head and passing it to the nearest squid butler. 'It's been great talking to you and I'm so glad that we've agreed to join forces against the Collector. But now we ought to be on our way to Pacifica.'

'Good luck,' the mermaids said. 'Travel safely.'

'What a great honour!' Gordon exclaimed. 'To have the first alliance between explorers and mermaids agreed right here in the Tiffin Room of Jaffles! A momentous occasion!' He beamed at the explorers and said, 'Please say you'll sign the guest book for our hall of fame before you go? We've had royalty and movie stars and famous writers and poets at the hotel before, but we've never had explorers! And while you're doing that I'll arrange for supplies from the kitchen to be sent to the dock for you to take away.'

The explorers knew it was a good idea to stock up on provisions where they could, so this seemed like a fair enough trade. They said goodbye to the other guests, then followed Gordon out into one of the hotel's corridors. Like the Tiffin Room, this was underwater and made from the same sea crystal that shimmered different colours in the light from the coral chandeliers.

'It's such a shame you can't stay,' Gordon said. 'We have entire suites specially designed for mermaids, with all the underwater furniture, clam beds and mermaid mirrors you could ask for. And we have human rooms too, of course,' he hurried to add.

'Perhaps some other time,' Jai said.

'It's pretty cool being able to breathe underwater,' Max said as they swam along after the squid.

Gordon soon led them into an impressively grand lobby, with giant pearls of all colours displayed on the walls and marble statues of magnificent rearing water horses. The sight of them made a familiar feeling of longing tug right in the pit of Ursula's stomach. It was too bad that they'd seen terrifying things like giant jellyfish and furious storm maidens but not so much as a single water horse.

'This way to our guest book.' The squid butler ushered them over to a large reception desk made from dark shiny volcanic rock. A couple of mermaids were checking in with the assistance of another squid butler. Once they'd finished, the explorers stepped forward and were shown to a big golden book sitting open on the counter.

'All our guests sign their names here,' Gordon explained. 'One of our cartographers recreates the famous signature in the hall of fame. You should see some of the names we have there!'

The explorers dutifully lined up to sign the book. Ursula was waiting for the pen when she thought she heard the faint whinny of a horse. She turned around but there were only the statues behind them. Max handed her the pen and as she was signing her name, the sound came again.

She looked back at the statues, wondering if they were making it somehow.

'What's that sound?' she asked Gordon.

'Why, that's the water horses, of course. Their stable is right next door,' he said. 'Most of the time they want to run and frolic on the surface of the sea, but every now and then they like to check in here to be looked after and pampered and have a bit of a rest.'

Ursula was staring at the squid with her mouth open. 'You have a water horse *stable*?' she managed. 'Here?'

'That's right. Would you care to see them?'

Ursula glanced at the others. 'I know we're in a hurry, but could we take a quick look? It's just that I've always wanted to see a water horse.'

'The kitchen will still be bringing the supplies up to your submarine,' Gordon said. 'We easily have time to pop in on our way there.'

'OK,' Jai said. 'I don't think any explorer has ever seen a water horse up close before. They sound quite something.'

They followed Gordon across the lobby and through a door that led back outside to the wooden boardwalk. The same magic that had kept the water inside the hotel also seemed to prevent any of it from leaving, for they all stepped outside completely dry. A squid butler seemed to appear from nowhere with a fluffy Jaffles robe for Ursula. As they walked towards the stable, the sea lapped at the wooden posts and filled the air with the smell of salt and brine and shells – Ursula thought it was the most wonderful scent in the world.

The stable was built on stilts over the water and

opened right up into the sea. Ursula heard the horses before she saw them. A mixture of snorting and playful whickering, along with the splash of hooves prancing upon water.

She found herself speeding up as they neared the entrance. She was aching to see the horses and Gordon seemed to be gliding along unbearably slowly. Unable to help herself, she overtook him right at the end, running the last few steps into the stable. And then she stopped short in amazement, her heart almost bursting with joy.

This was no ordinary stable. The floor was the ocean and the stalls were like a sandy beach, filled with golden sand and scattered with pearls and shells. But the most extraordinary thing was the horses themselves. There were four of them and they were all made entirely from water. Much larger than normal horses, they had frothing white foam for their manes and tails, swirling blue ocean for their bodies, shining shell for their hooves and wise, knowing eyes that were even bluer than the sea itself.

When the explorers entered, the water horses were dancing across the rippling waves in the middle of the floor, but as soon as Ursula raced over to the rail at the edge of the boardwalk, the horses all sensed the presence of a mermaid, paused what they'd been doing and turned around to face her.

'Hello,' Ursula said, beaming as she reached her hand out towards them. 'Oh, hello, at last!'

She'd tried so many times to call a water horse in her cave back home and to be faced with four of them now was an utter delight. To make it even better, the horses came straight over to her, seawater streaming from their large bodies as they nuzzled their damp snouts into her fingers and snorted softly into her palm. Ursula realised then that the water horses hadn't been ignoring her before. It was just that she'd been calling them too quietly, afraid of waking up the mermaid magic inside her. But now she could sense that same magic inside the water horses and it no longer seemed something to be afraid of. Instead it felt special, and wonderful, and beautiful, and she wasn't scared any more, she was proud and grateful instead.

Something deep inside her seemed to crack open like a shell, and she could suddenly feel her magic surging up in fizzing bubbles, making her fingers tingle where she touched the horses. At the same time, her clam necklace glowed a bright blue colour and with a soft click broke open slightly. Ursula prised the two shells apart and saw a glowing pink pearl nestled inside.

Instinctively, Ursula started to sing to the horses. Dozens of sparkling gold musical notes suddenly swirled in the air around them and the horses seemed utterly delighted, whinnying in pleasure. Ursula felt the song warming her in a way it never had before, as if she had music flowing through her veins rather than blood, and it felt glorious. Even the tips of her fingers seemed to fizz with the wonder of it.

One of the horses danced closer and suddenly the golden notes of Ursula's song were settling on its back, moving and shaping into a solid object, until they formed an entire glittering saddle. And this was no ordinary saddle – but one that was clearly designed for a mermaid. It was shaped for a tail rather than legs, and had decorative starfish all around the edge.

When Ursula finished the song there was total silence and she glanced back to see the others staring at her in wonder.

'That's the most beautiful thing I ever heard,' Jai said.

The others nodded their agreement, looking impressed, and Ursula smiled, relieved they weren't afraid of her voice but had seen the beauty of it instead.

When the horse with the saddle pressed its body right up to the boardwalk and whinnied at her, she glanced back at the others and said, 'I'll be right back.'

Then she vaulted over the rails, straight into the golden saddle. Although the horse was made of ocean, his back supported her well enough and Ursula felt the fresh chill of his body turning her legs into a mermaid's tail.

She just had time to throw her wet robe back to the others before the horse trotted straight out into the sunlight. It pranced across the surface of the water, its body sending sparkles of diamond light skittering over the waves.

Then Ursula had to wind her fingers into the horse's watery mane to keep from sliding off as he put down his head and set off at a gallop around the hotel. Ursula was delighted by the grace and glory of the horse. He felt strong and sure and swift beneath her, as though he would take her anywhere in the whole wide ocean she wanted to go. She adored the feel of the salty breeze in her hair and the sight of the dazzling sea racing by under the horse's hooves. But there was an important expedition to return to and Ursula knew she couldn't hold them up any longer. Reluctantly she whispered in the water horse's ear that she needed to return to the stable and he took her back at once, stopping right at the edge of the boardwalk before the rails started, allowing her to slide from his back straight on to the planks.

'Thank you,' Ursula said.

She gave the horse one last pat before he trotted off to join his companions. Ursula's teammates soon hurried over and Gordon produced a fresh, dry robe from somewhere for her to dry herself off.

'The blue streak in your hair has got a big bigger,' Genie pointed out.

'My mother said that would probably happen,' Ursula replied.

For the first time, the idea didn't scare her. After all, her secret was out now anyway, and it felt so good not to have to hide a part of herself away any more. She felt a surge of gratitude towards her new friends for accepting her exactly the way she was.

Gordon accompanied them back to the *Blowfish* where a team of squid butlers were carrying the last of the supplies on board. Then the explorers said goodbye and disappeared back into the submarine. It was duly released from the magnetic force field, leaving them free to journey deeper into the Bubble Ocean.

CHAPTER TWENTY

The explorers set the submarine on course for the mermaid ice-cream parlour shown on Ursula's map. They didn't plan to actually stop there, but once it came into sight they could use it as a navigation point to then take them on the final leg of the journey to the coordinates for the Sunken City of Pacifica.

'It'll take about four days to reach Pacifica I think,' Ursula said, looking at the mapping screen.

'That's as long as we don't come across any more sea monsters,' Max said.

'Right. Everyone keep their fingers crossed then,' Jai said.

'There's bound to be something looming up ahead out there,' Genie said, glancing towards the porthole. The dark ocean seemed to stretch on forever with no sign of life but for one of Bess's monstrous tentacles.

'We'll take it in turns keeping watch on the bridge,' Jai said.

They did exactly that for the next four days. Genie insisted on taking her shift with Ursula because she said Jai would only want to talk about his plankton and there were only so many plankton facts a person could take over the course of one expedition.

Ursula very much enjoyed the time she spent on the quiet bridge with Genie, keeping watch together out of the portholes as the submarine glided silently through the mysterious, unexplored sea. Bess would often join them – or at least as much of her as would fit. Ursula realised she'd gradually become accustomed to the great monster's size and didn't tremble in her presence any more.

'Kraken are terribly misunderstood creatures,' Genie said to her one time when they were taking the night shift and keeping watch in their pyjamas. 'They're quite shy and gentle, really. They don't want to fight anyone. They just want to be left alone. The problem is they scare people when they come to the surface, which they do quite a lot. It's because of the stars.'

The girls had spread a blanket out on the floor and piled cushions up to make their watch more comfortable. Genie also wore an octopus nightcap that she'd knitted herself. An assortment of papers, paints and glue were spread around her on the floor and she was using them to make a shark hat.

They'd also brought some food with them, since it seemed quite wrong to take the night watch without a midnight feast. Fortunately, they had a more exciting spread than tinned Spam and dried chicken dinners thanks to Jaffles. Each of the crates they'd been given was full of delicious treats, almost all of which were suitable for humans. Spread out on the blanket beside them now was a plate of little pink cakes in the shape of seahorses, some strange fruits that looked like grapes but tasted like fudge, a turtle whose shell was made from pizza and a big, tall jug of fizzy dolphin punch.

'The stars?' Ursula repeated, reaching for a pizza slice. 'What have they got to do with it?'

'Kraken are in love with them,' Genie said matter-of-factly. 'They come up to the surface whenever they can to gaze at the night sky in awe and wonder. It's strange that we're not all more amazed by the stars when you think about it. But to a kraken, a star is just the most extraordinary, wonderful, beautiful thing in the entire universe.'

Ursula noticed that one of Bess's tentacles was curled around Genie affectionately as she worked on her hat.

'That's kind of lovely,' Ursula said. 'I guess there's a lot we still have to learn about kraken.'

'People are scared of them and not interested in understanding them,' Genie replied as she glued a dorsal fin on to her shark hat. 'Which means they miss out. Kraken know an awful lot of secrets. Not just about the sea, but about our world and the stars as well.'

As they finished their midnight feast, Ursula reflected that it was nice to have a girl friend to talk to, especially one who knew she was part mermaid and that she felt relaxed enough to be herself around. She never felt like Genie was judging her, or was afraid of her, and she hoped the other girl felt the same way.

By the time Jai and Max came to relieve them in the early hours, the shark hat was just about finished. Max noticed it at once and said, 'Another excellent millinery specimen, Genie. You should open a hat shop. You'd make an absolute fortune.'

'I'm glad you like it because it's for you,' Genie said, presenting the shark hat to him proudly. 'After you admired my pirate ship hat I thought you might like one of your own.'

Jai winced and glanced at Max as if afraid he was going to sneer at Genie's efforts.

'It's an excellent hat, Genie,' he said to his sister. 'But perhaps not the most ... well, just not the most practical hat for an expedition?' He gave Max a pointed look. 'But I'm sure Max will keep it safe in his room until it's the right time to wear it, won't you?'

'Nonsense,' Max said cheerfully. 'A hat as superb as this is not made for sitting safely in one's room.' He took the hat from Genie and immediately placed it on his head. 'I can't think of a more suitable hat for deep-sea exploration. I shall be the envy of all my friends. Thank you, Genie. I'm utterly delighted.'

She beamed at him and even Jai smiled at Max, the first time Ursula had seen him do so. The boys stayed behind on the bridge whilst the girls returned to their bubble to get some rest. They snuggled up in their bunk beds and immediately fell asleep, only to be woken by the jolt of a sudden impact and the wailing of an alarm a couple of hours later.

They raced straight to the bridge in their pyjamas to find the boys at the harpoon cannons.

'What's going on?' Ursula asked.

'We're at the mermaid ice-cream parlour,' Jai said, glancing back at them. 'It's under attack.'

Ursula looked out through the front portholes and realised he was right. Looming before them was an undersea mountain, and perched on top was a building designed to look like a big conch shell. They could tell it was the mermaid ice-cream parlour from the map because of the bright pink neon sign over the top that read: *Mermaid Ice-Cream Parlour: Extra seahorse sprinkles with every sundae!*

There was also a big neon ice cream, the size of a person, flashing pink and white through the water at them. But Jai was right – the parlour was under attack. Cannonballs shot through the water in a stream of foaming bubbles, punching holes in the shell and knocking pieces off the sign. Mermaids were fleeing the building and many of them were families with small merchildren.

'Who's doing this?' Ursula gasped as another cannonball hit the *Blowfish*, making it shudder and groan in the water.

'The radar shows a ship on the surface,' Max said. 'We assume it's pirates.'

Ursula looked at the radar and saw he was right. There was a large object on the surface above them, big enough to be a pirate galleon.

'The Collector!' she said. 'The mermaids at Jaffles said Scarlett had made threats against them for refusing to join her.'

'Maybe,' Jai said. 'Either way, the ice-cream parlour is completely defenceless. We can't allow this to happen. We've fired warning shots at the ship but it hasn't stopped.' He looked back at Ursula and said, 'Bring the submarine to the surface. We're going to have to take more direct action.'

Ursula did as he said and the submarine quickly started to rise. She knew Jai was right and they had to do something to help the mermaids, but she was uneasy even so. An explorer's submarine wasn't designed for battle. It had the harpoon guns and sea cannon in case it ran into sea monsters, but it was outmatched against a pirate galleon, which was usually armed to the teeth and not afraid to fight dirty either.

Genie was obviously thinking the same thing because she said, 'We haven't got enough firepower to beat a pirate galleon, but Bess will scare them off.'

Before anyone could stop her, she turned and ran out towards the top fin. Ursula left the boys at the harpoons and followed. When she caught up with her, Genie grinned and said, 'Are you ready? Bess is a fantastic performer. She would have relished a life on the stage.'

With that, she pushed open the hatch and ran out on to the deck, which was dripping with seawater and sparkling in the sun. Their suspicion had been correct and a huge pirate galleon loomed before them. It was a triple-mast vessel with row upon row of big, white sails.

The nefarious pirate flag fluttered from the mast – in fact, there were two flags flying there and Ursula's heart sank at the sight of the Phantom Atlas Society emblem on the second one. As if the Collector wasn't dangerous enough without a fleet of pirates at her beck and call as well! The ship was too far away for her to see the crew properly, but there were lots of them at the rails and she got a worrying impression of flashing cutlasses and gleaming cannons.

That moment, a deafening boom seemed to rip right through the air and a cannonball landed horribly close to the submarine. It caused a great spray of seawater to surge up and fall across the deck, soaking Genie and Ursula in the process. Max and Jai fired the harpoon guns below but they were too far away to reach the galleon.

'Get lost!' one of the pirates yelled. 'We're on a mission for the Collector. We don't need no explorers poking their giant noses in!'

'You MORONS!' Genie shouted back. Ursula would never have believed she could yell so loudly. 'You've woken up the kraken!' she went on, waving her arms up and down in a panic-stricken fashion. 'Now she's on the warpath and looking for ships to gobble up whole!'

There was a moment of silence. Then another pirate shouted back, 'There ain't no kraken! Do you really think we're dumb enough to fall for that?'

'Wait,' Genie muttered under her breath. 'Wait, wait.'

There was another BOOM as the pirates fired the cannon and, once again, it created a huge splash.

'*Now*!' Genie hissed.

She must have been talking to Bess because the kraken immediately burst from beneath the surface of the sea. Ursula realised it would have looked very strange without the cannon explosion because Bess wouldn't even have made a ripple as she emerged, and then the pirates might have realised she was a shadow animal. But this way, she seemed to explode out in a great burst of foam and sparkling water droplets. And Genie was right about her being a good performer. All her tentacles flailed and her teeth bared in a way that was truly frightening.

Fortunately, it seemed the sight of her was enough to immediately convince the pirates, who didn't stick around long enough to notice that her tentacles didn't make any splash where they hit the ocean. There was suddenly a lot of running back and forth on deck, and a few panicked squawks from an unseen parrot, then the galleon was turning around in the water and sailing away from them as quickly as it could go. When they were a sufficient distance away, Bess reached one of her tentacles up from the water and playfully pretended to tickle the back of Genie's neck.

'Great job, Bess,' she said, beaming down at her.

The kraken slipped back beneath the water as the girls hurried through the hatch and returned to the bridge.

'Good work,' Jai said. 'It seems like you fooled them. They're going full steam ahead and they're not looking back.'

'We need to return beneath the surface,' Ursula said. 'Some of those shots hit the ice-cream parlour. There were mermaids inside – they might be hurt.'

Jai nodded. 'Of course,' he said. 'We'll see if there's anything we can do to help.'

CHAPTER TWENTY-ONE

Ursula went to the navigation controls and plunged the submarine beneath the waves once again. They returned to the top of the mountain, where the parlour's sign was broken and flashing intermittently. Mermaids were still coming out of the building, while others hovered in the water or hunched on the side of the mountain. Many of them looked round when the submarine appeared but they didn't seem to be afraid of it and Ursula hoped they realised they'd been trying to help.

'I should go out there,' she said. 'I can talk to them and explain that we're on their side.'

'I'll go with you,' Max said. 'We work in teams outside the submarines, remember? And I'll take the robot penguin in case we need to dig anyone out of any rubble.'

Max went to fetch the penguin while Ursula raced back to the bedroom to change into her bikini top.

The explorers met at the swim-out hatch to help Max into his diving suit and then the two of them went into the chamber together. It flooded with water and they opened the hatch. Ursula swam out, moving quickly and agilely in the sea. Max's movements were a little more cumbersome in his suit, but he followed after her as best he could.

Ursula rushed straight up to the nearest mermaid – a blue-eyed lady with two frightened merchildren clinging to her hands.

'Is anyone hurt?' she asked.

The mermaid turned large, worried eyes on her. 'I don't know,' she said. 'They're evacuating everyone now. Some of the pirate cannons went into the building.' She peered more closely at Ursula, then looked at the submarine in the water behind her and said, 'You're her, aren't you? The mermaid explorer? The one who's working against the Collector?'

'Yes,' Ursula replied. 'This is my friend, Max. He's from the Ocean Squid Explorers' Club too.'

'Why has he got a robot penguin under his arm?' the little mergirl piped up.

'It's in case we need to help rescue anyone,' Ursula said. She looked back at the adult mermaid. 'We met some other merpeople at Jaffles and they told us how

Scarlett had threatened you. We agreed an alliance. To try to work together.'

'We know,' the mermaid replied. 'All mermaids know. The news spread fast on the bubble tide.'

Before Ursula could reply, a small hand patted her insistently on the tail and she looked down to see the little merboy gazing up at her. 'I drew a picture of you at school,' he said. 'Would you sign it for me?'

'And can I get my picture taken with the robot penguin?' the girl asked.

'Oh.' Ursula was taken aback. 'Yes, but we need to see if there's anything we can do to help first. After that, OK?'

The boy nodded and his sister smiled shyly too. Ursula and Max made their way to the ice-cream parlour where the last few mermaids were coming out of the door.

'Is that everyone?' Ursula asked.

'We don't know,' a bearded merman replied. He glanced at her and said, 'Thank you for your assistance just then. I fear the pirates would have blown this place to pieces otherwise. We have no means of defence here. It's a family spot, mostly for children.' His eyes burned with anger. 'I suppose the Collector knew that when she picked it. It's lucky you turned up when you did.'

'We were glad to help,' Ursula said.

'Some of the roof caved in,' the merman went on. 'There may be people stuck inside.'

'We'll search with you,' Ursula replied.

She and Max went into the parlour, along with some of the other mermaids. Together they combed the place from top to bottom. It was a large building with several sections and in fact most of it was undamaged. The brunt of the attack had been taken by a couple of rooms at the back where the cannons had punched through the ceiling, smashing up booths and soda fountains.

The first room was empty but in the second one Ursula immediately heard sobbing.

'There's someone in here!' she exclaimed.

The room was in ruins where the cannonballs had torn through it and it was hard to search with the sand and rubble everywhere. They spread out and Ursula found him first.

'Over here!' she called.

The others rushed to where a big part of the ceiling had collapsed. Ursula was already heaving at the beam but it was too heavy to lift, even when everyone else joined in.

There was an impatient tap on her shoulder and she turned around to see Max gesturing with the penguin. With his diving helmet on he was unable to communicate with anyone, but Ursula quickly explained to the others that they needed to stand back.

Once they'd cleared some space, Max set the robot penguin down and it waddled over to the beam.

'It's all right,' Ursula called through the wreckage. 'We're coming to get you. Just hold tight.'

Everyone watched as the robot penguin tucked its wings beneath the beam and slowly lifted it. The great weight seemed to be no match for the penguin, but as the beam shifted, the other debris piled on top wobbled precariously and some of it slid down in a shower. The penguin froze and Max gestured frantically through the water at Ursula. Even without hearing his words, she knew what he was trying to say. If the penguin continued to lift the beam, the entire pile of rubble might tumble down on to the trapped child.

Ursula held up a hand to show Max she understood, then swam down to kneel on her tail at the penguin's side and peer through the small gap that had been made. To her relief, she could see the child now – a little merboy about five years old with bright blue hair that stuck up in spikes and a shimmering green tail. He didn't appear to be hurt, although he was still crying.

'Hey,' Ursula said. 'It's OK. We've come to get you. Can you swim through this gap?'

The merboy raised his head to look at her and shook his head vehemently. 'I'm scared,' he whispered. 'If I move it might all fall down on top of me.'

The tower of rubble gave another groan as a few more pieces slipped off and tumbled to the floor with enough force to crack the tiles. The robot penguin's wings seemed to shake a little beside her, and she wasn't sure how much more it could take the weight or how long the tower would remain stable. The gap was small – nowhere near enough for an adult mermaid to get through, but Ursula saw that she would just about fit and she didn't hesitate. She squeezed through the gap to the mermaid child, knowing she had to move quickly or else they'd both be flattened into pancakes.

'It's OK,' she said. 'I know it's scary but you can't stay here. It's not safe. You've just got to swim a short way through that gap, all right? I'll be right behind you the whole time.'

Ursula had hoped to coax him through, but in fact the little boy only moved to wrap his arms around her neck and then wouldn't let go. She swam with him back to the gap but it was too narrow for both of them to fit through together. There were some worrying creaks and rumbles above them and she knew they were running out of time.

'Listen,' she gasped. 'You've got to be really brave now and let go of me. Just swim straight past the robot penguin and I'll be right behind you.'

'Promise?' the boy asked.

'Cross my heart.'

She managed to prise his hands free from her neck and gave him an encouraging push forwards.

'Go!' she said.

To her relief, the boy swam through the gap and she followed. It was not a moment too soon. Ursula's tail fin had only just cleared the area when the rubble piled on top came crashing down into the space where she'd been. Max's hand gripped tight around her wrist and pulled her forwards. There was hardly any time to feel shock at her narrow escape because the little merboy immediately had his arms wrapped tight around her neck again and the assembled mermaids were all pressing forwards to clap her on the back.

At that moment, the boy's mother, having realised he was inside, burst into the room looking so wild with worry that Ursula thought she probably would have dug through the rubble with her bare hands to free her son if that's what it had needed. When she saw him unharmed in Ursula's arms she burst into tears and raced forwards to scoop him up. The next moment, Max, Ursula and even the robot penguin, were all being lifted up on to the mermaid's shoulders and hurried outside to be applauded and congratulated by everyone else.

A mermaid with a pearly-white tail and soft blue eyes soon hurried over to introduce herself as Selina, the owner of the ice-cream parlour.

'I can't thank you enough,' she said. 'My guests are all unharmed thanks to you.'

'We're glad we could help,' Ursula replied. 'And I'm really sorry this happened. My friend on board the submarine is a kraken whisperer. She used her shadow kraken to fool the pirates into thinking they'd woken a real creature. Hopefully they won't come back if they think one lives here. Can we lend a hand with the clear-up? It's bound to go faster with a robot penguin?'

'Thank you,' Selina said. 'We're in your debt.'

Max radioed to Jai and Genie on board the submarine and they put on their diving suits to come out and help, bringing another of Max's robots with them. With the combined efforts of all the mermaids, the explorers and the robots, the damaged parts of the ice-cream parlour were quickly made safe and as tidy as they could be for now.

'We'll soon have it rebuilt,' Selina said. 'We won't let the Collector win.' She looked at the explorers and said, 'In the meantime, will you please stay and have a sundae on the house before you go? As a special thank you?'

Ursula hesitated. The others couldn't communicate with her in their diving suits but she knew they were all eager to be on their way to Pacifica.

'Thank you,' she said. 'That's really kind, but I think we should probably press on. We're on a very important mission and—'

'I know,' Selina replied. 'That's what the sundae is for. Trust me. It'll be worth your while. And your human friends will be able to join in too.'

Ursula was intrigued by what she said and glanced at the others to gesture back towards the parlour, indicating that they needed to go inside. They followed Selina, able to take in the interior properly this time. The booths were striped in red and white and must have been made from the same materials as Ursula's mermaid furniture in her cave back at the club, because they seemed quite undamaged underwater. The menus were also printed on mermaid paper that didn't spoil, and drifted around the room from table to table. The floor was covered in black-and-white checked tiles and a gleaming silver counter took up one half of the room, with red stools set in front of it.

Beneath the glass of the counter they could see dozens of different types of ice cream in a whole rainbow of colours, with names like Mermaid Delight, Turtle Dream, and Starfish Disco. Lined up behind the counter were large glass jars full of multicoloured seahorse sprinkles. A white coral fountain poured out different types of sauce, from chocolate and caramel, to strawberry and bubblegum.

Many of the other mermaid guests had drifted back in and returned to their booths, but Selina waved the explorers over to the stools in front of the counter. Ursula perched easily on hers, while the others had to haul themselves up awkwardly in their diving suits.

She glanced at them and said, 'Selina, listen, you understand that my friends can't have any ice cream. If they take their helmets off they'll—'

'Drown within minutes, yes, I know,' Selina said, taking up position behind the counter. 'Humans are so delicate underwater, aren't they? Don't worry. I have a solution for that, if you think they'll trust me? Can they hear me in those suits?'

'I shouldn't think so,' Ursula replied. 'They're communicating with each other by radio.'

'OK, I'll write down the instructions then. Just let me get the sundaes first.'

Selina busied herself behind the counter, setting out four glass bowls and then taking out scoops of Ocean Discovery ice cream. It was bright blue and had little chocolate dolphins, candy starfish and sugar shells mixed in with it. By the time she'd added chocolate sauce, green seahorse sprinkles and a trident-shaped fudge stick, it looked absolutely delicious. Ursula noticed that her friends were all looking rather glum as they gazed at their ice creams through their helmets, obviously thinking they'd never get to eat them.

But Selina plucked a menu that was drifting by out of the water, scribbled a message on the back of it and then held it up for the explorers to see. It read:

IF YOU CAN REMOVE YOUR HELMET AND HOLD YOUR BREATH LONG ENOUGH TO TAKE A SINGLE MOUTHFUL OF ICE CREAM, THEN YOU WILL BE ABLE TO BREATHE PERFECTLY UNDERWATER.

Ursula looked at her friends. As Selina had said, it

really came down to whether they trusted her or not. If they removed their helmets here in the parlour, so far away from the submarine, and the ice cream didn't work, they'd be in a pretty serious situation. Just a week or so ago, trusting a mermaid would probably have been unthinkable to them all. But Ursula knew that their feelings about mermaids had changed since then, and they'd seen it was possible for humans to breathe underwater from their visit to Jaffles. So she wasn't surprised when Jai was the first to unscrew his helmet.

Holding his breath, he picked up a spoonful of ice cream and there was a horrible moment when he had to open his mouth to eat it and of course a whole load of seawater rushed in too. He choked and spluttered but managed to swallow the ice cream, and the next moment he was breathing through the water as easily as he had at Jaffles.

'Wow!' he coughed. 'That's some ice cream!'

'It lets you breathe underwater for twenty-four hours,' Selina said as the others quickly followed Jai's lead.

'Amazing!' Genie exclaimed, delighted.

'What I don't get,' Max said, 'is how we can now eat the ice cream without gulping loads of water down with it?'

'You *are* taking water in with it,' Selina replied. 'Just like you swallow air when you eat your food. You just don't notice because you can breathe through it.'

'It's delicious!' Ursula said. She'd never tasted ice cream like this before. It had all the salt and brine of the ocean but was somehow sweet and minty and chocolatey as well.

'You can take some with you if you have a way of keeping it frozen on your submarine,' Selina offered. 'As a special thank you for today, I'd like you all to consider yourselves entitled to a lifetime supply. And ...' She hesitated for just a moment, then went on. 'And once the Ocean Squid Explorers' Club has been rescued, if they want to come to some kind of business arrangement, then I'd be willing to talk about providing them with ice cream too.'

'How wonderful!' Jai exclaimed. 'This ice cream would be invaluable to Ocean Squid explorers. It could save many lives and allow us to explore places we haven't been able to reach before. And communicate with the people we find there.'

'I wonder if I could design some sort of tiny freezer robot to keep it cold?' Max said. 'It would be portable then.'

'The club could include it in all their explorer bags!'

Genie said excitedly. 'A mermaid ice cream that lets you breathe underwater would be far more useful than a flask of Captain Ishmael's expedition-strength salted rum.'

'Or a tin of his harpoon cannon polish,' Jai agreed.

The explorers finished their ice cream feeling very excited by the idea. What a proposition this would be to take back to the club, to say nothing of fostering good relations between explorers and mermaids.

'Just remember what I said about the time,' Selina said as they scraped their bowls clean. 'It doesn't matter whether you eat one mouthful or one gallon of ice cream, you'll still only get twenty-four hours of being able to breathe underwater. After that you'll need to breathe air for twenty-four hours before the ice cream will have an effect again.'

She fetched a big box of Ocean Discovery ice cream from the back room of the parlour for them to take away.

The explorers thanked her and began to leave but they were slowed down by all the mermaids wanting to speak to them and wish them well. Several of the children wanted their autographs and a picture taken, and finally Selina suggested that everyone gather together for a group photo so that the explorers would only have to pose once. They assembled in front of the ice-cream parlour, including the robots, and Selina took the photo.

'I'll print a copy for everyone,' she promised. 'And frame it for the wall of the parlour too.'

At last the explorers waved goodbye and returned to the *Blowfish*, feeling very pleased with how their rescue had gone.

CHAPTER TWENTY-TWO

Although they'd been slightly delayed at the mermaid ice-cream parlour, the explorers didn't have much further to go to reach the coordinates for the sunken city, where they'd be able to free Pacifica from its snow globe. Everyone felt rather elated by the mermaid ice cream and Max spent his time poring over ways to keep it cold in one of his robots. Finally, he managed to create a little fridge inside Ducky, which would keep a small amount of the ice cream frozen for a few hours.

Just two days later, they arrived at the coordinates Stella had given them. Unsurprisingly, they found nothing there except a vast expanse of ocean where the city ought to have been. The four explorers gathered on the bridge and there was an air of expectation as Jai unlocked the safe and brought out the snow globe.

Ursula peered into the glass sphere in wonder. They could see the most incredible city trapped inside, full of glittering glass skyscrapers, white marble streets and elaborate coral gardens set around a great underwater volcano at the centre. There were people moving around inside the globe but they were so small that they were barely more than dots.

'Amazing!' Genie breathed. 'What a beautiful place.'

'Can I hold it?' Max suddenly asked.

Jai handed it over and Max took it with a shocked expression.

'What?' Jai asked.

'It's just that I didn't think you'd trust me with it,' Max said. 'Not after what I said about the Collector.'

Jai shrugged. 'We're a team,' he said. 'In fact, I brought this for you.' He reached behind the captain's chair to pick up an explorer's cloak. 'I thought we should all be wearing them to greet the inhabitants of Pacifica.'

Max eyed the cloak with a look of longing. 'You don't have the power to reinstate me into the club,' he said.

'Not officially,' Jai replied. 'But we all know that you *are* a member. Besides, the club is still lost. The four of us are almost all that's left of it now. These are strange and unusual times. I think making up one or two of our own rules to fit the situation is allowable under the circumstances.'

Max passed the snow globe back and took the cloak,

wrapping it around his shoulders with a look that was truly happy.

'I know I complain about the club sometimes,' he said, fastening the cloak beneath his neck, 'but I want you all to know that I love the old place as much as you do. Warts and all. Stupid rules and all.'

'It's our club,' Genie agreed. 'For better or worse.'

'It'll be the greatest club in the world one day,' Jai said. 'I still believe that.'

'Me too,' Ursula said. 'It's the only club I want to be a member of.'

'Well,' Jai said. 'I guess we'd better go and save it then.'

'How exactly do you think we should do this?' Ursula asked. 'We're going to have to go outside the submarine to unscrew the globe, otherwise the city would rip the *Blowfish* apart.'

'I read Zachary Vincent Rook's Flag Report about when they released the Land of the Giants,' Max said. 'He described there being a great disturbance in the atmosphere when it reappeared. Winds ripping through their cloaks and tugging at their moustaches and all that.'

'It's a big thing to suddenly just pop back into existence,' Genie said. 'I guess it makes sense that there'd be some ripples.'

'Well, that could be even more of a problem underwater,' Max said. 'The shockwaves will toss us around like flotsam.'

'There's no way around it,' Jai replied. 'We've got to be outside the submarine when we open it.'

'I'll go—' Ursula started to say, but Jai was already shaking his head.

'It makes more sense for a diver to go. At least then they'll be protected by the suit. I'll do it.'

'I've got an idea,' Max said. 'I'll come as your back-up and bring my midget subs. Some of them have still got bubblegum coral stuck on them. We can use those to stick ourselves to the *Blowfish*. That way, we won't get separated if the currents come at us. And we can take knives to cut ourselves free afterwards.'

'Good idea.' Jai glanced at the girls and said, 'It won't be easy but you two will have to do the best you can to keep the submarine steady.'

With their plan agreed, the boys went to suit up while Ursula and Genie took their posts at the control panel. A few minutes later they saw Jai and Max swim past the portholes, with the fleet of miniature robot submarines in tow. The boys used the bubblegum coral to stick themselves to the sub and then Jai's suited hand appeared in front of the porthole in a thumbs up to let the girls know they were ready.

'We're in position,' his voice crackled through the radio.

'Hold on to your hats,' Max added.

Genie and Ursula looked at each other and hardly dared to breathe as Jai's arms reappeared in front of the window holding the snow globe. They watched as he carefully unscrewed the glass sphere until, finally, it came free from the base.

At once, there was a great explosion of green and blue light, and a surge of current as if a storm maiden had suddenly reached her massive hand into the sea to bat them away. The submarine wasn't just pushed back, but spun round and round, over and over itself. Genie and Ursula were thrown to the floor and didn't know what was up or down as thousands of tiny bubbles streamed past the portholes. They could hear things breaking in the other rooms within the sub, and lights and warning systems flashed all around them on the bridge.

Ursula was the first to drag herself upright to the control panel and engaged the reverse thrusters to try to stabilise them in the water. Genie soon joined her, and together they finally managed to get the submarine back in a stationary position, although the waves still came rolling towards them, battering at the *Blowfish* over and over again.

'Jai, Max, are you OK?' Genie asked, snatching up the radio.

Ursula's eyes went to the portholes anxiously. That had been even more of a shockwave than she'd expected and she prayed that the boys' suits had protected them.

'I dropped the empty snow globe but I'm all right,' Jai said. 'Max?'

There was a pause, then Max said, 'I think I might have thrown up in my helmet a little bit, but I'm OK too. And look, it worked.'

The hundreds of bubbles were finally starting to clear, allowing Ursula and Genie to see properly through the portholes. The sight before them was an incredible spectacle. The Sunken City of Pacifica glittered through the water, larger than life and astonishingly beautiful with its green-and-blue glass skyscrapers. Ursula had never seen buildings like them before. They must have been a hundred storeys tall at least. An arched golden gate marked the entrance and had the name Pacifica inscribed on it in twirling letters.

'We're coming back on board,' Jai said over the radio.

The boys soon joined them on the bridge and for a few minutes they just gazed speechlessly at the city.

'I guess we need to try to introduce ourselves,' Jai said at last. 'They're probably very frightened and confused about what's happening.'

'I wonder what kind of people they'll be?' Genie asked. 'They've been gone so long they've practically faded away into myth.'

'We know they're amphibious,' Max said. 'And that they're supposed to have psychic abilities. But that's about it.'

'They might not even speak human,' Ursula pointed out.

'Well, we won't be able to communicate with them at all in our diving suits,' Jai said. 'I think we'd better eat some of that mermaid ice cream so we can—'

He broke off with an exclamation of surprise as a bright, sparkling star shot up over the skyscrapers and then exploded into spirals of blue light that slowly faded away in the water.

'Are they *firing* at us?' Max exclaimed.

The first star was quickly followed by two more, only these ones gave out pink and green light.

'I don't think so,' Ursula said. 'I think those are sea fireworks.'

She was right. The city wasn't attacking them – it was celebrating.

'Perhaps we should take the sub in a little closer?' Max suggested. 'It looks like a technologically advanced city. They might have a submarine dock?'

'It's worth a try,' Jai said.

Ursula eased the submarine forwards slowly so as not to seem threatening. She needn't have worried though because the inhabitants sent out an escort to meet them in the form of a bright purple fish-shaped submarine. It hailed the explorers over the radio and a warbling voice came through, thanking them for freeing the city and requesting that they follow them to the docks where, he assured them, they'd be able to disembark and breathe without difficulty.

'It's almost like they were expecting us,' Jai said, looking pleased.

The boys changed out of their swimwear and into their explorers' cloaks as the *Blowfish* followed the purple submarine beneath the golden arch and into the docks. These took the form of a vast building with individual bay-like containers. Their submarine was ushered into one, and then to their surprise the ocean around them all drained away. They could see it sinking past the portholes until nothing but drips ran down the outside.

Once they were firmly anchored in place, the

explorers went to the top fin. They all felt a strange mixture of nervousness and excitement to have finally reached this big moment. Genie had asked Bess to make herself scarce so as not to frighten anyone, and the kraken had taken herself off to wherever shadow animals go when they aren't with their humans. Jai, as usual, had every one of his medals pinned to his cloak, Genie wore her favourite octopus hat, Max had Ducky tucked under his arm, and Ursula had a spanner in her pocket for luck, but they all matched in their black Ocean Squid explorers' cloaks.

'Well done, everyone,' Jai said as they paused inside the hatch. 'It wasn't an easy mission, but we did it.'

Ursula felt a sense of pride rush through her and was so glad that they hadn't listened to the adult explorers after all.

'Ready?' Jai asked.

The others nodded. He pushed open the hatch and they climbed out on to the top fin. They hadn't been able to see much of the container from the portholes and had expected that it would probably be empty but for one or two mechanics. They were therefore surprised to see that the space was much larger than they had imagined, and built around the dock itself was some kind of auditorium with rows and rows of seats spreading upwards in a semicircle. And every single one of those seats was occupied by the city's inhabitants, both young and old.

They were humanoid in shape but they had green skin and webbed fingers. Their faces were fish-like, with large, bulbous eyes, small mouths and gills on their necks. They all wore clothes made from some kind of metallic material that shone and flashed in the light, like scales. And before any of the explorers could say a word, the people of Pacifica were all on their feet, cheering and whooping and clapping their webbed hands together in a frenzy of excitement.

One of the inhabitants came forward on to the boardwalk below and they guessed he must be someone important because he wore a gold chain with a medallion around his neck. He held up a flipper-like hand for quiet and when the applause died away he looked up at the explorers and said, 'Welcome, my young friends. I am Magnus, the city's mayor. We have been awaiting your arrival for almost two hundred years. We'd almost started to think this day would never come, but we're so thrilled it finally has. We are forever in your debt. Please accept our thanks and our warmest welcome to the beautiful city of Pacifica.'

There was more applause at this and the explorers

made their way down the ladder on the side of the submarine until they joined Magnus on the boardwalk and introduced themselves.

'I have to admit, we didn't expect you to be so young, but naturally I am honoured to make your acquaintance,' Magnus said, beaming. 'Now, if you're not too tired from your journey, it would be our great pleasure to show you the extraordinary city you have saved.'

CHAPTER TWENTY-THREE

The audience filed out of the submarine dock and Magnus explained that they were going to prepare a great feast in the explorers' honour but they must see every inch of Pacifica beforehand. Jai tried to protest. After all, they were on a rescue mission and time was of the essence. Fascinating and spectacular as Pacifica undoubtedly was, they were all more concerned with establishing the location of Scarlett's headquarters so that they could rescue Max's sister and free the Ocean Squid Explorers' Club.

But when Jai started to explain about the time constraints, Magnus said, 'Naturally, young sir, we understand that you're doing extremely important work. Indeed, no one appreciates that more than the people of Pacifica, believe me. But please understand that we have been hoping and praying for this moment for a very long time. You must allow us to express our gratitude. One feast is all we ask. Something for my people to mark this auspicious day.'

Jai looked as though he might be about to argue further, but Genie nudged him in the ribs and said, 'We understand. And we'd love to see your city.'

Magnus beamed and gave her a bow. 'You are very gracious, noble lady,' he said. 'Rest assured that a place for all four of you will be made in our Hall of Heroes for eternity.'

Jai perked up at that and conceded that perhaps, after all, they did have time to stay for just one feast.

'Our chefs have been consulting the books in our library to learn more about what humans eat,' Magnus said. 'We hope to prepare all your delicacies. Pacifica is home to the greatest library in the world. In fact, I believe that would be the perfect place to start our tour.'

'Can I ask you something first?' Max said. 'How much of your city has air in it?' He hoisted the robot duck under his arm and said, 'Because we might need to eat some magic ice cream before we go on this tour if it's all going to be underwater.'

'Not to worry, young sir,' Magnus replied. 'I'm aware that humans only breathe air. Pacificans are like mermaids – we can breathe both air and water. The majority of the buildings in our city are dry, although the streets are submerged. But we have bubble cars that you will be able to use to travel safely through the water.'

He paused at the entrance to the docks where they found a platform with several of these bubbles lined up waiting for occupants. They were various sizes with some only big enough to take one person, while others were large enough for a group. Magnus selected one of the bigger ones now and indicated to the explorers that they should step inside. The thin skin of the bubble allowed them to pass right through and then closed up behind them again instantly. It had white benches in rows and the explorers took their seats on these.

Magnus entered the bubble last and said, 'To the library.'

The bubble obeyed his command instantly, moving away from the platform with surprising speed and then shooting out of a tube and into the streets of Pacifica. The explorers stared up through the roof of the bubble in wonder at the towering skyscrapers looming over them, which seemed even larger now they were so close.

'I've never seen buildings like these,' Jai said, shaking his head. 'I didn't even know it was possible.'

'We have some of the finest architects in the world,' Magnus said proudly. 'Yet another reason why it would have been so tragic if the city had been lost for good.'

The bubble set off very quickly down one of the streets, floating a little way above the white marble roads. The explorers saw that several of the local people were also using the bubbles to travel, and Ursula guessed this was faster and more convenient than swimming even though they could breathe underwater.

The bubble rounded a corner and the explorers gasped at the sight before them. At first, Ursula thought they were looking at some kind of slumbering ocean dinosaur, with humps on its back, a long graceful neck and large flippers.

But then Magnus said, 'Our library.'

Ursula realised that the creature was actually a building, fashioned from blue glass in the shape of a sea creature. Their bubble flew into a dry room inside and the explorers disembarked on the platform and followed Magnus into the main chamber, a cavernous space inside the animal's humps.

For a long moment they were all speechless as they stared around them. Ursula broke the silence first.

'But ... there must be hundreds and hundreds of books here!'

'Thousands,' Magnus replied with satisfaction. 'Like I said, it's the largest library in the world. Our collections on medicine, sea creatures and ocean history are unrivalled. This library has been collecting books for over five hundred years.'

The beautiful marble bookcases contained shelf upon shelf, rising right up to the ceiling. Ursula had never imagined so many books together in one place before. Not only that, but the library also contained spectacular globes of the world painted in intricate detail, as well as statues of some of the city's greatest thinkers. The stained glass bathed everything in a dappled blue light and the space had the reverent hush of all libraries everywhere. As explorers, the children had a natural respect for books and knowledge, and they found themselves grinning in delight. Ursula's fingers itched to go through the books, soaking up the wisdom and secrets they contained.

'We have some of the oldest books in existence here,' Magnus explained. 'Extremely valuable and rare volumes that you won't find anywhere else. They're housed in the flippers of the building as they need to be carefully preserved. And all of this has been saved thanks to your efforts.'

The explorers glanced at one another, feeling a deep sense of pride welling up inside them.

'Do you have any books about kraken?' Genie asked, fingering her whisperer's amulet.

'Of course, miss,' Magnus replied. 'In fact we have an entire room dedicated to kraken studies. Many see them as monsters but we believe they're one of the most noble creatures in our oceans.'

As if on cue, Bess appeared in the library beside Genie. It was one of the few spaces large enough that could fit her entire body unimpeded, but Magnus didn't react in surprise or fear.

'You're a whisperer!' he exclaimed. 'How extraordinary. Perhaps at some point you would care to consult our books and work with our kraken experts? I'm sure there must be additional insights you could add.'

'I'd love to,' Genie said, looking longingly at the books.

They left Bess floating happily around the library and returned with Magnus to the bubble car. He showed them their state-of-the-art hospital, with medicine and facilities far beyond what even the explorers' clubs had. Then there was the architects' guild and the scientists' labs, and the spectacular town hall where tables were being laid out for the feast.

Everywhere they looked there was innovative technology and fascinating artefacts and precious pieces of preserved history. The streets were made from white marble, or intricate mosaic tiles that must have required many hundreds of hours of work. It was clear that Pacifica placed a high value on knowledge and beauty. Their city was the result of centuries dedicated to the pursuit of these things.

'Now there's just one last place left to show you,' Magnus said as they climbed back into the bubble. 'Of course, you already know all about it but I imagine you'd like to see it close up for yourselves?'

Ursula frowned, wondering what he could be talking about. She glanced at Max, who just shrugged. Before she could ask, the bubble shot off, but instead of going along one of the streets, it rose straight up, higher and higher, until it hovered above the roofs of the skyscrapers.

And there before them was the volcano, steaming away underwater. It was absolutely gigantic – so tall that it towered over even the skyscrapers. It was located right in the centre of the city and Ursula had caught the odd glimpse of it as they'd travelled around. The buildings had obscured most of it and she'd only been able to see the top when she thought to look up. Now that they were faced with the sight, though, it was hard not to be awed by its great size.

When the bubble rose higher still, so that they

looked directly down on the volcano, Ursula saw that even the *Blowfish* could be lined up several times end to end within the crater and still not touch the sides. Most frightening of all was the fact that she could see the hot red gleam of molten lava bubbling and spitting deep within the volcano itself. Ursula felt a flicker of fear and unease as she stared at it. She knew from reports she'd read back at the club that underwater volcanoes could be ferocious and volatile and that they could take out entire nearby islands when they erupted. But then she thought of Pacifica's huge library, its science labs and technology, and all its specialists and experts. If they thought it was safe to be here, then surely it must be. Her fear eased a little, although being so close to the volcano still made her uneasy.

'Volcanoes are sacred to our people,' Magnus told them. 'Many of us believe that it's where the gods live. It's not uncommon for us to build our cities with a volcano at the centre. Of course, when our ancestors first chose this location for Pacifica, they believed that the volcano was extinct. It was only later on that we began to hear rumblings and detect signs of activity. Realising the potential danger, our scientists set to work immediately, working day and night, year after year, as time ran out all the while. Of course, in the end it proved to be quite hopeless. There was simply no way of preventing a volcano that wanted to erupt from doing so. Our scientists could tell that when this eruption came it was going to be a huge one, easily enough to destroy our entire city.'

Ursula frowned, wondering where this story was going. She was about to ask how they finally managed to solve the problem when Magnus gazed down at them with a look of respect and admiration and said, 'So tell me, how *did* you manage to stop the volcano from erupting?'

The explorers stared at him for a moment, wondering if they had misunderstood the question. Genie even glanced over her shoulder, thinking he might be talking to someone else, but they were the only ones there. There was a sudden weird silence that seemed to echo around inside the bubble.

'What do you mean?' Jai finally asked.

'I understand it may not have been one of you *personally*,' Magnus said. 'But someone else in the Phantom Atlas Society must have explained it to you? My people will be very eager to hear about the ingenious solution at the feast tonight.'

Max stared at the mayor. 'Do you think we're from the Phantom Atlas Society?'

Magnus blinked. 'Well, aren't you?'

'No, we're from the Ocean Squid Explorers' Club,' Ursula said.

'Oh. You mean you're working in partnership?'

'Absolutely not,' Jai said. 'We're working against the Collector. We only recently found out about what the society has been doing all these years. Now we're trying to rescue the places that were stolen. You're one of the first to be returned to your rightful place.'

Magnus didn't look pleased about this. He didn't congratulate them again or talk more about the Hall of Heroes. Instead, he looked utterly appalled and said, 'But ... but the Phantom Atlas Society didn't *steal* Pacifica. They saved it. We contacted them and *asked* to be put into a snow globe. It was the only way to preserve the city. Queen Portia came herself and promised that it would be released one day, as soon as they figured out a way to stop the volcano. She was only just in time too. Our scientists estimated that another day or two and the volcano would have blown.'

The explorers stared at each other in horror. Ursula wondered whether Scarlett had known the truth about Pacifica all along. As the Collector, surely she must have. She had said in her letter that there would be dire consequences if they released the city, but none of them had imagined this was what she meant. Ursula suddenly worried that perhaps Scarlett had *wanted* them to make enemies of the Pacificans all along.

'But we had no idea!' Jai almost wailed. 'We didn't know the volcano was about to erupt.'

Magnus grabbed his shoulder. 'Are you saying you haven't found a way to prevent it?'

'That's exactly what he's saying,' Genie said.

'Merciful heavens!' Magnus breathed, his eyes wild. He gripped Jai's shoulder tighter and said, 'Then you must put the city back in the snow globe. Immediately!'

'We can't,' Max said in a quiet voice. 'The globe was broken when we released you. It's gone.'

CHAPTER TWENTY-FOUR

Magnus took them back to the town hall. Instead of feasting and celebrating, guards were summoned and the explorers found themselves bundled off to a prison cell. Like everything else in Pacifica, the cell was clean and modern with pristine white sheets on the bunk beds and an immaculate bathroom. Ursula got the impression they didn't have much crime here.

The grilled door shut and locked behind them and the explorers were left alone. Bess tried to follow but there wasn't room for her in the cell, so she just poked one of her tentacles through the bars with them, while the rest of her large body remained sprawled in the corridor outside. None of the other citizens acted with fear towards her, and the explorers had already admitted to Magnus that she was a shadow animal, so there was no hope of trying to use her as a diversion.

'We've ruined everything,' Ursula said, sitting down on one of the bunks.

'We couldn't have known,' Jai replied, but he looked upset too.

'There must be something we can do!' Genie said, staring out of the window at the volcano.

But if a volcano wanted to erupt, it was going to erupt, and there was nothing in the world that anyone could do to stop it. They'd been in the cell for about half an hour before Magnus returned with two more of his people in tow. They both wore black uniforms and had extremely serious expressions on their faces.

The explorers all got to their feet at once and Jai began to apologise again, but Magnus cut him off abruptly.

'You say you have no more snow globes, and a search of your submarine confirms this to be true. In which case our only chance is to make contact with the Collector.' He stepped a little closer to the bars and said, 'Perhaps you do not know this, but my people have certain psychic abilities. We sense that the Collector we knew all those years ago, Queen Portia, has gone. The title must have passed to someone else. Give us their name and we'll be able to locate them.'

The explorers glanced at each other. This was what they'd hoped for when they'd come to Pacifica, but not under these circumstances.

'The society has changed since you knew it,' Ursula said. 'It doesn't just take endangered places any more, it takes ones that are perfectly fine and usually without their permission. That's why we assumed they'd stolen you too—'

'It makes no matter,' Magnus interrupted. 'All our dealings with the society have been positive. We owe them our lives. And now our only hope rests with them again. Give us the name. I should add that our psychic abilities mean we can draw it straight out of your minds if we have to.' He indicated the two men behind him and said, 'These are my inquisitors. If needs be they will suck the information from you, but it will be quicker if you simply tell us, not to mention less painful for you.'

'Her name is Scarlett Sauvage,' Jai said.

The explorers were all very aware that they were to blame for what had happened and if there was a chance Scarlett would, or could, do anything to help, then they owed it to the city to give them that chance.

'She probably won't help you, even if she can,' Jai warned. 'She's quite a villain.'

'To us, *you* are the villains!' Magnus snapped. 'Now please be quiet while we concentrate.'

The three of them turned away slightly, but the explorers could see their large eyes were suddenly glowing as they gazed ahead with intense expressions. Ursula realised they were using their psychic abilities to find the Collector, and indeed a moment later Magnus exclaimed, 'That is too far away! She'd never get here in time!'

'I don't suppose you'd mind sharing where she is with us, would you?' Max asked.

Magnus scowled at him. 'Not a chance. I won't do anything that aids your mission to stop the Collector.'

One of the inquisitors tapped Magnus on the shoulder. The mayor turned back and they had a brief, whispered conversation before the mayor looked back and said, 'How many Collectors are there now? Back when we knew the society, there were two of them – Queen Portia and a sorcerer named Jared.'

'They're both gone,' Ursula said. 'There's only one now and that's Scarlett.'

Magnus turned his bulging eyes on her. 'I'm not sure I believe you.'

'Well, that's your problem,' Max said. 'Because she's telling the truth.'

'For your sake, I hope she isn't,' Magnus said. 'We haven't time for this.'

He snapped his fingers and one of the inquisitors came forward. The explorers thought perhaps he was going to unlock the cell to come in, but instead he suddenly shot his arm through the bars, grabbed Max by the front of his cloak and dragged him closer.

The others rushed forward, protesting, but they couldn't stop the inquisitor from reaching through the bars with his other arm and grabbing the side of Max's head with his hand. For the first time they noticed there were tiny suckers along the Pacificans' fingers, and when these latched on to Max's skin they became glued so tight that the explorers couldn't prise them away.

Max yelled out an insult but then the inquisitor's eyes lit up, indicating he was using his psychic powers again and Magnus's words about it being painful were proved true. Max gave an awful scream, which quickly turned into a gasping groan.

'Stop it!' Ursula shouted as they all tried to prise Max free.

They simply couldn't loosen the inquisitor's grip, and Ursula felt despair bubble up inside her. But then Genie bit the inquisitor hard on the hand and he finally drew back with a yelp of outrage. Released, Max staggered, trembling from head to foot, even after Jai put a steadying hand on his arm.

'They're telling the truth,' the inquisitor said to Magnus. 'There is only one Collector.'

'And she's too far away to help us,' the mayor replied grimly.

'Now, look!' Jai said angrily. 'I understand that we've made a mistake releasing your city, but we acted in good faith and our only wish was to help. How dare you use those powers as a torture device?'

'Stupid boy,' Magnus replied, shaking his head. 'Can't you understand that you have doomed us all? Every person in this city, every book in the library, every piece of history we've preserved so carefully. All irreplaceable. We shall have to evacuate. Our great city will be lost.'

'Please let us out,' Ursula said. 'We can't undo what's happened. You know we were only trying to help you. We need to get to our submarine so that we can escape too.'

Magnus stared at her, but before he could reply there was a deep, loud rumbling from outside. They had even less time than they'd thought. The volcano was finally erupting.

CHAPTER TWENTY-FIVE

The mayor and the inquisitors hurried away, leaving the explorers alone in their cell once more. They all turned to the window to stare out at the volcano, which was now starting to trickle with lava. Unlike a land volcano, it didn't stay as hot red liquid for long. Once it came into contact with the ocean, a crust formed around the lava, making it look like grey rock. Some of it was clumping into large chunks that broke away and tumbled to the bottom of the volcano.

'What are we going to do?' Jai said. He ran his hand through his hair. 'There's got to be some way out of this,' he said. 'There's got to be.'

But no one could think of anything. Although they yelled for the guards until they were hoarse, no one came to let them out.

'There probably aren't any guards there,' Genie said. 'I bet they've all left the city with their families.'

'I think you're right,' Ursula said, staring out of the window. 'Even if we weren't to blame, no one is thinking about us at the moment.'

All around they could see the chaos and confusion of a city suddenly having to evacuate. Entire families went past on the street outside, some inside bubbles and some swimming, carrying what belongings they could. After an hour or so, the civilians were all gone and the only ones left were scientists and librarians, using the remaining time to fill up the last bubbles with books and artefacts. And the whole time, in the background, the volcano bubbled more and more.

Bess had disappeared when the mayor did, but she came back now, appearing in the sea beyond the window and spoke to Genie.

'This is bad,' the whisperer said, looking back at the others. 'Bess has been to look at the volcano. She thinks it's going to explode really soon. Less than an hour.'

They tried hammering on the window and yelling down to the last people in the streets, but even if they heard them, they were more concerned with their books and artefacts. Soon, even they had gone and the streets appeared quite deserted.

But then there was the sound of footsteps in the corridor and the explorers all hurried over to the bars.

A few seconds later they saw Magnus striding along the corridor towards them.

'Thank heavens! We thought you'd forgotten us!' Jai called.

Magnus gave them a look that was partly hostile, but partly pity as well.

'We've used every one of our bubbles to evacuate our citizens and take whatever treasures we can save,' he said. 'I am the last of us to go. As mayor, I wanted to see my people safely out first. There's one bubble left, which will take me and a few more books.' He went over to a control panel on the wall outside their cell and pressed some buttons on it. 'Your door will open in ten minutes,' he said, turning back to the explorers. 'That gives me enough time to get away. I can't have you trying to hijack the last bubble. My conscience would not be clear if I didn't at least give you a chance to escape, but in all truth the odds are very small and I do not expect you will survive.'

'Won't you reconsider and take us with you in the bubble?' Jai asked, gripping the bars. 'I know your books are precious, but surely our lives are worth more?'

The mayor was already shaking his head. 'We've saved only a fraction of our library. Less than one per cent of it. You brought this on yourselves and I won't sacrifice a single book for you. Good luck.'

And with that he turned and walked away, leaving them to wait helplessly for the cell to open. Through the window they could see that the volcano was belching out huge quantities of ash now, which swirled ominously in the water, making it hard to see what was going on.

'He said all the bubbles are gone,' Max said. 'That means we're going to have to swim to the submarine dock. It's too far to hold our breaths. We'd better hope Ducky has managed to keep the mermaid ice cream frozen.'

He pressed a button on the robot duck and a hidden compartment popped open revealing small tubs of the ice cream, still mercifully solid. Ursula, of course, didn't need it to breathe underwater, but the others swallowed theirs down quickly. A few moments later, the cell doors slid open. The explorers were ready and raced down the corridor, through the halls of the abandoned building until they came to an exit. They quickly stripped off their explorers' cloaks and other clothes down to their underwear so they wouldn't be weighed down in the water.

They stuffed their clothes in waterproof bags, then Jai pressed a button on the wall and the door slid open on to the street. It must have had the same charm as the doorways in Jaffles because the water didn't flood in, but they were able to step out into it and Ursula immediately transformed into a mermaid.

To their dismay, the water was full of clouds of ash, which made it difficult to work out where they needed to go. None of them were that familiar with the huge city, but this made it almost impossible to get their bearings and Ursula would have despaired of them ever reaching the submarine dock if Bess hadn't appeared in the water to guide their way.

The four of them followed the kraken through the abandoned streets, having to abruptly change direction several times in order to avoid falling pumice boulders flying out from the volcano. They could see fiery red explosions from within the ash now, which was coming thicker and faster. Some of the boulders were gigantic – the size of carriages – and where they crashed into buildings they broke off pieces of glass and metal that flew around the explorers too.

Ursula's heart beat so fast in her chest that her ribs ached. *We'll never get out of this alive,* she found herself thinking hopelessly.

She knew that explorers had near misses and close shaves sometimes – she'd read enough about their escapades in the Flag Reports back at the club – and she'd never heard of any explorer being involved in a situation quite as desperate as this and living to tell the tale. But she also knew that an important part of being an explorer was to keep going, even when things looked hopeless. You'd never escape if you didn't believe there was a chance.

She saw the same fear and determination reflected in the others' eyes as they followed the shadow kraken through the crumbling city. Great piles of Pacifica were already in heaps of rubble, but to their relief they saw that the submarine dock was not too badly damaged. Part of a wall was gone, but they could see the *Blowfish* through this and it still seemed to be all in one piece, although it had broken free of the dock and now floated in the middle of the space.

They swam towards it quickly and tumbled in through the swim-out hatch, leaving Bess in the water outside. There was no time to lose so they didn't even wait for the chamber to drain, but opened the hatch to the rest of the submarine straightaway, causing water to flood into the corridor. There were no towels for Ursula to dry herself so Max scooped her up and carried her as the explorers ran towards the bridge. They turned the engines on, switched them to full speed and broke through part of the dock's wall as the sub burst out in a shower of glass and metal shards.

Max set Ursula gently down on the floor by the window as Jai and Genie went to the control panel and pointed the sub in the right direction. It began to move out of the city, breaking through the cloud of ash into the clear blue ocean beyond.

'Perhaps we'll make it after all,' Max said after a few minutes, when it seemed as if they were managing to get clear.

But Genie had been talking to her kraken through the portholes and turned back looking stricken. 'It's no use,' she said. 'Bess can tell from the volcano's rumbles that the main eruption will be here at any moment. If we could go just a little faster it might be possible to clear the blast zone, but we're already moving at full speed.'

Jai raised the periscope to look at the volcano behind them, and when he turned to the others his expression filled all their hearts with dread.

'I think she's right,' he gasped.

'No!' Ursula said. 'Not when we've come this far. Not when we're so close. If we need just a tiny bit more speed, then I think I know how. If I can call the water horses, they might be able to help.'

'You'd better do it quickly then,' Max said.

Ursula curled her tail beneath her, squeezed herself

close to the window, pressed her fingers against the cool glass and concentrated with all her might. She recalled the sight of the incredible creatures at Jaffles – how their great bodies had churned and foamed and their eyes had been a deeper blue than even the ocean itself. She sensed their majesty and the incredible magic inside them and the pearl in her necklace glowed brightly as she found that same magic inside of her. Ursula remembered the song she had sung and when she summoned them with it this time, her voice rang out loud and clear, filling the air around her and the sea beyond with those glittering musical notes.

To her delight, the water horses came at once. She saw them forming in the ocean on the other side of the portholes, tossing their heads and rearing up to kick their front hooves through the sea, already anticipating the desperate race ahead.

'You did it!' Genie exclaimed.

Ursula's tail had dried and she gathered her robe about her as she stood up and ran for the door. 'I've got to go out there!' she cried.

'You can't be serious!' Max moved to block the door. 'As soon as the volcano erupts there'll be showers of rock and clouds of ash for miles. You won't stand a chance if you're outside the submarine.'

'I *have* to!' Ursula said. 'The horses can't move the submarine without my help. And if I don't try we'll all be swept away in the eruption anyway.'

Max opened his mouth to speak but Ursula held up a hand. 'No one is coming with me either. The submarine is moving too fast – you wouldn't be able to keep up. There's no time to argue, I have to do this.'

She glanced back at the others, desperate for them to understand and to let her go. Her friends looked stricken but then the volcano gave another terrible rumble that they could all feel through the soles of their feet.

Max squeezed her arm and then let her go. 'If anyone can do it, it's you,' he said, stepping out of her way. 'Just make sure you come back.'

Ursula flashed him a smile and then she was running through the corridors of the submarine as fast as she possibly could. By the time she reached the swim-out hatch she was so out of breath she could hardly drag in air, but there was no time to stop. She slammed the door closed, pressed the button to fill the chamber with water and tossed aside her robe. On the other occasions when she'd exited the submarine this way it had been stationary in the water. She realised that this was going to be a completely different experience and yet she still wasn't quite prepared for the ferocity of the sea racing past in a storm of white bubbles. They lifted her up the moment she exited the hatch, tossing her about like a piece of flotsam. Mermaids could swim extremely quickly, but the submarine was going even faster than that and Ursula quickly found herself in the water alone, watching it shoot ahead of her.

She glanced back towards Pacifica just once, taking in the angry cloud of ash getting larger and larger around it. Then she straightened her shoulders and started to sing again. The bright golden notes surrounded her and quickly brought one of the water horses galloping to her side. Ursula put her hand on his muzzle, silently thanking him for coming to her aid as her song made a saddle on his back, just like it had at Jaffles.

She leaped on and wound her fingers in the horse's mane, urging him to follow the submarine. The great horse immediately wheeled around and went after the *Blowfish* at a full gallop. It was the fastest Ursula had ever travelled in her life. They seemed to move through a churning tunnel of tiny bubbles in their race to catch up with the other horses. When they drew level with the submarine, Ursula heard her mother's voice inside her head: *Magical things can happen sometimes when mermaids and water horses come together . . .*

She knew she needed every glittering sparkle of that magic now. She closed her eyes for a moment and concentrated on blocking out the collapsing city behind them, and the rumbling volcano and the fact that everybody was counting on her. All that mattered was the music and she focused all her thoughts on the song. Mermaid magic still felt so new to her and she had not yet had the chance to practise and become familiar with it, yet deep in her soul she could sense how it worked and knew what she needed to do.

The pink pearl in her necklace shone brightly as she opened her eyes and moved into a new melody so powerful that a little explosion of golden notes seemed to burst around her like fireworks. Concentrating with all her might, she guided these into the shape of long golden ropes that attached themselves to the water horses as harnesses at one end and tied themselves into knots on the submarine's fins at the other.

Now, Ursula thought her instructions into the song, *you just need to FLY!*

The horses responded to her immediately, putting their heads down and galloping through the water as fast as their magical bodies could go, dragging the submarine with them while Ursula clung on for dear life. She felt a great surge of hope that perhaps

they really would be able to outrun the volcano after all . . .

But then there was a huge *BOOM* as if a chunk of the world had just been torn away. The entire ocean glowed red and Ursula could feel the heat on her bare skin. The volcano had finally erupted. The next second a great wave of ash enveloped them and gigantic pumice boulders flew past. The water horses could re-form if a boulder burst them apart but Ursula, of course, could not, and her whole body ached with fear as she clung to her horse, praying that he would be able to dive and weave around the terrifying chunks of rock. She could hear the awful *thump, thump, thump* of boulders smashing into the roof of the submarine and her heart was with her friends on the bridge.

'Come on,' she whispered in her horse's ear. 'We're so close. Just a little bit more.'

Then she drew in her breath and sang again, her golden notes glittering through the ash as she urged the horses on. And they continued to gallop through the storm of boulders, not stopping or slowing down for a moment.

And finally, just as Ursula began to think she was too tired and scared to sing for a moment more, the horses cleared the ash cloud, bursting back into the welcome blueness of the ocean. They didn't stop running until the *Blowfish* was a safe distance away from the danger zone, then they slowed to a canter and then a brisk trot, and finally stopped, the submarine floating stationary alongside them.

The golden ropes and saddle melted away and the four horses gathered around Ursula, nuzzling her. She clung to each of them in turn, offering her heartfelt thanks, almost crying in relief. Then all too soon, the horses tossed their large heads in farewell and melted away back into the sea. Ursula returned to the swim-out chamber and as she waited for the water to drain, she noticed her own reflection in the porthole and saw that a purple streak had appeared beside the blue one in her hair.

The door slammed open the moment the chamber had drained and her friends burst in to help her out to the corridor, where she soon dried herself off in a fresh robe. The moment she got back her legs, Max, Jai and Genie were all enveloping her in crushing hugs that squeezed the remaining breath from her.

'We made it,' Max yelled. 'Against all the odds.'

For several minutes, they simply rejoiced, slapping Ursula on the back and exclaiming over the extraordinary water horses, and how worried they'd been when ash covered the portholes, and the relief and delight of finding Ursula unharmed. She felt a glow of warmth deep down in her belly at her friends' joy and realised they really were a proper team, just as she'd always dreamed.

When they returned to the bridge, however, they examined the monitoring screen and their jubilance faded. Pacifica was gone. Where the city had been, was now just a mass of solid lava and smouldering stones.

'At least no one was hurt,' Genie said quietly. 'Magnus said he was the last to leave, didn't he?'

'Still,' Ursula replied. 'All that history and knowledge destroyed.'

The explorers were silent for a long time as they gazed at the screen. Each of them felt the great weight of terrible responsibility pressing down on them. They'd gone in thinking they were rescuing the city and now it had been obliterated and all its citizens displaced because of them.

'I wonder where the Pacificans went,' Jai said.

'I guess they'll make their way to one of the nearby islands,' Max replied.

'Perhaps they'll build a new city eventually,' Genie said hopefully.

Ursula sighed. 'Well, we're going to have to make

contact with the Sky Phoenix Club and tell them what's happened.'

The explorers felt even more glum at this. They'd disobeyed a direct order in coming here, and perhaps that would have been all right if they'd successfully completed their daring rescue mission and returned in triumph with the coordinates for the Collector's headquarters. Instead they had nothing to show for their disobedience except for a destroyed city and an angry group of citizens who were now refusing to help them.

'It was always the mission to return Pacifica,' Jai pointed out. 'So the adult explorers would have made the same mistake we did. Hopefully they'll take that into consideration.'

'And we've got the beginnings of an alliance with the mermaids,' Max said. 'They might be pleased about that.'

CHAPTER TWENTY-SIX

The explorers brought the submarine to the surface and radioed the Sky Phoenix Explorers' Club, but the president wasn't happy about any of the things they had to say. He ranted and lectured them for almost an hour about what had happened to Pacifica, and he wouldn't even consider the idea of an alliance with the mermaids.

'I'm astounded,' he said over the radio. 'Frankly astounded to hear Ocean Squid explorers, of all people, speak in such a way. Don't you realise that mermaids are responsible for more deaths in your club than shark, squid and kraken attacks put together?'

'Excuse me, sir, but we don't think that's actually true—' Jai began, frowning.

'Why, if you've been colluding with mermaids then there might very well be treason charges brought to bear,' President Jacob went on.

'We weren't colluding with them,' Max said. 'We were trying to work together in order to—'

'Good grief, is that the pirate-conspirer speaking?' President Jacob exclaimed. 'Next thing you'll be telling me the mermaid girl is there with you too.'

Jai sighed. 'Naturally, sir,' he said. 'She's been a valuable member of our team and has proved her loyalty over and over again. If you would only let me explain how we—'

'I've heard enough!' President Jacob snapped. 'I won't listen to any more of this. You are to return to our club's headquarters at once, hand over the submarine and submit yourselves for questioning. You're in plenty of trouble as it is. Don't make things any worse for yourselves.' And with that he ended the call.

For a long time, the explorers just stared at each other, feeling glum. This wasn't how any of them had pictured their adventure ending.

'Well,' Jai finally said. 'What are we going to do?'

'Maybe we should go back to the Sky Phoenix Club,' Genie said. 'We might be able to get them to see reason about the mermaids if we can talk to them face to face.'

'And the submarine could get a proper crew, at least,' Jai said. 'And a new mission that might achieve something in the fight against the Collector. We'll have to face the music for what we've done eventually.' He looked at Ursula and said, 'I'm not sure whether it's safe for you to come back with us, though.'

'You mean we should split up?' Genie asked, horrified.

'I don't want to,' Jai said. 'But you heard what President Jacob was saying about mermaids, and most explorers would agree with him. There's no guarantee that Ursula will be treated decently when we arrive. She might be dragged off to prison for all we know.' He turned his gaze back on her and said, 'It's up to you either way. We'll support your decision. I just want you to think about it. You said your mother lives in this ocean. Perhaps you'd prefer to go and find her?'

Ursula felt as though her heart was being squeezed tighter and tighter at the thought of losing her ties with the explorers' clubs.

'I could,' she said. 'But mermaid cities are too deep for me to live in for long. I'm only half mermaid, remember, so I need access to both the sea and land. And some mermaids might not accept me because of my father being human. If I run away now, then I'll probably never be able to go near a club again. Besides, I can't just abandon Joe. He's still stuck in the snow globe. I've got to do *something* to try to rescue him.'

'I don't know what to suggest,' Jai said helplessly.

'It's all so unfair, but if we can't get the adults to listen to us then I don't know how to fix this.'

'I don't think you can,' Max said. 'But whatever Ursula decides to do, I can't go back to the club. I don't have time to answer their endless questions and get involved with meetings and investigations. Jada is still out there with the Collector and I've got to find a way to free her soon, or I'll lose her for good. I hope you won't mind if I take one of the mini submersible pods?'

'It won't get you very far,' Jai said. 'It's not meant to be a long-distance craft, but you're welcome to it, of course.'

'Thanks.' Max looked at Ursula and said, 'You can come with me if you want? If we find the Collector and my sister, then we'll also find the Ocean Squid Explorers' Club.'

'I think we should *all* go,' Genie protested. 'I'd much rather help you try to find your sister than be stuck in the Sky Phoenix Club.'

'I'd agree with you if we had any leads,' Jai said. 'But we're no nearer to knowing where the Collector is than we were before. She could literally be anywhere on the planet. What are we supposed to do – just wander the world searching?'

'It's better than doing nothing, isn't it?' Genie asked.

'What are the adults going to do if we take the submarine back? None of them are Ocean Squid explorers so none of them knows a thing about deep-sea exploration. They'll probably crash the submarine the first time they take it out.'

There was a long pause and Ursula could tell Jai was battling with his deep aversion to breaking the rules.

'You said before that President Jacob isn't your president,' Ursula pointed out. 'Well, that's still true, isn't it?'

'I guess so,' Jai said. 'But if we're to defy orders again, then we need some kind of mission. Otherwise we're just renegades drifting aimlessly.'

'We could continue building our alliance with the mermaids,' Ursula suggested. 'They live through all the seas and can communicate using the bubble tide. We know they want to find the Collector and that they're willing to work with us. They can help with the search. Someone, somewhere must have spotted Scarlett or come across her headquarters.'

'I suppose that's true,' Jai conceded. 'If we're out of the picture then none of the other explorers will put any effort into establishing this new relationship. And I guess we're more likely to earn the mermaids' trust if Ursula is with us.'

'Are we agreed then?' Max asked, an eager, hopeful expression on his face. 'Are we going to continue on together as a crew?'

'Bess and me are in,' Genie said immediately.

'Me too,' Ursula said.

They all looked at Jai, who was hesitating.

'Come on,' Max said, nudging him in the ribs. 'Don't be a spoilsport. I promise not to make fun of your medals any more, even your yodelling turtle one.'

Jai rolled his eyes. 'I don't care what you say about my medals,' he said. 'That isn't the point. I'm just trying to work out what's the right thing to do in this situation. One of us has to be sensible. And cautious. We don't want to cause another disaster like we did this time.'

Before anyone could reply, there was a little burst of flame and a small puff of smoke, and the firebird appeared on Max's shoulder with a scroll clamped in its beak.

Max immediately stiffened. 'I suppose Scarlett has found out about Pacifica somehow,' he said, reaching up to take the message from the bird.

Everyone stayed grimly silent as Max unrolled the message, but to their surprise it wasn't Scarlett's spidery scrawl across the page, but large, looping handwriting instead.

Max gasped. 'It's from Jada!' he said.

The others crowded round the message, which read:

Max,

Where on earth are you? Scarlett's told us time is running out unless someone comes up with a weapon for her soon. Me and the other kids are getting worried. I told them you'd come, but as you still haven't, I realise I have to sort things out myself and risk sending this message in secret.

I haven't got long, but the only thing you need to know is that Scarlett's keeping us at her HQ on Pirate Island. I've written the coordinates at the bottom of the page. Now all you have to do is come and get us. I can't make it any easier for you than that, Max, so please stop messing about.

Lots of love,
Jada.

P.S. Be careful. There are lots of pirates here.

'Well,' Jai said. 'Your sister sounds like she knows what she wants.'

'She does,' Max replied, grinning. 'I'm surprised she hasn't rescued everyone herself already, but I guess sometimes you just need your big brother to come and help.'

'But this is fantastic!' Ursula exclaimed, looking at the coordinates. 'Now we know exactly where to go.'

Max looked at Jai. 'So are you in?' he asked.

Jai didn't hesitate. 'Of course,' he said. 'I said I'd do all I could to try and help your sister and I meant it.'

'Good,' Max said. 'Because you never know when an expedition might call for a plankton expert. I'd hate to set off without one.'

Jai narrowed his eyes. 'You're making fun of me again.'

'Only a little,' Max replied. 'But I'm glad you're coming. All of you.'

'We should tell the other clubs what we've discovered,' Genie said. She glanced at the firebird, poking its beak into the corners of the bridge. 'Maybe we should send a message by bird rather than radio? That way we won't have to have another argument about coming back.'

'Good idea,' Jai said.

'We should contact the mermaids too,' Ursula said, gazing at the sea beyond the portholes. 'They said they'd help us, after all. And I think we'll need every bit of help we can get if we're going to Pirate Island.'

Once the messages were duly sent, the explorers put the coordinates for Pirate Island into the navigation system. Despite the setbacks they'd suffered and the mistakes they'd made, Ursula was glad that the team were staying together, and pleased they had another chance to make things right. All the rule breaking and the disaster with Pacifica couldn't be for nothing.

She knew there would be challenges ahead but she was sure they could achieve great things if they continued to work together and make the most of their individual strengths. After all, they weren't just four children lost in the ocean – they were a mechanic, an inventor, a kraken whisperer and a leader. And first and foremost they were explorers; the last remaining members of the Ocean Squid Explorers' Club. And they would never give up until they had found and rescued it.

And so the *Blowfish* glided on through the dark water, carrying them ever closer to Pirate Island, with a great shadow kraken swimming happily in its wake.

POLAR BEAR EXPLORERS' CLUB RULES

1. Polar Bear explorers will keep their moustaches trimmed, waxed and generally well-groomed at all times. Any explorer found with a slovenly moustache will be asked to withdraw from the club's public rooms immediately.
2. Explorers with disorderly moustaches or unkempt beards will also be refused entry to the members-only bar, the private dining room and the billiards room without exception.
3. All igloos on club property must contain a flask of hot chocolate and an adequate supply of marshmallows at all times.
4. Only polar-bear-shaped marshmallows are to be served on club property. Additionally, the following breakfast items will be prepared in polar-bear-shape only: pancakes, waffles, crumpets, sticky pastries, fruit jellies and doughnuts. Please do not request alternative

shapes or animals from the kitchen – including penguins, walruses, woolly mammoths or yetis – as this offends the chef.

5. Members are kindly reminded that when the chef is offended, insulted or peeved, there will be nothing on offer in the dining room whatsoever except for buttered toast. This toast will be bread-shaped.

6. Explorers must not hunt or harm unicorns under any circumstances.

7. All Polar Bear Explorers' Club sleighs must be properly decorated with seven brass bells, and must contain the following items: five fleecy blankets, three hot-water bottles in knitted jumpers, two flasks of emergency hot chocolate and a warmed basket of buttered crumpets (polar-bear-shaped).

8. Please do not take penguins into the club's saltwater baths; they *will* hog the jacuzzi.

9. All penguins are the property of the club and are not to be removed by explorers. The club reserves the right to search any suspiciously shaped bags. Any bag that moves by itself will automatically be deemed suspicious.

10. All snowmen built on club property must have appropriately groomed moustaches. Please note that a carrot is not a suitable object to use as a

moustache. Nor is an aubergine. If in doubt, the club president is always available for consultation regarding snowmen's moustaches.

11. It is considered bad form to threaten other club members with icicles, snowballs or oddly dressed snowmen.

12. Whistling ducks are not permitted on club property. Any member found with a whistling duck in his possession will be asked to leave.

UPON INITIATION, ALL POLAR BEAR EXPLORERS SHALL RECEIVE AN EXPLORER'S BAG CONTAINING THE FOLLOWING ITEMS:

- One tin of Captain Filibuster's Expedition–Strength Moustache Wax.
- One bottle of Captain Filibuster's Scented Beard Oil.
- One folding pocket moustache comb.
- One ivory–handled shaving brush, two pairs of grooming scissors and four individually wrapped cakes of luxurious foaming shaving soap.
- Two compact pocket mirrors.

Ocean Squid Explorers' Club Rules

1. Sea monsters, kraken and giant squid trophies are the private property of the club, and cannot be removed to adorn private homes. Explorers will be charged for any decorative tentacles that are found to be missing from their rooms.

2. Explorers are not to fraternise – or join forces – with pirates or smugglers during the course of any official expedition.

3. Poisonous puffer fish, barbed wire jellyfish, saltwater stingrays and electric eels are not appropriate fillings for pies and/or sandwiches. Any such requests sent to the kitchen will be politely rejected.

4. Explorers are kindly asked to refrain from offering to show the club's chef how to prepare sea snakes, sharks, crustaceans or deep-sea monsters for

human consumption. This includes the creatures listed in rule number three. Please respect the expert knowledge of the chef.

5. The Ocean Squid Explorers' Club does not consider the sea cucumber to be a trophy worthy of reward or recognition. This includes the lesser-found biting cucumber, as well as the singing cucumber and the argumentative cucumber.

6. Any Ocean Squid explorer who gifts the club with a tentacle from the screeching red devil squid will be rewarded with a year's supply of Captain Ishmael's Premium Dark Rum.

7. Please do not leave docked submarines in a submerged state – it wreaks havoc with the club's valet service.

8. Explorers are kindly asked not to leave deceased sea monsters in the hallways or any of the club's communal rooms. Unattended sea monsters are liable to be removed to the kitchens without notice.

9. The South Seas Navigation Company will not accept liability for any damage caused to their submarines. This includes damage caused by giant squid attacks, whale ambushes and jellyfish plots.

10. Explorers are not to use the map room to compare

the length of squid tentacles or other trophies. Kindly use the marked areas within the trophy rooms to settle any private wagers or bets.

11. Please note: any explorer who threatens another explorer with a harpoon cannon will be suspended from the club immediately.

UPON INITIATION, ALL OCEAN SQUID EXPLORERS SHALL RECEIVE AN EXPLORER'S BAG CONTAINING THE FOLLOWING ITEMS:

- One tin of Captain Ishmael's Kraken Bait.
- One kraken net.
- One engraved hip flask filled with Captain Ishmael's Expedition-Strength Salted Rum.
- Two sharpened fishing spears and three bags of hunting barbs.
- Five tins of Captain Ishmael's Harpoon Cannon Polish.

Desert Jackal Explorers' Club Rules

1. Magical flying carpets are to be kept tightly rolled when on club premises. Any damage caused by out-of-control flying carpets will be considered the sole responsibility of the explorer in question.
2. Enchanted genie lamps must stay in their owner's possession at all times.
3. Please note: genies are strictly prohibited at the bar and at the bridge tables.
4. Tents are for serious expedition use only, and are not to be used to host parties, gatherings, chinwags, or chit-chats.
5. Camels must not be permitted – or encouraged – to spit at other club members.
6. Jumping cactuses are not allowed inside the club unless under exceptional circumstances.
7. Please do not remove flags, maps or wallabies from the club.

8. Club members are not permitted to settle disagreements via camel racing between the hours of midnight and sunrise.

9. The club kangaroos, coyotes, sand cats and rattlesnakes are to be respected at all times.

10. Members who wish to keep all their fingers are advised not to torment the giant desert hairy scorpions, irritate the bearded vultures or vex the spotted desert recluse spiders.

11. Explorers are kindly asked to refrain from washing their feet in the drinking water tureens at the club's entrance, which are provided strictly for our members' refreshment.

12. Sand forts may be constructed on club grounds, providing explorers empty all sand from their sandals, pockets, bags, binocular cases and helmets before entering the club.

13. Explorers are asked not to take camel decoration to extremes. Desert Jackal Explorers' Club camels may wear a maximum of one jewelled necklace, one tasselled headdress and/or bandana, seven plain gold anklets, up to four knee bells and one floral snout decoration.

UPON INITIATION, ALL DESERT JACKAL
EXPLORERS SHALL RECEIVE AN EXPLORER'S BAG
CONTAINING THE FOLLOWING ITEMS:

- One foldable leather safari hat or one pith helmet.
- One canister of tropical-strength giant desert hairy scorpion repellent.
- One shovel (please note this object's usefulness in the event of being buried alive in a sandstorm).
- One camel-grooming kit, consisting of: organic camel shampoo, camel eyelash curlers, head brush, toenail trimmers and hoof-polishers (kindly provided by the National Camel Grooming Association).
- Two spare genie lamps and one spare genie bottle.

Jungle Cat Explorers' Club Rules

1. Members of the Jungle Cat Explorers' Club shall refrain from picnicking in a slovenly manner. All expedition picnics are to be conducted with grace, poise and elegance.
2. All expedition picnicware must be made from solid silver, and kept perfectly polished at all times.
3. Champagne-carrier hampers must be constructed from high-grade wickerwork, premium leather or teak wood. Please note that champagne carriers considered 'tacky' will not be accepted onto the luggage elephant under ANY circumstances.
4. Expedition picnics will not take place unless there are scones present. Ideally, there should also be magic lanterns, pixie cakes and an assortment of fairy jellies.
5. Oriental whip snakes, alligator snapping turtles, horned baboon tarantulas and flying panthers

must be kept securely under lock and key whilst on club premises.

6. Do not torment or tease the jungle fairies. They *will* bite and may also catapult their tormentors with tiny, but extremely potent, stink-berries. Please be warned that stink-berries smell worse than anything you can imagine, including unwashed feet, mouldy cheese, elephant poo and hippopotamus burps.

7. Jungle fairies must be allowed to join expedition picnics if they bring an offering of any of the following: elephant cakes, striped giraffe scones, or fizzy tiger punch from the Forbidden Jungle Tiger Temple.

8. Jungle fairy boats have right of way on the Tikki Zikki River under *all* circumstances, including when there are piranhas present.

9. Spears are to be pointed away from other club members at all times.

10. When travelling by elephant, explorers are kindly asked to supply their own bananas.

11. If and when confronted by an enraged hippopotamus, a Jungle Cat explorer must remain calm and act with haste to avoid any damage befalling the expedition boat (please note that the

Jungle Navigation Company expects all boats to be returned to them in pristine condition).

12. Members are courteously reminded that – due to the size and smell of the beasts in question – the club's elephant house is not an appropriate venue in which to host soirees, banquets, galas or shindigs. Carousing of any kind in the elephant house is strictly prohibited.

UPON INITIATION, ALL JUNGLE CAT EXPLORERS SHALL RECEIVE AN EXPLORER'S BAG CONTAINING THE FOLLOWING ITEMS:

- An elegant mother–of–pearl knife and fork, inscribed with the explorer's initials.
- One silverware polishing kit.
- One engraved Jungle Cat Explorers' Club napkin ring and five luxury linen napkins – ironed, starched and embossed with the club's insignia.
- One magic lantern with fire pixie.
- One tin of Captain Greystoke's Expedition–Flavour Smoked Caviar.
- One corkscrew, two Scotch egg knives and three wicker grape baskets.

ACKNOWLEDGEMENTS

Many thanks to the following wonderful people:

My agent, Thérèse Coen, and the Hardman and Swainson Literary Agency.

The lovely team at Faber – especially Natasha Brown, Leah Thaxton and Sarah Lough.

My two Siameses, Suki and Misu, and my husband, Neil Dayus.

All of the children's booksellers and teachers who take the time to champion books and nurture a love of reading in young people.

And, finally, to all of the children who have read and enjoyed Polar Bears. When you dress up as the characters, or write letters to me, or create things in the classroom, or share your amazing ideas at events, you remind me of what a special thing it is to be a children's writer. I hope you enjoy this book too.

Other Fantastic Faber Reads

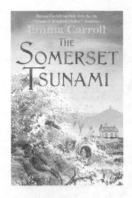

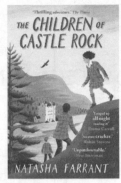

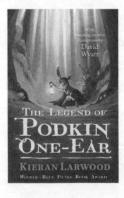